REIGN OF TERROR
A Chance Barnette Story

REIGN OF TERROR!
A Chance Barnette Story

Timothy Bowe

Inspiration Pointe
PRESS

Editor: Rick Benzel
Creative Director: Susan Shankin & Associates
Cover Design: Tim Kummerow

Published by Inspiration Pointe Press,
an imprint of
Over and Above Creative Group, Los Angeles, CA
www.overandabovecreative.com

Copyright © 2016 by Timothy Bowe. All rights reserved.

This book contains material protected under International and Federal Copyright Laws and Treaties. No part of this publication may be reproduced, distributed, or transmitted in any form or by any means, including photocopying, recording, or other electronic or mechanical methods, without the prior written permission of the author, except in the case of brief quotations embodied in critical reviews and certain other noncommercial uses permitted by copyright law. For permission requests, please email the publisher at following address: rickbenzel@overandabovecreative.com.

All characters, organizations, and events in this book are a work of creative fiction. Any resemblance to current or past persons and events is strictly coincidental.

ISBN: 978-0-9968406-2-0
Library of Congress Control Number: 2015959678
First edition

Printed in the United States of America

Visit Timothy at: timothyboweauthor.com

Dedicated to Willie and Clara Bowe

In loving memory of Al and Ada Moore

NOBODY LIKED THEIR JOB AS MUCH AS CHANCE BARNETTE. He craved action and reveled in the dangers of his occupation. He had stopped counting the number of times he had been shot, but if he really wanted to know, he could simply count the scars. Being stabbed with a knife was different. Only one man had gotten close enough but on that day Chance just happened to be wearing body armor. He punched his assailant in the throat, put his left arm behind his neck and reached over his face grabbing him by the chin with his right hand. In one final motion he pulled his chin upward snapping his attacker's neck.

Chance was an imposing figure, standing six foot five with a heavy, ripped muscular build. He was as handsome as he was big with a military style crew cut and a clean-shaven face and piercing black eyes.

Even as he made his way up the street that ran parallel to, and directly behind the building where the hostages were being held, the adrenaline surged throughout his body, giving him a familiar high. He moved in the shadows, ducking into alleyways as he advanced, not because he feared the marauders who roamed about the town in the darkness, but knowing that any skirmish he might have with them would slow his approach.

He waited in the shadows, as he often did, with his back against a wall and hung his turbaned head, waiting for his mission to begin.

Six Months Earlier

Three heavily armed men made their way into a narrow tunnel that had been carved into the mountains by elements and time. They wore camouflage desert fatigues and were equipped with goggles and aspirators to protect them from the sandstorm raging outside the entrance. One member of the trio used a battery-powered lantern to illuminate the path, while the others pointed the barrels of their Heckler & Koch MP7 submachine guns into the dark unknown before them.

Eventually, the narrow, winding passage opened up into a large subterranean chamber, illuminated by several battery-powered lanterns. With their MP7's level, they surveyed the cavern's interior. One man raised his hand in the air and clenched his fist in an okay signal. They quickly removed their head coverings, goggles and aspirators, while continuing to survey the various openings in the cavern walls, with weapons ready.

Several figures eventually emerged from one of the passageways on the far wall of the chamber. Wearing head wraps and long robes, they were equipped with AK-47s. All but one stopped upon entering the chamber. He approached the waiting mercenaries.

"You must be Stryker."

Stryker recognized it as a dialect that heralded from the mountainous regions of western Pakistan.

"Where is Ahmad?" he demanded sharply.

"My name is Sair." He extended his hand toward the battle-hardened mercenary, who completely ignored the gesture. "I am sorry; Ahmad was not able to make the trip."

"Ah. That's too bad. I guess we're done here then." Stryker turned back toward his men.

"Wait!" Sair grabbed Stryker's arm. Stryker spun around to Sair and trained his cold sinister eyes on him, causing him to immediately release his grip.

"I have your merchandise," Sair said. He turned to the passageway from which his group had entered the cavern. He clapped his hands and two robed men came forward carrying a metal chest by steel poles attached to either side.

"That's nice but I only deal with Ahmad."

Stryker turned again to leave, just in time to see four robed men approach through the narrow passageway from which he had led his men into the cavern. They were armed, with their faces covered as protection from the storm. The fighters paused at the tunnel opening to get their bearings in the dimly lit chamber. They readied their weapons and approached the mercenaries, standing with their weapons at the ready.

"As you can see you are outnumbered, so you will deal with me." Sair smiled.

Stryker turned and looked at the fighters between his small group and the cavern exit. He raised his hand in a beckoning gesture. One of his men removed his backpack and handed it to him. He took the backpack, unzipped it, and tossed it at Sair's feet. Several stacks of money fell out.

"It's all there, one million." Stryker signaled to one of his men, who approached the chest with a Geiger counter. He scanned the seams of the chest, then turned to Stryker and nodded approval.

Sair reached down, picked up the backpack and looked inside. He smiled and signaled to his crowd. One of them approached and asked, "How much is there?"

"He says it's a million. We'll count it later."

"Okay. We'll take our package now." Stryker demanded.

"Not so fast," Sair instructed. "Are you aware that this package was stolen from the Iranian government?"

"That's not my concern."

Sair continued giving Stryker a stern look. "Unfortunately for you, the Iranian government wants their property returned. Can you imagine how pleased they were when I told them that I could recover it quietly, without incident?"

"So why didn't you return it to them?"

"Well, when we found it was in the hands of... you said his name was Ahmad?" Sair smiled and touched his knife that was attached to his belt. "We had to use his family to persuade him but eventually he told us about your arrangement."

Sair kneeled down and began to push the stacks of money that had fallen out into the backpack. Suddenly, the fighters who had entered the cave behind the mercenaries removed the coverings from their faces and began to fire their MP7's over Sair's head killing his men, leaving him alone.

Sair did a double take, realizing the shooters were not his men. He covered his head with his hands. "Please don't hurt me," he begged. "You appear to be reasonable men. Please. The box is yours. Take it and leave. I don't even want to know what it is." His hands trembled as he nervously began to put the stacks of money in the bag while keeping an eye on Stryker and his men.

Stryker kneeled down in front of the stunned rebel. "You're not very brave for a freedom fighter."

"No, no, I'm not a freedom fighter. I'm a businessman like yourself."

"You and I are nothing alike. Ahmad, now he was a soldier. We fought on the same side in some campaigns and on opposite sides in others. He was driven by honor and belief, not greed.

"Two of the mercenaries lifted the container and headed out of the cave. Stryker rose to his feet and pulled Sair up by his arm as he clutched the backpack tightly. He looked into Stryker's eyes and saw no glimpse of humanity.

"Please do not rob me. I have a wife and children to feed."

"Like Ahmad?" A long uncomfortable silence followed as Stryker looked into Sair's eyes. Sair looked away, avoiding eye contact.

"If you don't mind, I will take my money and just leave now, okay?"

Stryker pried the backpack from Sair's arms with his left arm while shoving him with his right, causing him to fall to the ground.

"Please don't kill me." Sair scrambled to his knees and clenched his hands upward toward Stryker, begging for mercy.

"I wouldn't give you the honor." Stryker used the sole of his boot in Sair's chest to shove him to the ground, before turning and walking toward the exit. He looked in the direction of one of his men, nodded, and headed back up the tunnel while pulling his goggles over his eyes and the respirator back over his nose and mouth.

The sound from the gunshot echoed past him as he exited the tunnel stepping over four dead rebel bodies that lay across the tunnel entrance.

Present Day

The sniper sat in the darkness on the roof of the three-story clay building. His back leaned against the three-foot wall that surrounded the entire rooftop. After opening his rifle case, he removed the main assembly attached to the black composite stock. He took out the black rifle barrel, screwed it onto the assembly, then withdrew a dark-colored towel from his belt.

"It's hot as hell out here," Brock complained in a low tone as he peeled off his PTM, laid it in the padded rifle case and wiped the sweat from his face and then his hands. Brock removed a rifle scope from the leather case that lay on the floor next to him. Turning his body and kneeling up onto one knee, he set the scope to night vision and peered over the edge of the wall. The sniper began to scan all the rooftops within sight and then focused on the front of a two-story building across the street from his location.

The structure, constructed of hand-made earthen bricks, was similar to all of the other buildings in the Afghan village, located in the Nahrin District. The homes and businesses, which had survived numerous earthquakes, attacks by the Russians, the Taliban, Al-Qaeda, the Americans, and the drug lords, bore the scars caused by the decades-long cycle of damage and repair. Many of the structures had been abandoned, displaying various stages of neglect and decay. Some had simply crumbled to the ground.

Those villagers who remained had seen many aid workers come and go. The only constant in their lives was the oppression brought on by the various militant groups and drug gangs who used the area to hide from Allied troops. In the light of day, the villagers went about their daily hustle and bustle, but they would bolt themselves behind their wooden doors as soon as the sun began its descent behind the mountains in the distance. The pinging of gunshots typically accompanied the darkness, adding to the fear and helplessness shared by those still living in the community.

Brock shifted the crosshairs of his scope toward the front door where two robed men stood talking. They each had an AK-47 slung over their shoulders, telling Brock that he could easily drop his targets before they would be able get a single shot off. He was amused, knowing they would not even know what had happened to them before they expired. The door was open, but even with his night vision goggles, Brock had only a limited view of the interior.

He sat back down and attached the scope to his rifle, then pointed it at the small rectangular structure at the center of the roof where he was seated. A door on the structure concealed the steps that led down from the rooftop. He smiled as he anxiously looked through the lens and reminisced about one of his proudest moments a few years back.

Brock and a spotter lay prone on a ledge overlooking an insurgent camp on the desert floor below them, waiting for the missiles to strike. He had been embedded in an Army Recon unit on observation missions. He peered at the camp, which his unit had tagged with a missile location laser through his binoculars.

"Bet I could drop one from here," he quipped to his spotter.

The spotter laughed. "That's probably at the edge of even my range."

"The one with the red turban."

The spotter raised his scope and peered. "He's over two kilometers away. You'd never make that shot. Especially not with that old rifle. What is it anyway?"

"An M40A1, with a sound suppressor, circa 1980." Brock reached into a side pocket on his backpack next to him. "My M40 and this." He held up a brass-jacketed shell with a dull alloy tip.

"That's bigger than standard munitions for that weapon, huh?"

"I always say, go big or go home."

"What is it?"

Brock laughed. "If I tell you, I gotta kill you. Fifty bucks says I can drop him from here." Brock laid down his binoculars and loaded the shell.

The spotter checked over his shoulder if anyone was there. "Are you serious? We can't do that."

"They're about to get blown to shit, anyway." Brock looked up at the soldier. "Nobody will ever know. They'll all be friggin' camel food in a minute, bro."

The Ranger looked over his shoulder once more and turned back with a smile. "Ok. Fifty. The red turban guy. One shot. Go for it."

The spotter looked back through his scope as Brock took aim. The red turban made the target easier to see, as he concentrated on the rhythm of his own heartbeat. He took a shallow breath and gently squeezed the trigger. The shell left the barrel with a thud and in a moment, the insurgent fell to the ground, twitched a few times, then lay motionless on the desert sand. Several of his comrades immediately ran to his aid while others looked out over the desert, babbling and pointing in various directions. Seconds later, Brock and the spotter were temporarily blinded by the flash of a cruise missile exploding just above the insurgents' heads resulting in a cloud of smoke and dust.

"That was a hell of a shot, man." The soldier laughed and patted Brock's shoulder.

Brock Mentor, known as The Prairie Dog, had small, piercing blue eyes peering out like lasers from his wide, ruddy, and heavily bearded face. His scruffy red beard and long red hair perfectly portrayed his fiery rambunctious personality. He was not a tall man but he was thick, bulky and strong. He was also deceivingly agile with a reputation for being fearless and confrontational, with an extremely short fuse. He had been blessed with perfect vision and a wickedly deadly aim. He was the agents' favorite sniper when they needed coverage.

Brock laid a much newer rifle down and took a drink from his canteen. He wiped his face and eyes once more before hearing a lone vehicle approaching from the south on the crater-filled street. He rose up on his knee once more and watched the proceedings through his rifle sight. The vehicle was a dark, late model American-made SUV. It stopped in front of the door, allowing five men wearing dark-colored robes to get out. Three of the men carried various model AK-47s. One of the unarmed men opened the back of the SUV and removed a tripod; the other lifted a video camera from the hatch.

Two of the men with AK-47s and the two carrying the camera equipment all went inside and closed the door behind them. The driver remained outside with two other men who were guarding the door. One of the SUV men came back out of the building and talked to the driver, who got in the vehicle and backed it into a narrow alleyway before getting out and going inside. Sitting back down, Brock wiped the sweat from his face with the towel once more. "Damn, I'm sweating like a pig up here," he mumbled to himself.

Brock removed a military-style knife from a sheath on his belt and reached over to the dead body that lay on the roof not far from him. After cutting a strip of cloth from the robe of his prior victim, he tied it around his head just above his eyebrows. "Ah, much better."

"Ops to Prairie Dog," his earpiece buzzed.

"Go for P Dog," Brock replied to his controller on the other end of the line.

"We have company approaching from the south at one kilometer."

Brock peered over the wall. To his right, a pair of headlights approached from the far end of the street. The silence was eventually broken by a windowless white '70s-era Econoline van. Brock watched as it made its way down the crumbling street, the driver making little effort to miss the potholes. The van stopped just past the door guards who looked on with extreme interest. A passenger got out carrying an AK-47, and was greeted enthusiastically by the guards, before walking to the rear of the van and opening both doors.

"Do you have a visual on the van?"

"Affirmative." He leaned his weapon on the wall next to him and picked up a cylindrical device that fit comfortably in his hand. He looked into the night vision scope that offered a clear green image of the action on the street below. He watched two armed men climb out, then roughly yank three hooded hostages out. Their hands were bound behind them. As each one stood on the ground, they were shoved out of the way.

"We see three hostages with hoods being taken from the van."

"Tagging three hostages now."

Brock aligned a white dot inside the device on the first hostage, then pressed a button on top. His controllers, who were viewing the events from a satellite, would be able to see thermal images once the hostages and guards entered the building. From the images they would not be able to distinguish the individuals from each other, but as Brock tagged each hostage, a computer memorized and tracked each of their positions in reference to their captors.

Brock returned the device to his backpack and raised his weapon. He readied himself to take any shots necessary to secure the perimeter of the entrance.

The Assistant to the President for National Security Affairs, Howard Neal, was a man whose career was in jeopardy. Not because his college friend, the president, was dissatisfied with his performance, but because the highly unpopular president's tenure had been plagued by accusations of greed, corruption and incompetence. He had been accused of taking campaign contributions from The Humanitarian Aid Alliance for Developing Nations (HAADN), a humanitarian organization with alleged secret ties to some Middle Eastern terrorist organizations. Several of the group's workers had been accused of recruiting young men for various terrorist groups, then deploying them throughout the world under the guise of volunteer workers. When the story got leaked by a Washington Post reporter, the president quickly returned the money, while publicly voicing his outrage at the organization.

On many occasions, Neal had been made to take the blame for the president's failed foreign policies. He knew from the beginning that he would sometimes be used as a scapegoat, but not like this. Neal was not a likeable man, eliminating his chances of a long political career, but he accepted the position knowing that the immediate rewards could be very lucrative. He was arrogant, sarcastic, vindictive, and hated by subordinates as well as peers. Although he was known for holding grudges for decades, he was also known for his loyalty to the current administration. He protected his friend, the president, at all costs.

Although he was not officially part of the president's Cabinet, many called him Secretary Neal and he had no shortage of enemies on Capitol Hill. He was typically brought in to strong-arm political opponents when negotiations had broken down. It was said that Neal kept notes on everyone he had ever met, and would constantly seek out new methods of gathering personal information. He was not above leaking sensitive and even personal information to the press about anyone who dared stand up to him. It was rumored that he secretly used friendly operatives in various agencies to gather data on anyone who rose to any level of power or authority. In earlier years, he kept notes on his enemies in a black leather-bound binder. More recently he stored the information on his laptop which was never out of the reach. But in meetings where he was met with resistance, he would still remove his black leather notebook from his briefcase and place it on the table in view of everyone as a reminder.

When all else failed, he was not above threatening or even destroying the careers of his opponents' family members and friends. The reporter who broke the HAADN story and her editor were both fired and blacklisted from all of the mainstream news agencies.

Needless to say, Secretary Neal was excited to visit and learn more about the Homeland Security Agency (HSA) today. The agency, an autonomous organization that fell under the direction of no other security agency, possessed unparalleled information gathering capabilities. Neal himself was unaware of the organization until, while searching for soft money, he questioned a rather large line item that was being filtered through the Department of Defense budget for black ops. He wondered why, as National Security Adviser, he had not been made aware of this intelligence-rich organization that surely should have fallen under his authority. When Neal questioned the president about the agency, he was told to leave it alone. His own exploratory meetings with the heads of the US Senate Select Committee on Intelligence, as well as the US House Permanent Select Committee on Intelligence, both proved to be fruitless. Neither was willing to discuss the HSA and advised him not to pursue the path he was following. The instructions only made Neal more adamant about knowing.

The flight from Baltimore-Washington International airport had proven to be uneventful as the pilot lined up for his final approach to MacArthur airport on Long Island. Secretary Neal sat in the fully upright position, with his elbows planted firmly on the armrests, and his hands folded in front of him while fixating on the power of the intelligence that could be gathered by this, until now, elusive source of information. His heart pounded in his chest as he contemplated how he could use it for his own personal gain. He looked down at the laptop case that had been placed under the seat in front of him. He smiled before turning to his aid, Jennifer Stockton, who was seated next to him. After a quick scan to make sure no one was watching, he gently touched her bare thigh, revealed by her skirt that had risen up as she slept.

It was long rumored that Neal used his position to take advantage of young female aides, but because of his reputation for ruthlessness, his opponents rarely followed up. He, himself, operated with relative impunity, using the peccadillos of others to draw attention away from his own salacious deeds. A good rumor, even when false, would raise questions about the integrity of a politician long after his or her career was over. Neal concentrated on the sexual indiscretions of anyone who was unwilling to support the president's directives in the wars on terrorism and crime. He knew that nothing could raise the ire of the voter more than sex and fear.

Jenny, a recent law school graduate, had heard the whispers about Neal, but could not resist the temptation of having such a powerful lover. She justified the affair by the fact that Neal's marriage was already on the rocks following numerous affairs. He kept his wife home and quiet with drugs and alcohol, and by threatening to reveal painful secrets involving her family.

"Jenny. Wake up, we're landing."

"Oh, sorry. I didn't realize that I had fallen asleep."

"And when we get off the plane, go fix yourself up. You look terrible."

"Sorry. You rushed me out this morning." She looked at her watch. "It's nine fifteen. How did we get here so fast?"

Secretary Neal checked his watch, rubbing her thigh one more time. "Hmmm. It was a smooth ride, I guess."

The plane taxied to the jetway and came to a halt. Jenny grabbed her briefcase and purse from under the seat as Neal grabbed his laptop and slung the strap over his shoulder. He rushed Jennifer to her feet and pushed her toward the door so they would be among the first to exit. He smiled and shook the flight attendant's hand as they exited. To their surprise, they were met in the jetway by a TSA supervisor.

"Good morning, Mr. Secretary. Ms. Stockton." He extended his hand to the confused secretary.

"Excuse me if I'm a bit surprised," Neal said, shaking the TSA officer's hand. "I didn't announce this trip."

"We got word about an hour ago when the helicopter that came to pick you up landed. This way please."

"Helicopter?"

"Yes, a Marine Corps helicopter is waiting for you across the runway, sir."

He led them out the jetway through a side door and down a set of steps to the tarmac where a van was waiting. He opened the back door allowing them to enter the vehicle which had a military driver behind the wheel.

"Enjoy your visit, Mr. Secretary." The TSA supervisor looked at Jennifer and back at Neal, then smiled to her, making her uncomfortable.

The TSA supervisor closed the door and patted the roof of the van. The driver said nothing as he drove them to the opposite side of the airport where they boarded a waiting Seahawk helicopter that whisked them across Long Island to the Calverton Naval Proving Grounds. It landed in the center of a large yellow circle painted on a concrete pad, just as a late-model black SUV with heavily tinted windows approached. The SUV turned off of the road and drove across the grass, stopping at the edge of the landing pad. Neal exited the helicopter squeezing his laptop case tightly against his body. He was followed closely behind by Jennifer, who clutched her burgundy leather briefcase tightly with her purse slung over her shoulder. A tall, well-built officer with salt and pepper hair stepped out of the vehicle and extended his hand.

"Good morning Secretary Neal, and welcome to Calverton. I'm Commander Ron Crayton."

"Hello Commander," Neal responded, shaking his hand. Wanting to show his authority, he added, "The president sends his regards." Neal knew that this was a lie since he didn't tell the president that he was coming, but it was a good political move.

"Thank you, sir."

"This is my assistant Jennifer Stockton."

"Hello. Nice to meet you," she said, extending her hand to the commander.

"Pleasure ma'am." He gently shook her hand. "This way, please." He stretched his open hand toward the SUV where a sailor stood beside the open door.

As they approached, Jennifer noticed that the sailor, an ensign, was about her age. His eyes locked on hers and held contact until she finally had to look away. He appeared to be more experienced and worldly than any of her male college friends. There was a certain confidence which showed in his body language, that she had so far only seen in older men.

"Let me help you, ma'am," the ensign said, reaching out his hand to offer Jennifer help into the vehicle. As she climbed in, he touched her lower back when her ascent purposely faltered.

"Thank you so much," she smiled graciously, accepting his help.

"No problem," he smiled.

Jennifer felt warm and weak as she slid across the seat. She could no longer connect with his light brown eyes and looked away. The ensign's token offer to assist Secretary Neal into the vehicle was waved off as Neal took the door handle himself and closed it once he was inside.

The ensign slid into the driver's seat while the commander, now seated in the front passenger seat, signaled him to go. They turned left at the road, then headed toward the woods at the edge of the base.

"I take it you expected us," Neal said, half asking.

The Commander turned to face them. "Yes sir, we were advised by the Homeland Security Agency that you were coming."

"That's odd, considering that I didn't tell anyone that I was coming today. I didn't even alert the Secret Service until we were on our way to the airport." He turned and stared at Jennifer, who looked back into his eyes and hunched her shoulders, indicating she didn't know either.

The road ended at an entrance with a double steel gate, forming a sort of holding area. Between the outer and inner gates, there was enough room for only a single automobile. On either side of this inner area stood structures built of cinder block. The one on the right had a metal door and a large, heavily tinted window. The area between the gates was now empty, but a lone black SUV sat idle on the far side of the inner gate. Two armed guards stood on either side of the SUV, wearing black fatigues and matching sunglasses. The two standing at the rear of the vehicle, closest to the gate, carried fully automatic rifles.

The soldiers themselves stood at attention while their faces lacked any show of expression. Secretary Neal and Jennifer eyed the spectacle as their SUV came to a halt at the gate. Signs on the gate and along the adjacent perimeter fence that disappeared into the woods warned that this was government property, the fence was electrified and violators would be subjected to a lethal dose of electricity.

"Well folks, this is it. The end of our jurisdiction," the commander turned and said. He got out of the vehicle and opened Secretary Neal's door. The ensign opened the opposite side door for Jennifer. "I would imagine what you're looking for is on the other side of that gate." Commander Crayton pointed to the other vehicle.

Neal walked toward the gate as the SUV drove away.

"What is this place?" Jennifer asked.

"This looks like the place where we need to be." Neal put on his political smile as they walked closer. "Why aren't they opening the gates since they're so aware of us coming? The bastards know who I am," he said while trying not to move his lips.

The outer gate began to slide open. Neal walked through while Jennifer followed closely behind. The gate closed behind them and a metal door leading in to the guard house opened. A woman wearing the same uniform as the men came out to meet the pair. Her face, like the men, remained expressionless.

"Secretary Neal, welcome to HSA headquarters. We've been expecting you. You're a little bit behind schedule, so you'll have to hurry," she said in a monotone voice.

The inside gate began to slide open and the woman motioned for them to proceed. They looked at each other and walked toward the vehicle parked there, apparently waiting for them. The armed guards standing at the rear doors of the SUV slung their guns over their shoulders and opened the doors. Neal pointed for Jenny to enter on the opposite side. Once they were in the car, the guards closed the doors and the remaining two guards entered the vehicle on the front seat. Not a word was said.

The driver started the SUV and drove it to a narrow roadway that entered into the woods. Just past the tree line, the road veered sharply right, followed by a left turn, after which they entered a parking lot full of cars. At the edge of the opening stood a small tan metal multipurpose building, hardly large enough to hold all of the drivers of the cars parked in the lot. The driver stopped in front of a set of double doors, and exited the vehicle. He opened the back door beckoning Jenny, then Secretary Neal to exit. They followed him to the double doors where he stopped and peered into a retinal scanner on the door jamb.

The door clicked and he opened it, then directed Neal and Jennifer to enter. Once inside, the door slammed shut behind them. Neal turned and looked through a narrow wire-mesh window in the closed door where he could see the guard returning to the SUV.

"What now?" he asked.

He looked over at Jennifer who was pointing to the right side of the foyer where another guard dressed in the black uniform stood behind bullet resistant glass. The guard pointed to a set of opening elevator doors on the opposite wall. As they approached, they saw another set of double doors leading into a dark gym, illuminated only by the light spilling in through a skylight, and the exit signs. They looked inside as they walk past it and into the elevator.

Neal entered the elevator first and Jennifer followed. When she entered, the doors quickly closed and the elevator jolted downward. Neal noticed that the buttons next to the doors showed only two choices: G with a star, and M. Seconds later, the elevator slowed to a halt, and the doors opened up into a dark hallway.

Secretary Neal panicked and quickly reached for the G floor selection button, but got no response. He had many enemies and now wondered if the covertly planned trip had been a wise decision or a trap of some kind. He slowly turned and looked at Jenny who was staring out into the darkness. Nervously doing a gentlemanly gesture, he placed his hand on her lower spine and gently pushed her out into the hallway. As soon as she stepped out, florescent lights directly overhead surged on, illuminating a ten-foot section of the arched hallway. Neal continued to push Jenny forward and once he had stepped out, the elevator doors closed. They both paused, staring down the dark hallway.

As they started to walk forward, still not sure where, the lights in each ten-foot section of hallway flickered, then came on, illuminating just that one section of the passageway. Neal kept pressing Jennifer forward until they reached the next section. Whenever he turned around to monitor the hall behind, the lights in the section that they had come from went dark.

After several sections of hallway, Secretary Neal removed his hand from Jenny's back and began walking beside her.

Then lights in the next section revealed an intersection with several arched hallways left and right. Neal motioned for Jennifer to stay put while he turned down one of the side hallways. He wandered about ten feet into the dark hallway, but no lights came on, so he turned around and walked back to the main hallway.

"This way, Secretary Neal," a woman's voice faintly called out.

Neal turned to Jenny. "What did she say?"

Jennifer pointed down the hallway to a light that was seeping out of an open doorway. A female figure could be seen standing in the threshold. Neal and Jennifer walked toward her, passing several more doors on either side. The lights before them continued to brighten with each step until they could finally see clearly.

Standing in the doorway was an attractive middle-aged woman. Her short, dark hair was punctuated with natural streaks of gray, spaced so perfectly that they looked planned. She wore a gray suit with a tapered jacket, revealing a trim waistline, and under it she wore a tailored blouse. Around her neck was a white silk scarf with a burgundy and gray floral pattern. On her feet she wore a pair of burgundy low-heel Manolo Blahnik shoes.

"I'm definitely paying these people too much money," Neal thought.

"Good morning, Secretary Neal. Your timing could not have been better. I'm Marge, the director's executive assistant." Before Neal could reply, she shook his hand and turned to Jennifer. "Nice to meet you too, Jennifer."

Neal caught himself giving her a perplexed look. "Yes, hello Marge. That's quite a hallway that you have," he said with a confused smile.

"We conserve energy as much as we can. We feel that it's important for us to save the government money wherever we can."

"So, can you tell me . . . "

Marge interrupted him. "May I take your coats?" She hung their coats on a coat rack next to the door. "I imagine that you'd like to freshen up after your trip? You have a little time."

"No, I'm fine," Neal replied abruptly. "Time for what, exactly?"

"I certainly could use it." Jennifer interrupted, handing her briefcase to Secretary Neal. Marge pointed to a rest room in the vestibule and Jennifer disappeared.

Turning back to Neal, she instructed him, "If you would wait in here, sir, Dr. Moore, the director, will be in momentarily. Marge smiled and opened a door on the far wall leading to a plush conference room.

Neal entered. The room was dominated by a long table in the center. On the wall was a credenza with a tray of bagels, four pitchers of a variety of juices, and three silver urns. In front of each urn was a silver plaque listing its contents. Neal read them in sequence, noting that one urn held decaffeinated hazelnut coffee, his morning coffee of choice.

He removed his laptop from its case and set it up at the head of the table in front of the credenza. After removing his black notebook from Jennifer's briefcase, he sat it on the table in front of his computer, ready for combat with this Dr. Moore whom he knew nothing about. He pressed the power button on, then focused on the continental breakfast. He turned over one of the coffee cups which sat upside down on a saucer, and poured himself a cup of the hazelnut. With no warning, he was suddenly startled by the low baritone voice booming coming from the doorway at the other end of the room.

"You're an enemy of the United States of America, and you have breached our outer perimeter security. We allow you to continue into the building and down the elevator. As you progress down the hallway, several highly trained guards lay in wait in the darkness. The darkness behind you fills with more guards. You are trapped, alone and a secret prisoner of the United States."

Neal recovered his breath and sat his coffee down on the credenza. Turning, he saw a tall, muscular, bald man approach from the opposite end of the room. He wore a crisp white shirt under a red tie. The collar and the tie were loosened informally, and on his lapel was an American flag pin.

"Of course, you are not an enemy of the State," the voice said in a friendly tone. "Welcome to HSA headquarters. I see you've found the coffee and bagels. I believe there is cranberry juice there. Can I get you some vodka?"

"No thanks," he snapped. The rumor about the vodka was true but he dismissed it as common knowledge." I'm fine with the hazelnut coffee. Thank you for preparing this."

"Please make yourself comfortable. I'm Dr. Shelby Moore, director of the HSA." He had a big grin on his face as he approached and extended his hand to Neal.

"Dr. Shelby Moore? That name doesn't ring a bell," Neal responded as they shook hands.

Dr. Moore looked down at the black binder and tapped it a few times. "Trust me, Secretary Neal. You don't know me and I'm not in your book."

Neal fought off the urge to grab it away by reminding himself that in regards to this meeting, the pages were still blank.

"Hmmm. Dr. Moore, you say?"

"Yes. I have a PhD in psychology from DeSales University."

Neal took his coffee and sat in the chair at the end of the table. "I understand that you've been expecting us. That's odd, considering that I never told anyone that I was coming."

"Here in the HSA, surprise is the equivalent of failure, Mr. Secretary. We live or die by that motto."

"I must admit, I've never heard of your agency but you seem to know a lot about me. You even know what kind of coffee I like to drink in the morning?"

"You'd be surprised at what we know."

"And how is it that you have so much information?"

"We're very proud of our unparalleled intelligence gathering capabilities. But trust me, Mr. Secretary; you don't want the answer to that question." He looked sternly into the Secretary's eyes.

"Hmmm. Maybe it is best, but . . . " Neal looked around the room to see if anyone had come in. "But until early this morning, I didn't even know that you, or any of this, existed."

The grin quickly disappeared from the director's face. "Good. We're going to keep it that way," he snapped before pouring himself a cup of coffee and plopping himself down at the opposite end of the table.

"How long exactly has this agency been around?" Neal made an effort to gain control of the conversation.

Dr. Moore smiled. "In some form, functionality or name, since the Revolutionary War. It was actually formed to gather information about the governing officials of the original thirteen colonies in order to use it against them if they didn't stay true to the cause. During the Cold War with the Soviet Union, our intelligence gathering ability overseas surpassed even that of the CIA and the KGB."

"How is that?"

"When you don't exist, you don't have boundaries of any kind. We were the ones who alerted officials that the U.S. Embassy in Moscow had listening devices embedded right in the concrete wall sections." He paused and looked at Neal, waiting for a response. "When Saddam Hussein invaded Kuwait, we added military personnel cells, and after 9/11, we were called into service to use those assets to combat enemy terrorists. That was when our name was changed to the Homeland Security Agency."

"So you're telling me that this organization is older that the nation itself?"

The director laughed. "You know the eye on the dollar bill? Many think it's a Masonic symbol, but it actually represents us watching over our national interests."

"That's ridiculous. You expect me to believe that all of these decades, you people have been watching us? What about the laws against spying on our people?"

"Don't be naive, Secretary Neal. I know why you're here. Besides, the organization has its own constitution that predates even the Articles of Confederation and the Perpetual Union. Quite simply, the rules don't apply to us."

"Who do you report to?"

"Your boss, the president, but only after the fact. That allows him a certain level of deniability."

Secretary Neal folded his hands, leaned back in his chair and thought for a moment.

"How many people make up the HSA?" he demanded, again trying to reassert some authority over the situation.

Dr. Moore paused and smiled, "If I tell you, I'll have to kill you."

Secretary Neal placed his elbows on the table and leaned forward. "I didn't come here to get into a pissing match with a subordinate. I want answers, Dr. Moore."

The doctor relaxed in his chair.

"The sole purpose of this organization is to protect the way of life of the most powerful nation on earth without them knowing that they need to be protected. We keep the nation safe from international and domestic terrorist organizations and other enemies of the state. The men and women of HSA are not first responders. When the first responders arrive, we've already done our job and left."

He took a slow sip of coffee, then continued, "We have constructed the most advanced surveillance system in the world. Not only do we have access to the NSA, CIA, FBI and DARPA networks, but the federal government has funded our own multi-billion dollar surveillance network. We also have complete latitude when doing surveillance and performing interrogations. All of this has accounted for our unparalleled ability to gather information."

He paused and looked at Secretary Neal, waiting for his next questions. When Neal said nothing, he continued.

"Another advantage we enjoy is our technology, which thanks to the generous funding practices of your boss and his predecessors, we're able to consistently upgrade and innovate."

The director swiveled around in his chair to a cabinet, mounted on the wall behind him. He opened it and removed a pair of glasses, turned back, and slid them down the length of the table to Neal.

"This is our third-generation Personal Tactical Monitor, or PTM as we call it. Though they look like ordinary sunglasses, they are not, and they are light years more advanced than the commercially available wearables. They give us the ability to view what our agent is viewing, to hear what he or she hears, and to send audio or visual data directly to them."

Secretary Neal inspected the PTM, then placed it back on the table.

Dr. Moore began again. "The PTM is the key to our agent's ability to share vast amounts of information with our controllers and other agents. The inside of each lens is a plasma display monitor. The outside of the lens is made of thousands of individual photocells arranged in a convex configuration to give agents a 270-degree range of view. An outer protective coating, which makes them appear to be one single glass lens, also gives the lens the ability to pick up sound waves. A built-in transmitter sends the data collected by the PTM to mission control. The PTM is held snug against the agent's face by an elastic safety strap. A small, round, convex cluster of photocells, attached to the center of the strap, completes the 360-degree range of sight.

"Images transmitted back to the mission control can be enhanced by computer and sent back to the agent. Computer enhancements include glare filtering for operations done in bright light, thermal-aided night vision when working in complete darkness, and magnification for enlargement or distance. Many of the photocells are thermal sensors that allow agents to see thermal images, even through walls. The mode can be used by a series of eye blinks, or by voice command. Each agent has a mission controller who also can control the PTM.

"Communication between PTM's and mission control typically uses cell phone towers to transmit and receive low-frequency coded transmissions in the form of digital data. In remote areas, both government and private satellites can transmit and receive the data. Prior to their launch, we fit even private satellites with communication equipment that we can use for our agency missions."

His speech over, Dr. Moore poured himself another cup of coffee. Neal sat silent, toying with the PTM on the table in front of him.

"One thing is certain," Dr. Moore continued, "you picked the perfect day and time to show up. We did have to clear some airspace to get you here faster though."

"You cleared air space?"

"Yes, we had to. We're on a live mission as we speak. We wanted you to get an inside look at some of the work that we do."

The director stood up as Marge and Jennifer entered the room.

Neal stood to introduce Jennifer. "Dr. Moore, this is my assistant, Jennifer Stockton."

"I know. Hello, Ms. Stockton." He turned to his executive assistant. "Marge, why don't you entertain Ms. Stockton here in the conference room while Secretary Neal and I step into my office and view the mission."

"No, she goes where I go," Neal snapped.

The director shrugged his shoulders. "Suit yourself." He sat back down in his seat. "Have a seat, Ms. Stockton." The director pointed to two high back leather chairs situated around the conference table.

"I must remind you both that what you are about to see is one of our nation's most guarded secrets. This facility, as well as this organization does not exist, and what you are about to witness, never happened. We are authorized to use whatever methods we deem necessary in order to protect the secrecy of the organization." He paused giving them each a moment to think about his warning.

"I'm the National Security Adviser," Neal blurted out. "I have a right to be in the loop."

The director laughed. "We are aware of that, but might I also remind you that any discussion of what you see here will be considered a breach of national security."

"That sounds like a threat."

"I trust you won't be careless enough to test my resolve." He turned and reached into his credenza once more removing three additional PTM's.

"You're aware of the five British aid workers who were taken hostage last week?"

Secretary Neal looked at Jennifer, who responded. "They were taken ten days ago when their convoy was attacked."

"Yes, that's right," Dr. Moore interjected.

"Let me bring you up to speed though. We've located the aid workers. Our people have been monitoring their transmissions and heard they plan to execute them today."

"Unfortunately, we have many enemies who consider executions to be encouraging for their cause," Jennifer interjected.

"Yes, and fortunately for us, public executions take a little bit of logistical planning. The British military had put out a plea to all Allied information gathering agencies, to help with locating them. Yesterday we located the hostages, and since we had some agents embedded in a recon group in the area on a training mission, we requested to have our agents enact the rescue."

"You can't imagine how happy the president will be to get this information."

"The president is well aware of the events that have been unfolding," the director asserted.

Secretary Neal took a deep breath and exhaled while looking visibly annoyed that his long-time friend had kept him in the dark. He began to wonder what other secrets had been withheld from him.

"You seem a bit surprised?" Dr. Moore probed.

"This whole morning has been full of surprises. At least this one will be good for our national morale. The American public needs to know that their safety is our priority, that we have everything under control."

"Let me remind you, Mr. Secretary. This program is classified. As far as the public is concerned, we do not exist. Arrangements have already been made to credit a British Recon unit. I'm sure we will all be better served if you folks in DC would concentrate on the deficit."

Moore walked around the table and placed a PTM in front of each lady, then sat in a vacant seat near Neal. "If each of you would put on your PTM."

"Ready sir?" A voice resonated from the conference call box located at the center of the conference table.

"We're all set here."

The satellite image of a small town surrounded by desert appeared on each PTM. Many different conversations could be heard coming through the speaker on the table but very quickly narrowed to just those of the mission participants. Even though Afghanistan was shrouded in darkness, the images shown in real time appeared to be occurring in broad daylight.

At the command of his controller, Chance rose to his feet and began to walk up the unlit alley that led between two buildings and terminated at the street where the building with the hostages was located. At the alley's end, he paused and peered out into the main street.

"Honey Bee for Hellcat," a female voice called out softly.

"Go for Hellcat," Chance replied.

"Stand by for my count."

"Roger that, Honey Bee." Chance's controller, Jasmine used the satellite, which had moved into place high above the village, to locate and watch Chance's movements. She scanned the rooftops and the activity going on outside the building that contained several insurgents.

"Smile guys. I'm taking your picture now."

"You got my good side right?" Brock replied.

"You don't have a bad side, P-dog. You handsome guy, you," Jasmine laughed.

"Who you kiddin'? I know my limits, but I make up for it in other ways, if you know what I mean." He laughed and stroked his scruffy beard.

"Let's keep it clean. We have guests observing us today," the lead controller informed them.

"Ok. I have four guards outside. Prairie Dog, can you confirm?"

Brock peeked over the wall of the rooftop he sat on. "Four bodies. Confirmed." Looking down on the street, he then began to watch Chance advance through his PTM.

"Dog to Ops."

"Go for Ops."

"When we get through this mission, let's celebrate with dinner, Honey. You could come over to my place. I'll open up a bottle of wine. We can sit in front of the fireplace."

"Cut the chatter Prairie Dog Brock," a male voice commanded.

"Sorry. Just trying to lighten the mood a little. Besides if I get killed on this mission, the last voice that I want to hear is The Honey Bee. Ain't that right, bro?" Brock waited to hear what Chance would respond, but no reply came.

Brock laughed. "That's what I like about my man Hellcat. He don't say much but he's to the point."

"We're all set here?"

"Hellcat's a go."

"Let's get it on then."

Chance felt a warm rush throughout his body. He began to calculate his options for making kills at various distances as he closed the distance between the guards and him. Brock used a series of blinks to set his PTM to the same satellite view used by Jasmine. He could see everyone's thermal image, including that of Chance who was closing in and now about only one hundred meters from the guards.

"Ops. Give me one hundred X with night vision, and scale back as I get closer."

Without another word being spoken, the image in Chance's PTM changed to the eerie green of night vision, magnified one hundred times.

"Begin op. On my mark in five, four, three, two, one, mark."

Chance stepped out of the alleyway and headed quickly toward the unsuspecting guards.

The first guard had noticed the robed figure in the distance, a lone silhouette moving up the otherwise deserted street. As he got closer, Chance attracted the interest of the remaining guards. They watched as he walked up the opposite side of the street. As he got closer, he veered and headed directly toward them. The guards became uneasy as he closed the distance between them and when he was within twenty feet, the two guards closest to him leveled their weapons and yelled for him to stop. One of the guards immediately tried to contact the other that they had posted on the rooftop across the street.

"He's dead," Chance calmly said before dropping his robe to the ground. He was now wearing black fatigues, with full body armor. On each thigh, he wore holsters that contained Colt .45s, and a sheath containing his military knife was attached to his belt. On each shoulder was an empty holster, and in each hand was a silenced Sig P226 HSP 9 millimeter handgun.

A bullet from the rooftop across the street ripped through the head of the guard standing closest to Chance, causing a massive exit wound. Chance immediately shot the other in the neck, severing his artery, while simultaneously hitting another guard in the heart. The next bullet from the rooftop hit the remaining guard at the base of his skull.

"All done, brotha," Brock reported.

"Hey Dog, why don't you get your lazy ass down off that roof? I don't wanna miss our jump outta this hell hole." Chance turned his attention back to the house.

"Hellcat to Ops."

"Go Hellcat."

"Give me a layout."

Within seconds a diagram of the building layout was relayed to his PTM. A white dot appeared at the location of each hostage and a green dot represented each terrorist. A dark green dot represented the guard on the first floor.

"Kill power."

"*Negative. They have a generator. You'll have to do this one with no cover.*"

"Must be out back," Brock added as he repelled down the wall from his rooftop to the street below. "Want me to get it?"

"*Negative. No time.*"

Chance slowly pushed the door open. Clearing the threshold, he dropped to one knee and shot the guard standing at the foot of the steps in the chest before he could even raise his weapon. The silenced shot went unheard by the inhabitants behind the door at the top of the stairs who were yelling commands in Arabic. Three females were sobbing, while a male voice was reading out loud. Chance rose to his feet just as Brock showed up, backing into the doorway. He gestured with his fingers that he would go up the steps. Brock dropped to one knee, and settled into his position guarding the front door. Chance stepped over the body and cautiously ascended the stairway, lit by a single incandescent bulb above the top landing.

"Ops, refresh," Chance whispered.

The image refreshed allowing Chance to see that there was a guard directly in front of the door.

When he reached the door, Chance could hear a female hostage begging for her life. He placed the Sig P226's back in the shoulder holsters and strapped them in. After removing the Colt .45 from his right thigh holster, he heard a male voice commanding the hostage.

"Read it," he yelled to his sobbing hostage. "Read it."

"You're hurting me," the hostage struggled.

"Read it, you bitch."

Chance tapped lightly on the door with the barrel.

"Not now," yelled an agitated voice from inside.

Chance broke the light bulb directly overhead and tapped once more.

The man guarding the door flung it open angrily, and was immediately hit in the head with the butt of Chance's gun. One of the hostages was being held in a kneeling position by her hair ten meters from a video camera on a tripod. Her assailant held a large knife in his free hand. A man standing behind the camera was holding up a cue card for her to read. Chance wrapped his left arm around the semi-conscious man's neck, keeping him from falling to the floor, while quickly scanning the room. He pushed his gun forward and shot at the guard standing directly to his right, hitting him in the chest, just as he had begun to raise his AK-47. He immediately fired a second shot at the guard, once more striking him in the head.

Even though the collapsing guard whom Chance was holding up for cover took the brunt of the ensuing automatic gunfire that rang out from across the room, he could still feel the force of shells being absorbed by his body armor. He slid his left arm away from his human shield's neck, and replaced it with his right hand so he could grab the AK-47 slung over the dying man's shoulder. With the weapon still strapped to the guard's shoulder, Chance flipped it upside down with the barrel facing in the direction of the gunshots headed his way. He returned a volley of ammo in the direction of the automatic weapon fire from across the room, immediately silencing it.

As the life slipped from the guard in his arms, it became harder for Chance to keep the limp body from falling to the floor. He glanced at the hostages who were now huddled on the floor in the corner to his right, let go of his dying captive, and dove in the direction away from them. As he rolled, he felt the powerful force of a few shells hit his Kevlar, but was able to remove the .45 from his left thigh holster. Firing several shots from both guns in the direction of the shooters killed the remaining two guards.

Chance leaped up to his feet just in time to see the masked terrorist leader raise his knife into the air over his hostage with the intention of beheading her. He immediately fired a short burst in the direction of the knife, striking the assailant's wrist and causing the knife to fall on the floor. He lowered his weapon and fired one shot in the leg of the masked man. The bullet entered the terrorist's leg, shattering bone and causing his body to crumble to the floor. Chance turned his weapon on the camera man who looked horrified.

"I am only the camera man," he said, trembling while peeking over the sign.

Seeing no weapons, he turned his attention back to the masked man, now writhing in pain on the floor. He pulled the hostage away, quickly holstered both .45's and removed a 9mm from each shoulder holster. He pointed one at the man who was on the floor and in pain. He pointed the other to the camera man.

"Excellent job. Who is that man?" Secretary Neal asked, clapping at the intense action.

"I'm sorry but that's highly classified. Keep watching."

"Who are you?" Chance demanded of the camera man.

"They just pay me to operate the camera."

"Is your camera still running?"

"Yes it is. Would you like me to turn it off?"

"No. Take it off the tripod. I'm going to give you something to take back."

Chance turned to the hostages. "Is everybody accounted for?"

"You're American..." One of the women yelled as they all slowly rose to their feet.

"Yes, I was sent to get you out of here. Anybody hurt?"

"No. We're all okay."

"Stay low and hold on for a few more seconds," Chance instructed them. "Jasmine. I need transport ASAP!"

"ETA in two minutes."

He helped the woman who had been kneeling in front of the camera to her feet, then picked up the terrorist's knife and cut the bindings from her wrists.

"Prairie Dog, you clear?"

"I got ya, brotha. Send 'em down.

Chance looked at the woman he had just freed. "Cut your colleagues loose. Can you use this?"

The middle aged woman smiled at Chance who noticed that she had a black eye. "Oh they didn't take us without a fight."

Chance smiled in admiration. "That a girl. Free your colleagues and go downstairs. The big handsome guy in the door is a friend. Your ride is on the way."

"What about you?"

"Be right down."

He turned back to the man who once wielded the knife and waited until the last woman started down the steps. He grabbed the terrorist by the collar and pulled him to his knees.

"I demand that you let me go. You'll soon find out who I am," the masked man yelled.

"No, let's see who you are right now." Chance pried at the mask while his captive struggled to continue to hide his identity.

Chance tightened his grip on the collar causing his captive to release his grip on the mask. Chance finally ripped it from the kneeling man's head.

Secretary Neal leaped to his feet. "That's Omar Shakeef, he's a member of the royal family." He turned to the director. "Tell your man that he's not to harm him. We've been searching for him for months."

"With all due respect, Mr. Secretary, Omar Shakeef is a wanted terrorist. He's a former protégé to bin Laden. We'll deal with him our way."

Neal barked back, completely ignoring the remarks made by the director. "I want him alive. We can pay back a few favors with this one. The president will be pleased. You have to be able to look at the bigger picture." He grinned, "Turning him over to his family could very well force them to enter into some of the trade agreements that we've been seeking. Imagine with the election coming up we can offer five cents savings per gallon to drivers and another ten cents per gallon to the oil company. That's good for the economy."

Shakeef immediately lowered his head rather than face the camera, his downfall being recorded for all the world to see. With his right hand, Chance grabbed him by the hair and lifted his head. With a smile, he pointed his .45 at his temple and pulled the trigger.

"What the hell was that?" Neal yelled and banged the conference room table with both clenched fists. "I told you we needed him alive. We can't show the entire world that this is how we handle prisoners."

"I'm sorry, Mr. Secretary. There's no way that we were going to spare the life of Omar Shakeef."

"Damn it. Somebody's gonna pay for this," he yelled, slamming the PTM to the table.

Chance removed his knife from a sheath and cut off the dead man's thumb, placing it in a plastic bag that he put in a pocket on his vest.

He looked straight into the camera, tilted his head to the right, and smiled before following the hostages down the steps. Brock held the freed hostages at the doorway until two UK military vehicles stopped in front of the building. The hostages were quickly hustled out of the building and into the waiting transports. One of the British soldiers looked at Chance and Brock.

"Are you gents coming?"

"Nah, but thanks. We've got a flight to catch."

"Who are you?" the British soldier asked.

"Brothers." Brock smiled and saluted the soldier.

The soldier entered the transport through the open rear door. He took one last look in their direction, then pulled the door shut. Chance and Brock watched them turn at the next corner on their way to the fire base. Just as the vehicles disappeared, Chance and Brock headed down the desolated street.

Brock put his arm around Chance's shoulder. "You know brotha, I been thinkin'. You need to get out more. You know. Maybe open up a little. There's more to life than all this runnin' and gunnin'."

"I'm not real comfortable in crowds," Chance replied dryly.

"You gotta just relax. Let it just flow, ya know?" Brock turned to Chance, "Hey man, you got a little blood spatter on your cheek."

Chance wiped his cheek. "Did I get it?"

Brock inspected Chance's face. "Yeah, you got it, bro."

Professor Kimble disconnected his laptop from its docking station and slid it into its case on his desk. He walked over to the coat rack, grabbed his wool scarf and wrapped it around his neck twice, crossing it neatly in the front. After slipping into his camel cashmere coat, he turned back toward his desk, double-checking if he forgot anything. Tess, his lab assistant, had come into the office unnoticed and was now standing behind him. The professor shuddered as he turned to see her.

"Sorry, Doctor Kimble. Did I frighten you?"

"Oh no, that's okay, I've just been on edge lately. I don't know why."

He eyed his assistant, secretly admiring her beauty. She stood just over six feet tall, with a jet black pony tail that reached half way down her back. Her long frame was toned and muscular, resulting from many years of martial arts and fitness training. High cheek bones accented her radiant black eyes. A small permanent scar on her left cheek, caused by an old knife wound, was the sole reminder of her rough background. Dr. Kimble made a special effort to suppress the physical attraction that he had for the young grad student, hoping that she would never recognize his desire for her.

"I just get that feeling that I'm being watched lately." He lifted his laptop case from the desk and draped the strap over his shoulder. He then grabbed his briefcase.

Tess smiled. "They're always watching someone as brilliant and important as you, you know that."

"You're too kind, Tess. I came along during a time when people with our experience were considered invaluable."

"Are you heading home now?"

"Yes. Why don't you go home, too? Life has much more to offer than just research. I sometimes wish that someone had given me that advice when I was young."

"I know professor, but I really appreciate the fact that working as your assistant is paying for my education. I wouldn't have been able to do it any other way without this job." She smiled widely, her eyes displaying what he took for her deep gratitude.

"How's your part-time job coming anyway?"

"Not too bad. It'll be coming to an end though soon."

He put his hand on her shoulder "You're too young and too pretty to spend your Friday evenings in a lab. Go."

"Once I complete my PhD, I'll take some time off to relax."

"Promise?"

"Yes professor, I promise." She let out a small giggle. "Actually, you'll be proud to know that I have a date tonight."

"Oh really. A new man in your life?"

"No, just some old friends. We'll see. Oh, how's Megan?"

"It's Friday, so I'm sure that she's at home asleep right now. All she does is sleep, eat and party. I wish that she were more like you, Tess."

In addition to her beauty, Dr. Kimble admired his lab assistant's determination and work ethic. She had gone to undergrad on a Judo scholarship, maintained a 4.0 average and still managed to graduate with a physics degree in four years. She then worked her way through grad school, finishing it on schedule.

Tess was about the same age as his daughter Megan, who lacked drive and ambition. She was completely content to sit around the house all day eating and sleeping before going out and drinking all night with her friends.

"I may not be as good a girl as you think, Professor." Tess winked.

The professor chuckled, but then a concerned look came across his face. "Megan has this new boyfriend, and I don't know why, but I get the feeling that he's bad news."

Tess laughed, "Don't worry about it professor. I'm sure Megan will realize it eventually. She just doesn't know how lucky she is to have a dad like you."

"I don't know if it's luck, Tess. Maybe I've spoiled her too much."

Tess looked down. "If I had a father like you, my life would have been so much different."

"Cheer up Tess. I see such a bright future for you. You tell those friends to take you out and do something exciting."

"I'm sure they will." She smiled and, on impulse, kissed him lightly on the cheek. "Go home professor. I'll lock up."

"Thank you, Tess. See you on Monday."

Tess watched as the professor left. He turned and waved another good-bye. She blew him a kiss and laughed, then took out a cell phone from her pocket and dialed.

"Hi it's me . . . I'm leaving now, I'll be there soon. Okay, see ya." She hung up her phone, put it in her lab coat, and proceeded to lock up the lab.

The drive to Professor Kimble's Chestnut Hill home took him along Lincoln Drive, a narrow, winding roadway through the expensive Fairmount Park neighborhood. Though it was a dark and treacherous-to-drive road, it was a welcome relief to go home from the Philadelphia University campus located in University City, Philadelphia, where he had worked since leaving his top secret research position at Brookhaven Labs on Long Island. His specialty and expertise, nuclear decontamination, had provided him with an extremely comfortable life, having been well paid to work at the highest levels of government research. He regretted the fact that his wife, who had stuck with him through his long hours of work, and the loneliness of his being away from home on government missions for months at a time, was no longer alive to enjoy their prosperity. She had given him one daughter, for whom he was now determined to make up the time that he missed during her childhood.

Dr. Kimble continued along Lincoln Drive as it exited the park, and turned onto a narrow, obscure road barely wide enough for two cars. Thick, stately trees lined both sides of the road, and the lights from the large estate homes could be seen flickering here and there through the leaves. Mailboxes marked the gated entrances to the long driveways that ended at the front door of Tudor mansions. Some of the driveways were paved with asphalt while others were paved in cobblestones or carefully laid red bricks. Kimble turned into the driveway at his mailbox, stopping first to get the mail. He drove between the two brick columns and up the solar lantern-lined driveway. He circled around on the drive that, going to the right led to a three-car garage, or to the left curved past the front steps and looped back onto the street. Rather than heading into the garage, the professor parked behind Megan's Porsche at the foot of the tiled steps leading up to the double front doors with stained glass patterns in each one.

He suspected that Megan would be leaving soon. He grabbed his briefcase and laptop from the passenger side, got out of the car, and bounded up the steps. After unlocking and opening the front door, he was greeted by the shrill of the alarm system. Entering his code, he closed the door and stood in a large marble foyer.

"Megan, are you awake?" his voice echoed through the vaulted ceiling.

He walked through the foyer, past the living room on his left and the dining room on his right. Just past the living room were stairs that climbed up to a landing. Kimble turned right and crossed over the back entrance at the rear of the house where the marble floor turned to inlaid wood. Dr. Kimble turned right into the kitchen and sat his briefcase and laptop case on the island in the center of the room. The television in the family room adjacent to the kitchen was turned off, but he could see someone seated in the large swivel chair with its back to him. Perhaps Megan was sleeping. Dr. Kimble reached for the light switch, but when he flicked it on, nothing happened, and he tried unsuccessfully a few more times.

"Megan, are you okay? What's wrong with the light?" he said suspiciously looking in the direction of the family room.

The chair swung around, and immediately the professor was blinded by a beam from a flashlight that was now shining in his face. A raspy male voice spoke from behind the light. "Good evening Dr. Kimble."

"Who are you?"

"My name is Stryker."

"I don't know who you are. It's been a long time and the government assured me that as long as I never discussed the project that they would leave me alone." Because of the nature of his research, Dr. Kimble suspected that there was always the possibility that one day, the government would want to erase all traces of his project, including him.

"Sorry to disappoint you, but I'm not with the government."

"Who are you then?" He began to walk toward the seated Stryker and pointed toward the back door. "Get out of my house."

Dr. Kimble's momentum was halted when he heard the door behind him swing open colliding with the door stop. His head instinctively turned back toward the sound. Footsteps shuffled through the doorway, and the beam of light moved from the back of the professor's head to the commotion going on behind him. In the doorway, his daughter, Megan, struggled with Brandon, the tall, thin young man whom she had been dating. His left arm was wrapped tightly around her neck and his right hand covered her mouth. The doctor lunged toward them but was immediately met by a third man who sprang at him from the garage. He was a large muscular man and had very little trouble lifting the professor off of his feet and slamming him to the floor. The full force of the assailant's five-foot ten inch, two hundred eighty-pound frame came crashing down on the middle-aged college professor, squeezing every ounce of air out of his lungs.

Megan immediately bit the hand that covered her mouth. "Don't you hurt him!" she yelled, while struggling with her captor.

"Ouch! You little . . . " Brandon aggressively slapped the side of her face with a swift open hand.

"Please don't hurt my daughter," Kimble gasped. "She doesn't know a thing. She's innocent," the professor pleaded, trying to breathe under the tremendous weight that was pressing down hard on his body.

Stryker chuckled. "Innocent? Hardly." He raised his eyebrows, grinned widely and turned the beam of light back onto the professor's face. "But it is true she doesn't know anything about your research. In fact, she doesn't know too much about anything. I suspect that you kept her that way for this very reason."

"Please let her go; it's me that you want." Dr. Kimble made an attempt at reasoning.

"Now you're a very bright man, Doc. You know we can't do that. But here's what we'll do for you. Let him up, Mr. Hodges," Stryker said to the assailant sitting on Kimble.

The large man with the military haircut pushed against the professor's body to get himself up. He yanked Kimble up by the arm, nearly separating his shoulder. The professor grunted, then winced in pain. But his assailant didn't loosen his grip. The professor struggled but was no match for the muscled guy, especially with an injured shoulder.

Stryker stood up. "Be careful with him. If he's dead or too injured to work, we don't get paid. Let's get them out to the truck." He looked at his watch. "We've got only thirteen minutes, so let's get a move on."

Kimble and Megan were forcefully led out the back door onto the large deck, down the steps to the back yard where a white, windowless work van was waiting. The professor was still being held by his injured arm, though he offered no resistance. Megan struggled to free herself from Brandon, who was aided in holding her by Stryker as they bound her wrists with tie wraps. They opened the rear doors and used her wrist bindings to forcefully pull her inside. A third tie wrap was used to secure her to the metal framing inside the cargo van. Megan continued to pull violently at her bindings like an animal stuck in a trap.

"Don't cuff him," Stryker commanded. "He's not going anywhere as long as we have her." Hodges helped the professor get up into the van where he slumped on the floor next to Megan, holding his injured arm.

Stryker got into the van on the passenger side and pointed his gun back at the young woman who continued struggling unsuccessfully to free herself. Hodges got in the back and sat on the floor across from the hostages. Brandon closed the cargo doors and walked around the van to the driver's door. Megan stopped struggling and began to cry. Stryker grinned at her as Brandon got in on the driver's side and put the van in gear.

Stryker glanced at his watch. "We're cutting this kind of short. Let's get out of here."

"Daddy, I'm so sorry. I should have known that Brandon was up to something."

Hodges who sat across from the pair of captives was untouched by the display of emotion. His face remained cold and void of emotion.

"No honey. This isn't your fault, and there is nothing that you could have done to prevent what's happening. My past has finally come back to haunt me."

Their guard remained silent except for occasional grunts he made each time that the van hit a bump. He exhibited no sense of urgency guarding the cargo doors since both captives were incapacitated. The van moved quickly around the house and down the driveway making a right onto the narrow road on the way back to Lincoln Drive. But because the van had no windows, the professor eventually lost track of the turns and could not tell which direction they were heading.

Dr. Kimble put his uninjured arm around Megan to console her. Hodges kicked his foot and motioned for him to take his arm away from her. Megan continued to cry as the van kept making left and right turns to confuse Kimble and Megan.

Eventually the van came to a stop. They sat for what seemed to be a lifetime before continuing. The next time that they stopped, Brandon got out, walked around to the back of the van and swung the rear doors open. Hodges slid out the rear of the van onto his feet, and performed several stretching routines before motioning to Brandon to help the professor exit the van. After Kimble climbed out, Brandon held him by the back of his collar. The professor was in too much pain to even struggle. Stryker came around to the rear of the van and he and Hodges cut the tie wraps that were holding Megan inside.

With her hands still tied together, they dragged her toward the door of the van by her ankles. She tried to kick herself free, but they pulled her onto the concrete ground, landing her on her back. Hodges used her hair to pull her up to her feet. He grabbed her by the upper arm and they all walked behind Stryker through a large empty warehouse. The smell of mildew and dust permeated the air. Each footstep echoed through the large empty chamber. In the shadows along the far wall, they could see the silhouette of a big rig.

In the darkness, they were ushered to the doorway of a large empty room, lit only by the moonlight that trickled in through enormous windows at least twenty feet up from the floor. Megan's hands were cut loose and both she and her father were pushed into the room, a metal door slamming behind them. All light was now gone as they huddled on a crate and held each other, unaware of what would become of them.

Chance sat in a dark, late model car parked in the middle of the block, admiring some couples walking past him, holding hands. One man pushing a stroller with a woman clinging to his arm stopped beside the car, unaware of Chance's presence. The mother released her grip on her husband's arm, moved around to the front of the stroller and lovingly adjusted the blanket protecting their baby from the early evening chill. She noticed Chance in the window of the car and smiled. Life as he knew it was far too complicated to have such pleasures, and he acknowledged them with a fake smile. Their lives were as foreign to him as his was to them. Most people have no idea that people like Chance exist at all, let alone coming so close to and affecting their daily lives in the ways that he did.

As the evening sunlight faded toward night, the good was fading to bad. Chance looked at the unlit street light, which stood as a sleeping sentinel, waiting to guard the corner as soon as the sun fell below the roof tops. A scream punctuated the silence though, and a few seconds later a young thug ran down the street with a woman's purse flailing in tow. Chance watched the woman chase the purse snatcher but she soon stopped and bent over as if something had removed all of the air from around her. On this chilly spring evening, evil had finally awakened, and soon it had come out to play. Chance had no fear of the impending evil, as he had faced it many times before. The evil did, however, have reason to fear Chance Barnette whose sole purpose for being was its elimination.

Only a third of the sun could be seen remaining over the roof lines, when he saw the two policemen walking up the sidewalk. *Keep walking guys. Don't stop. Not now. Not today.* Chance's luck had run out. One of the officers walked out into the street and approached the car from the right rear. The other remained on the sidewalk and approached from the driver's side. Chance removed a small unmarked gray can from his coat pocket and tucked it into his black leather-gloved hand. He lowered the driver's side window and watched the officers release the safety straps on their 9mm side arms as they stepped into the car's blind spots. Chance hung his left elbow out the driver's side window with the cylinder tucked in his palm.

One officer stopped just behind the passenger side door while the other, just behind the driver side door, positioned his leg to impede its opening. His right hand was now on his gun, sensing that the mysterious loiterer may be a threat. His partner waited and watched from the opposite side of the car just behind the front door. The officer lowered his face and peered into the car, finding Chance's dark eyes.

"Could I see your driver's license, registration, and insurance card please, sir?"

Chance slowly turned to look at the officer, then unleashed a powerful stream of immobilizing invisible gas on him. On contact, the officer gasped for a breath, grabbed his throat, and then fell to his knees holding his throat. His partner drew his weapon but Chance immediately cried out for his help. "Don't just stand there. He's having a heart attack or something."

The partner ran around the car with his weapon drawn and pointed at Chance. Seeing no blood, he lowered his gun to his side and frantically asked "What happened?"

"Looks like a seizure to me."

The officer fell to the ground completely as Chance got out of the car to aid his victim.

"Don't just stand there. Give me a hand. Let's sit him up on the seat."

The assisting officer holstered his weapon and helped Chance lift his partner to his feet and sit him in the car. The immobilized policeman sat silent and completely motionless, except for his eyes that were opened wide in horror and following the movement of the two men who were helping him. His eyes fixed on his partner as if pleading for help, or warning of danger. After sitting the disabled officer down, the assisting officer turned slightly, looked over to his shoulder and reached for his radio microphone attached to his right epaulette. Chance immediately sprayed the second officer's face, then caught him in his left arm before he could fall to the ground. With his right hand, he opened the rear door and sat him on the back seat. The officer had the same look of horror as Chance pushed both men all of the way into the car, then locked it. Many passersby watched the events unfolding in front of them but in their attempt to avoid involvement, they continued passing by as though they saw nothing.

Chance was unconcerned about the policemen, knowing that the chemical used on them would cause only temporary paralysis and permanently erase their short-term memory. The lapse would only be a few hours, though they would have an extreme headache. His job entailed avoiding harm to civilians whenever possible.

After safely locking the police officers in the car, Chance retreated to the back of the car and opened the trunk. After donning his Kevlar vest, he removed two shoulder holsters, each containing his Sig P226 HSP 9 millimeter handgun. He strapped those on, then put on two thigh holsters. The right one contained an M-1014 combat shotgun, and the left, a Colt .45. His last piece of gear, before slipping into his three-quarter length black Kevlar-lined canvas coat, was his utility belt lined with spare clips for each of his handguns, various types of shotgun shells, percussion grenades, and the saif from his first kill. Last, he put on his PTM and looked up at the camera that sat atop the light pole. He acknowledged the mission controllers with a wave.

He blinked his eyes and set his PTM to night vision, and quickly moved down the street toward his assignment, a known terrorist cell's headquarters. A few blocks away, sirens could be heard racing to the area where the two police officers had been left locked in the car. Upon reaching the apartment building that contained the headquarters, he slipped into an alley between two abandoned houses on the opposite side of the street and trained his eyes on the front door.

"Hellcat in position," Chance reported.

The voice of a male controller transmitted the message, *"All containment personnel are in position. All agents hold for further instructions."*

Thirty-two minutes passed and once more the male voice rang out over the PTM. *"Hold all positions. We have one suspect leaving the structure."*

"Containment agents standing by," Jasmine replied. *"Which exit?"*

"Front door."

"I have a visual on the subject. He's mine," Chance replied as the front door swung open and a young man wearing a black backpack and a Yankees baseball cap exited the building.

"Hellcat is in pursuit, all other agents stand by. Honey Bee, go private with Hellcat."

"Going P-COM. Hellcat, do you need support?"

"Negative. Do I have a green light on the subject?"

"Negative. You'll have to get close enough for a density scan on that backpack."

The young man who didn't realize he was being followed disappeared down the steps leading to the subway, along with a steady stream of unsuspecting commuters. Though it was the end of rush hour, there were plenty of riders still trying to make their way home.

"He's going down into the subway. Do you have visual?"

"I've picked him up on our feed from the subway surveillance system."

Chance continued to tail his target from a safe distance, walking past a paperboy selling his newspapers.

"Paper, sir?"

"Nah, kid," Chance waved him off.

"Help the kid out, buy a newspaper. You'd be smarter if you read more. The suspect's not going anywhere."

"Hey kid. Paper. Here." He paid for the paper, folded it and put it under his arm "Feel better now?"

"Excuse me, sir."

"Oh, I'm talking to my wife." He pointed to the ear on the opposite side of his head indicating that he had an earpiece on the side of his head facing away from the paper boy, who leaned forward to see his earpiece.

Chance turned his head not allowing the paper boy to catch a glimpse of that side of his head.

The paperboy waved, turned and headed toward the stairs leading down into the station.

"Hey kid, where you going?"

"In the station to sell the rest of my papers. It's getting cold out here."

"Three minutes."

"How many papers?" Chance rushed.

"Three. I'll sell them on the subway, on my way home."

"Look, here's ten bucks. I'll buy the rest of your papers. You run over to that pizza shop and get a couple of slices. Then catch the bus home. They're having problems with the train tonight."

"Thanks." The paperboy took the ten dollar bill and offered the remaining papers to the generous stranger, who refused with a wave.

"Uh, where you going kid?"

"I ate already so I'll just catch the train home. Maybe I can sell the rest of these papers."

"Do me a favor. Catch the bus."

"The subway's quicker."

"Two minutes thirty seconds."

Chance opened his jacket and displayed his arsenal.

"Do yourself a favor. Catch the bus, kid, like I said."

"Don't you shoot him!"

The paperboy dropped his remaining papers, turned and ran up the block.

"One minute thirty seven seconds."

Chance ran down the steps and through the turnstile, which Jasmine released as soon as he entered the gate. As he reached the platform, he saw his visibly nervous target standing against the wall with his back to the edge of the track.

"We're running out of time."

"Let me get a little closer."

Chance paused about 20 feet from his prey. He took the newspaper from under his arm and unfolded it allowing him to inconspicuously lift the watch to the level of the subjects backpack. He began to read, paying close attention to the article about a missing college professor. He put his head down and walked briskly toward the suspect, coming to within a foot of him. The suspect bristled in Chance's direction. Chance turned toward him and postured causing the smaller man to back down.

"Yeah. It was just some asshole in my way. I'll be home in a little while, so don't put dinner away yet, honey." He turned and continued to walk down the platform.

"Hate to tell you sweetie, I wouldn't cook for you even if I knew how."

Chance glanced back toward the man. "Whaddya got?"

"Scan's complete. It's RDX composition B." Jasmine immediately terminated all cell phone activity in the area and began scanning for any transmitter signals.

"The train is coming. Please advise," Chance said excitedly.

The lead controller broke in with the command. *"Green light. Terminate the subject."*

Chance reached into his coat for his gun but the commuters were already surging to the edge of the platform, completely filling the space between him and his prey. He tried to push his way through the crowd, but they resisted his efforts, as everyone was jockeying for a good spot on the platform. When the train stopped, Chance entered the forward set of doors while the suspect walked back and entered the rear doors. They each held their positions in their respective doorways as the doors closed and the train pulled away from the station.

"Opportunity lost," he reported.

"Stand by."

The subway car was packed, with little room to move. All of the seats were taken and even the aisle was filled with standing commuters. The hunter kept a close eye on his prey using the 45-degree camera mounted on his PTM. The suspect appeared to be very nervous and his eyes reflected the terror of a man who was about to be executed.

"Hellcat?"

"Go," he said in a soft voice.

"We've secured the airwaves so there's no way to detonate remotely, but look at the left strap." Jasmine used the PTM camera and zoomed in on a device located on the strap and relayed the image back to Chance.

"Looks like a switch. Hold for a second; let me zoom in even closer. Yes, it's Model H237," she continued.

A male voice chimed in. *"Model H237 normally open toggle switch."*

"It's a suicide bomb and it looks like he's going to detonate it himself," Jasmine continued.

"What's he waiting for?"

The train sped through the tunnel, screeching and lunging and jerking from side to side. It was noisy and the lights flickered continuously as it sped along.

The first of five masked figures dressed in all-black military fatigues and wearing PTM's picked the front door lock of the building. In a matter of two seconds, he eased the door open and all five silently slipped in. One went through the door leading to the basement while the other four crept up the stairs to the third floor with their MP-5 submachine guns poised and ready. Four agents in police uniforms entered the building and began to evacuate the residents on the lower floors. In the rear of the building were three similarly dressed figures. One snagged the bottom of the fire escape with a rubber-coated grappling hook attached to a rope. Together they pulled the ladder down and climbed up to the metal stairs to reach the third floor. All seven were heavily armed, in constant contact with the controllers.

In the third floor hallway, Dalton Hardaway, the lead agent who had formerly been a US Marine and a CIA interrogator, switched his PTM to thermal imaging. The primary controller received the image. With each of the terrorists' exact locations within the apartment revealed, the controller tagged and assigned an agent to each of them. He transmitted the image with the tags back to each agent and began a three-second countdown. With one second left, the agent who had entered the basement used bolt cutters to rip through the power main. At zero seconds, the building was plunged into darkness. Each agent switched their PTM to night vision, while the door and window that led out to the fire escapes were simultaneously compromised, giving the agents access to the apartment. Each agent quickly captured his assignee without incident, and they were immediately stripped, gagged, bound with tie wraps, and forced to huddle in the middle of the floor. One agent stood with his MP-5 trained on the captives, while the others searched for bombs, weapons and other contraband.

The Special Information Network Technician (SPIN Tech), Clarisse McMillan, entered once the all-clear signal was given. She was responsible for documenting the raid, documenting the identities of the terrorists, recording any intelligence gathered, and later, designing the best cover story for the press if needed. She conferenced with Hardaway, the lead controller, and one of the other agents as the group of naked men huddled in the middle of the floor, making an effort to cover themselves.

"You're all aware that Hellcat has a confirmed saboteur cornered in a subway car right?"

"Affirmative. We need to be quick and efficient," Hardaway, otherwise known as Ripper, informed the group.

McMillan responded, "Our guys will just have to put in some overtime before the AM news. Controller, contact SPIN supervisor and inform her that we need all hands on deck ASAP."

"Copy that. Ripper, you have full authority to proceed as necessary."

An agent emerged from the bathroom. "We've got cyclotrimethylenetrinitramine and a powder keg in here."

"We've gotten the building evacuated, and I'll alert the scrub team."

"Yes, sir."

Hardaway grabbed a chair, placed it in the center of the living room void of furniture. He unholstered his Colt .45 and nodded at one of his subordinates who grabbed one of the terrorists by the tie wraps binding his wrists. He forcefully guided the enemy combatant to the chair and tie-wrapped him to it. Hardaway knelt down on one knee and spoke calmly in his ear.

"Where is your associate headed?"

"I don't know what you're talking about." The terrorist remained calm.

"The man carrying the bomb."

"I don't know anything about a bomb."

"I bet you do." Hardaway stood to his feet, removed his side arm, turned off the safety, and pressed it against the man's temple. The remaining hostages all looked away.

"Talk to me."

The hostage closed his eyes and began to breathe very heavily. "I have rights you know. I want to call my lawyer."

Hardaway laughed and turned to McMillan who also laughed. "The piece of garbage wants a lawyer."

He signaled for an agent to bring another hostage to the center of the room. The gun barrel was then pointed at his temple.

"Ok, if you don't talk, I'll kill him."

Getting no response, Hardaway shot the hostage once in each knee. He fell to the ground in pain. Another agent immediately shoved a rag into his mouth. He groaned as he lay on the floor writhing in pain. McMillan held her watch up to the seated hostage's face.

"Look at it," she yelled.

"This is the United States. We have rights here. You cannot do this to us."

McMillan showed no emotion. She looked at the scanner, then had the identity information relayed to the team leader's PTM. He motioned to one of the other agents.

"Cut this one loose."

After the straps were cut, the seated hostage was pulled to his feet and pushed back into the huddle. Another was pulled out and immediately scanned.

"I'll be damned. Scan them all," Hardaway said after looking at the data.

The third one scanned was also pulled from the huddle and placed in front of the others.

"Looks like we've got us a family here," Hardaway smiled. "And a familiar one, at that."

One terrorist was seated and strapped to the chair and another was pushed directly in front of him. The leader pointed the barrel of his gun at the temple of the seated man and looked into the eyes of the other. The standing terrorist closed his eyes. The leader turned his weapon on the standing hostage and held the barrel inches from his left eye and looked at the seated terrorist.

"Do you want your little brother to die?" He moved the barrel down and pointed it at his groin. "Or worse? You two are the last males in your family." He smiled "I know, because I killed your other brother last year."

Both hostages seethed with anger.

"If you tell me, I'll let you both go. I'd hate to see your family line die off."

The standing terrorist opened his eyes and looked toward the huddle at the man who had been seated earlier and had been identified as the cell leader.

"No don't worry about them. They're all going to hell with him." He pointed to the bloody corpse lying on the floor. "And if you don't tell me what I want to know, you'll be there before them."

"Just shoot me then," the terrorist yelled, looking directly into Hardaway's eyes. Hardaway responded by pressing the barrel hard against his temple. "Don't think I won't shoot you," he yelled back.

"Go ahead, you don't have the balls. Coward dog." He spit on Hardaway just as a knock preceded the entry of a man dressed in green mechanic's overalls. He was dirty as if he had just left the garage. He had a small unintimidating frame and sported a military crew cut. A blue and white oval name tag sewn to his overalls read, 'Joe.'

"What's he doing here?" McMillan inquired.

"Somebody call for road service?" He spoke with a slight southern drawl.

"These people are holding me hostage."

"Ohhh. Sorry, but I'm with them." He smiled while kneeling down in front of the seated hostage.

"Oh god, I hate this part." McMillan said while turning toward the door. "Just keep recording and let me know what he says." She walked out into the hallway.

Joe removed a red rag from his back pocket and unfolded it on the floor in front of the hostage. He looked at her as she exited the room, then turned to him and laughed.

"Nice ass, huh?" he smiled. "Between you and me, women just don't understand mechanic talk. Too complicated, know what I mean?" he laughed.

Hardaway interrupted, "Come on, let's get on with it. We've got business to take care of."

"Ok. Ok." Joe stopped smirking and turned his attention to the seated hostage who was sweating profusely. He reached into his overalls and removed a ball-pen hammer, laying it gently on the rag. He looked into the eyes of the hostage as he removed a medium-sized flat screwdriver and a pair of pliers from his overalls. "You know why they call me the mechanic? Well, it's like this. A lot of guys have all these special information gathering gadgets. I just believe that keeping it simple is better."

Joe stood up in front of the hostage. "Remember when you used to open the hood of the car and there it was. All engine. No frills. No emissions. Just engine. Now everything is a mess. You can't even fix one without a diagnostic computer. Now don't get me wrong. You do know what I'm talking about? Awfully quiet. Do you even speak English?"

He tapped the hostage's forehead several times with the screw driver.

"Yes, yes. I speak English."

"You know what I'm talking about?" Joe yelled angrily.

"Yes. Yes," the hostage replied excitedly while trying to free himself from the restraints.

Joe smiled. "Ok, let's talk now. You have a comrade. He doesn't have to be a comrade. I'm just thinking that he stole your stuff and is acting on his own," he said in a low calm voice, then smiled. "Where is he going?"

The hostage looked away. An excited expression suddenly crossed Joe's face. He dropped his tools and reached into his top pocket and took out a murky liquid-filled syringe.

"Know what this is?"

"Some kind of truth serum?"

"No, it's morphine." Joe smiled. "You'll beg for it right before you tell me what I want to hear. But you won't get it until I know the truth. You're going to talk to me," he yelled angrily, picking up the hammer and slamming it against the man's kneecap.

The hostage screamed in pain. Joe immediately shoved the pliers up the hostage's nostrils and plied them open, crushing the interior cartilage and splitting the skin. The hostage's mouth filled with blood.

"Where is your mule going?" Joe yelled while removing the pliers.

"Go to hell." The hostage yelled, spitting out blood that poured from his nose into his mouth.

The hostage shrieked as Joe forced the pliers back into his nostrils.

"Ops for Hellcat."

"Go ops"

"Green light on the subject. There's a protest march going on in the square, lots of people, lots of press."

"That's the next stop. Stand by."

Chance quickly assessed the situation and sprang into action. He removed his saif from its sheath and gripped it firmly in his right hand. The razor-sharp saif, which had been taken as a trophy while on his first mission, glistened as he held it in the air and allowed the light to hit it. A rider, who was sitting next to the doorway where Chance was standing, saw the knife. Just as Chance hoped, she jumped up and screamed. "He's got a knife!"

The passengers immediately leaped to their feet and ran to the doors at each end of the car. Amid the chaos, Chance ran down the aisle toward the bomber, pummeling any commuter who was unfortunate enough to be in his path. The confused terrorist stepped out of the entryway into the aisle, closed his eyes, and reached for the switch attached to the strap of his backpack. With one clean swipe, Chance slashed both straps on the backpack and grabbed it with his left hand before it could fall to the floor. He then dropped the knife, unholstered the Colt .45 from his right thigh and ran with the backpack toward the rear of the car. He shot out a rear window as he ran toward it, then threw the backpack through the broken glass, turned and ran in the other direction.

The bomb exploded in a bright blue flash on impact with the subway tunnel floor. The train shook and screeched to a violent stop. The force of the explosion sent Chance airborne, while the forward momentum of the train propelled him up the aisle. He landed hard enough to dislodge his PTM from his face. The sound of shrapnel could be heard ricocheting between the tunnel floor and the subway undercarriage. The impact was so painful that he knew his body was being stressed to its physical limit. All motion stopped and little sound could be heard except for the faint screams of the passengers who had escaped.

Chance heard his mother, Tracy, call his name and looked up just in time to see his father, Stan, reach out his hand help him to his feet.

"Wow look at my baby. You're a mess." Tracy grabbed Chance and embraced him in a hug, while tears flowed down her cheek.

"I'll be okay, mom."

"No, look at your leg, you're bleeding," she cried.

"Oh, Tracy. He'll be okay, remember?"

She kissed his cheek and stepped back wiping the tears from her eye. "I know, but he's still my baby."

"We're so proud of you, son." Stan hugged Chance.

"Thanks, dad. I'm proud of you, too."

Stan took Tracy by the hand. "We have to go now, son."

"No, not again. Don't leave me this time." Chance tried to walk with them but was unable to lift himself up onto his legs.

The couple turned and walked away. Chance could hear another voice calling his name. The Barnettes stopped and looked back at him.

Tracy smiled, "Look, I think she likes him."

The floor of the train felt warm and somewhat comforting as his mind drifted back to consciousness and he realized that the voice he was now hearing was Jasmine's.

"Hellcat, do you need medical assistance?"

The ringing in his ear was starting to subside, but a piece of jagged metal from the floor had impaled his thigh. He freed himself from the metal though it had plunged deep into his flesh.

Except for the emergency lights the entire train was dark and filling with smoke. The smells of molten metal and burning oil filled the air, and Chance could feel the searing heat through his glove as he probed the floor for his PTM. After locating the strap, he yanked it toward him, bringing the PTM within reach. He put the PTM on and found that the right screen was blank while the left one flickered. He slowly rose to his feet, bloody and still shaken by the violent explosion.

"Hellcat, I'm sending in a medic."

"No, just give me some lights Honey Bee," he grunted.

"No lights. I think the bomb hit the third rail. That's probably what set it off. It caused a power failure in the tunnel."

"My PTM is not functioning."

"I can see it. I'm sending help ... your vitals are out of whack."

He breathed hard and touched his pant legs, soaked in his blood. "No, I'll be ok."

"Should I call in a scrub team?"

"Affirmative. It's a mess down here. SPIN is gonna have to put in some overtime on this one."

Chance looked toward the front of the car. Several commuters were slowly getting up from the floor, but most were already in the next car running toward the front of the train. He made his way to the spot where he remembered dropping his knife. Not seeing it, he slowly lowered to his knees and searched under all the seats in that area, but it was nowhere to be found. He got up and managed to push his way through the escaping crowd from car to car, finally exiting out the front of the train. The crowd surged up the tunnel to the station where small emergency lights shone through the smoky air.

"Be careful. Two police officers are rushing down to the platform, and lots more are on the way. The crowd should offer you plenty of cover to escape."

As Chance reached the platform, he heard the officers yell "Freeze." Most of the passengers continued to climb onto the platform and run toward the exit. Chance noticed that the police officers had the terrorist cornered against the wall. Their guns were drawn, but the bomber had taken a young woman hostage with the saif that Chance had dropped. The blade was at her throat and the bomber held her tightly by the hair. The officers were yelling for him to let her go. His shirt was slashed completely exposing his bloody chest. Chance knew that the terrorist was desperate to salvage his mission and that his hostage would die unless he intervened. The terrorist had nothing more to lose.

Chance put on his PTM. The right screen was still completely blank while the left screen flickered off and on. He shut his right eye and approached the abduction.

"Can you see that?"

"We're working on a plan now."

"No time."

One of the officers, who was trying to reason with the horrified terrorist, noticed Chance approaching with his gun drawn. She yelled for him to drop it and stop, then turned her weapon on Chance who continued to move toward them.

"Lights, Jazzy."

"The PTM..."

The first bullet struck Chance body armor.

"Lights, now!" he demanded as the second bullet from the officer's gun ripped into his arm.

The emergency lights were turned off and the platform dropped into darkness. Jasmine switched Chance's view to night vision. Just as he took aim, the left screen went blank. Chance had, however, already memorized the landscape. Despite the pain and darkness, he felled the bomber with one shot from his silenced 9mm. The saif fell to the ground with a clank. He moved swiftly and silently, spraying the officers, and the hostage with the can of immobilizer.

When Jasmine restored the platform lights, the two officers had both dropped to their knees, the young woman was sitting on the ground crying, and the bomber lay next to her with blood trickling from a single bullet hole in the middle of his forehead. Chance picked up his saif and the officer's gun, which seconds earlier had been pointed in his direction. He fired a shot from it over the edge of the platform where the bullet lodged itself into one of the railroad ties, then placed the gun next to the officer who was now in excruciating pain.

"Chance! Your blood pressure is dropping."

"Must be a malfunction. I'm ok." he grunted.

"Are you sure you don't need help?" Jasmine asked frantically.

"I'll be ok but tell 'em I won't be in tomorrow."

"Listen. Be careful. The place is crawling with police."

Chance secured his weapons, zipped his coat, caught up with the crowd, and clumsily made his way across the dimly lit platform to the steps heading up and outside.

The commuters flowed up in a steady stream, frantically seeking the safety of the street. They pushed past a thick line of police officers making their way down the steps into the subway. Chance ran with the crowd up the steps to the surface. He sought cover in a dark alleyway a half block away, where he collapsed.

Chance heard the faint voices seeping out of the shadows, just as he had many times before. His mind drifted between various states of unconsciousness, while his body, weak from the blood loss, slumped on the curb.

"He's bleeding badly," a male voice said.

"Let's get him in now. Oh, he's friggin' heavy."

"Get all his stuff off, too. Hey, make sure to get everything, and put it in the van."

Chance struggled to open his eyes but couldn't. He realized he was in a moving vehicle. Inside was dark but he could hear several male voices. The vehicle eventually stopped and the male voices were replaced by two familiar ones, one male and one female.

"He looks terrible."

"He needs blood."

"He's a bloody mess."

"Start the transfusion. I'll try to get the bleeding stopped."

"He's coding. Get the paddles."

"Clear! Clear!"

Then the room was white, and the brightness seemed to make everything shine. He saw himself as a small child screaming and struggling violently, as his life was being ripped away. Chance looked down into his own eyes and cried helplessly, reaching out as his small body was carried away into the darkness by an angel, dressed in all white. The sound of his voice eventually faded away, and he was left with just a whimper.

Chance opened his eyes and could see only bright white light. Once again he could hear the voices, and as his vision cleared, he could no longer stare into the light overhead. He turned his head and looked at the liquid from the IV bag dripping into the tube that put lifesaving fluid directly into his veins.

"He's awake."

"Already?"

"Hurry, get him sedated again. It's better for him."

Chance watched as a pair of bronzed hands with long slender fingers used a syringe to inject something into his IV tube. He faded into a dream.

He was riding the bicycle his parents had given to him for his birthday. Little Chance pedaled as fast as he could, leaving his father who had been running beside the bicycle. He heard his father laughing and yelling for him to slow down, but the wind felt so good on his face, he couldn't manage to pedal fast enough. The wind whistled around the little blue helmet that shielded his eyes from the sun. The white fence was approaching fast and he heard his father yell.

"Turn, Chance, turn!"

Chance turned too quickly causing the front wheel to stop immediately, while the rear wheel flew up, launching Chance over the handlebars. Before his body hit the ground, he was impaled in the thigh by a broken slat from the fence. He screamed in pain, and could see his father running toward him with a cell phone raised to his ear.

Stan Barnette dropped the cell phone and quickly assessed the situation. He lifted Chance from the broken slat and covered the gaping wound with his hand. He ran to the house, carrying Chance and applying pressure to the bleeding. Tracy Barnette met them at the door and held it open as Stan entered. They laid Chance on the living room floor, where Stan continued to apply pressure to the profuse bleeding.

"Did you call them?" Tracy frantically inquired.

"Yeah, they should be on their way now."

Chance looked up at his father and gave him a wide grin. "Did you see me, Daddy? I can ride like a big boy."

"Yes, you can. You ride very well." Stan forced a fake smile, not letting up on the pressure.

"Aren't you proud of me, daddy?" Chance beamed.

Sliding back into consciousness, Chance made an attempt to sit up. His body was numb, but he tried his best to make his muscles work. He pressed hard until, even with the pain killers, he felt excruciating pain in his arm.

"Stop, Chance!" The short, portly man ran to the bed where Chance was laying. "Let me raise the bed so you don't re-injure yourself."

"Uh, yeah," Chance replied, trying to mask the pain.

The back of the bed rose slowly, allowing Chance to survey the space illuminated by bright fluorescent lights. He lay in the middle of the room on a hospital bed under a surgical light. The ceiling, the walls, and even the floor tiles were white. Counters, cabinets with stainless steel doors and a large stainless steel sink lined the walls. There were also three stainless steel rolling tables and two stools. Then someone approached his bed, coming from behind.

"Well, if it isn't Dr. Frankenstein. How did you find me this time?"

Chance stared into the eyes of the short, portly doctor. Dr. Busby immediately looked away, then nervously looked down and inspected his spotless white lab coat. Chance turned to the tall, lean woman who had also come to his bedside. They each wore white lab coats over their green scrubs and stethoscopes around their necks.

"And you've brought Igor, how lovely." Chance stared into Edwina's cold eyes for a moment, then scanned down her five-foot eleven inch, toned frame to her feet and back to her face. He admired her slender pecan-complexioned face, but she returned only an icy stare back.

"Look at you, so beautiful." He shook his head at her. "But so evil."

"And right now, Chance, you look like shit."

Chance turned to Dr. Busby. "Hey Buzz. Think you can get a heart for Edwina here?"

She tightened her glistening lips until they formed a slight pout, her eyes squinting slightly.

"Actually you'll probably be happy to know that I actually feel worse than I look."

"You seem to ignore the fact that you are mortal," Dr. Busby reported.

"How bad was it this time?"

"The blood loss was massive."

"Well I did get blown up and shot all in the same mission."

"We had trouble finding you. Had to dispatch several teams of contractors just to track you down. I have no idea how you got so far with so little blood. And you managed to avoid the cameras on the street."

"Instinct."

"He looks like a mess," Edwina said, pointing to the slow stream of blood that began to gush from the artery in Chance's arm.

"I'm starting to feel a little dizzy."

"We need to get some blood in him right away."

"Get some blood while I suture the wound."

Edwina's heels clicked as she walked across the sterile white room to a small refrigerator. She returned with several bags of blood. She hung one and connected its tube to the catheter that remained in Chance's arm.

Chance was losing consciousness but managed to look into Edwina's eyes. She smiled at him and gently held both sides of his face between her hands. Chance reached up and placed his hand over hers.

"Who am I?" he mouthed as a tear ran from his eye and down his temple before everything went dark once more.

The doorbell startled Tracy when it rang, but she quickly composed herself and ran to answer it.

"Daddy? Is that the doctor?"

"Yes, buddy. It is."

The tears returned to Chance's eyes. "I don't like him, daddy."

"Why not?"

"He's a mean man."

"He'll make you feel better."

Chance grabbed Stan's arm, squeezed tightly, and looked away when he saw the doctor enter the room. He was carrying an aluminum briefcase.

"Barnette," the doctor said calmly, giving Stan a forced smile.

"Hello, Dr. Busby." Stan nodded with a stern look on his face.

The doctor looked at Chance's wound. "Take him up to his room."

Stan carefully lifted Chance up into his arms and took him up the stairs to the room. Tracy and the doctor followed as Stan laid Chance on his bed. The doctor opened his briefcase on a desk in the room and removed rubber gloves and put them on. He took scissors from the case and began to cut Chance's pants leg off.

"No!" Chance screamed.

Dr. Busby placed his hand on Chance's head and shoved it down onto the pillow.

"Don't do that to him," Tracy yelled.

"What the hell does he care? He's just a kid, sort of."

Stanley Barnette grabbed Dr. Busby's collar and yanked him, causing him to cower and raise both hands in submission. "Ok. I'm sorry."

"Don't you ever forget what I could do to you!"

"Ok, Barnette. I get it." He straightened his collar and tie when Stan released his grip.

Dr. Busby cleaned the wound, then filled it with a clear analgesic gel before suturing it closed.

"This one is pretty deep so it may take a few days to heal, but he'll be alright. Keep him still and resting. Remember, if he gets infected, there's nothing that we can do for him," he said to Tracy before turning to Stan. "Listen, I'm sure this was just a misunderstanding, but I don't want any trouble."

Dr. Busby hastily put his instruments into the metal briefcase before closing it. Stan looked at Tracy and nodded his head toward the door.

"Come on, Dr. Busby, I'll walk you to the door," Tracy said coldly.

Stan sat on the edge of the bed and put his hand on Chance's head. "I'm sorry that I had to talk mean to Dr. Busby, but always remember that it's your mom's and my job to keep you safe, okay buddy?"

Chance reached up and rubbed the top of Stan's head. "And I'll always protect you and mommy, too."

Stan smiled and rose to his feet. "You get some sleep now. Tomorrow we'll fix the bike, alright?"

"Ok, daddy. You and mom get some sleep too," Chance grinned.

Stan turned the light off and closed the door.

Chance opened his eyes. The bright light above his head was off. He lay completely still as he panned the room with his eyes. He saw several figures dressed in white moving about. He panned the room once more but this time moving his whole head.

"He's waking up," an unknown voice whispered. Chance watched everyone leave the room just as Edwina entered.

She quickly walked over to the bed and placed her hand on Chance's forehead. She waved an electronic thermometer across his forehead.

"98.6, right?" Chance asked resolutely.

"Not exactly," she chuckled. "But you're alright. Let's get you up."

Edwina raised the head of the hospital bed a bit, and Chance sat up the rest of the way. He swung his legs over the side of the bed.

"I'll have to help you up. You may feel dizzy because you lost a lot of blood, but take this first."

She stood in front of him and handed him a small cup containing two pills and then a plastic cup of water. When he finished swallowing, she took the cups and turned to place them in a trash can at the foot of the bed. Just as she did, Chance rose to his feet but fell into her body. He wrapped his arms around her at the shoulders to cling on, and she grabbed his waist tightly. She always wore a loose fitting lab coat so to Chance's surprise, he found her body trim and firm. He felt her large round breasts pressed against his body. His heart started to pound and she breathed heavily as she held him there. Chance was tall, so he didn't have to look down for his cold, dark eyes met her laser-like green eyes. Stunned, they stared into each other's orbs and instinctively their mouths drew closer.

Edwina suddenly closed her eyes, took a deep breath, turned her face defiantly to the side and lifted him back onto the bed. "Just sit for a moment, Chance. Get your equilibrium," she said. Then she walked out of the room. Chance rose to his feet again but this time he used the bed to balance himself. Feeling stronger, he pushed himself away from the bed and began to walk slowly, then paced a bit faster around the room. He felt his power coming back. He flexed his heavily muscled arms and then his chest. He lifted his right knee and then his left. He jumped into the air, then assumed a boxing stance throwing a few punches into the air. The door opened and Edwina returned to the room. Her face was expressionless.

"Looks like things are back to normal for you, huh?" She pointed to the bed. "Let's get you ready to go home."

Chance returned to the bed and lay down. Edwina removed a hypodermic needle and an alcohol pad from a cabinet. She injected him, then took him by the hand. As his consciousness slipped away, Edwina whispered in his ear. "I've been doing this for too long Chance, and I can't stand to see you hurt like this anymore. Goodbye, Chance."

Chance woke up to the sound of waves crashing onto the beach. He immediately spotted the shadowy figure sitting silently in the corner of the room. A sliver of light shone around the closed window curtain, indicating that it was daytime. He lifted his head and looked in the direction of the petite figure.

"Good morning, Chance." Her slightly broken English was accompanied by an engaging smile.

"Hi, Cintia," he replied, trying to sit up "How long was I . . ."

She jumped up and ran over to the bed.

"Sixteen hours." She handed him his robe and walked toward the French doors leading outside.

Chance put on his robe and slipped out of bed. He limped into the bathroom and hung his head over the sink. After rinsing his face with a handful of cold water, he opened the medicine cabinet and grabbed the bottle of ibuprofen. He shook the bottle, removed the top, then poured the entire contents into his mouth and threw the empty container into the trash can. He turned and looked at his reflection in a full-length mirror behind the bathroom door. Besides the scars on his chest, his side was bruised and his leg was covered with dried blood. He had other old scars elsewhere on his body, and he knew that these most recent ones would heal just as the others had.

Chance looked at his face in the mirror, and considered that his fatigue was worse than his injuries. He removed one of several bottles of rubbing alcohol from under the sink, and limping over to the spa tub, he swung his leg over its side. With a grimace, he opened the bottle of alcohol and doused his leg with it. He felt the burning sensation of the alcohol on his wounds, but he clenched his lips tight and poured until the bottle was empty. In the corner of his bathroom was a small freezer, and from it he removed two bags containing frozen blue gel. Then he limped back to the bedroom just in time to see Cintia changing the bed linen. Bright sunlight now shone through the opened French doors, causing him to turn his head away from the light and shield his eyes with his hand.

"Oh, I'm sorry." Cintia rushed over to close the French doors. "I guess it's been a while since you've been out in the sunshine?"

"No. Leave them opened please. The air feels good."

Chance had known Cintia Vargas since his childhood. She had been employed by his aunt Mary who was briefly Chance's caretaker after the death of his parents. After the death of Aunt Mary, Cintia married, divorced and returned to work for Chance once he became an adult. Cintia had become the closest thing to a relative that Chance had.

Beyond the French doors, the deck extending outside boasted a wide view of Long Island Sound over the tree tops. Chance stood in the doorway with his eyes closed and took several deep breaths of the moist air.

"Why do you do this to yourself?" she asked as she approached and took him by the hand.

"I don't know. Loyalty. Duty..."

"Stupidity. Your aunt left you well off. She even saw to it that I'd never have to work again, and you go out and put your life on the line constantly."

Chance looked down at her. "I really don't know. It's a drive of some sort. Why do you even stay?"

"We're family Chance. You know I love you as much as I love my own brother. You're our family and we want you to settle down and start a family. You act all tough, but beneath it all you're loving and caring and gentle..."

"Alright. I get it. I just don't see anything like what you're talking about in my future."

Chance wrapped his arms around her and pulled her toward him with her head resting on his chest. "I'm sorry Cintia."

"No you're right."

"I didn't mean it that way."

"It's ok, Chance," she said as she backed away. "I'm going to go shopping. The nurse should be here in a little while."

"What nurse?"

"Dr. Busby scheduled a nurse for you."

"I don't need a nurse."

"Dr. Busby said that someone should be here to watch you."

"I'm fine. Get out of here and get some air. I know you've been sitting here the whole time."

"But Dr. Busby told me that I should keep an eye on you till the nurse gets here."

"Just go get some air, and don't forget to cancel that nurse and any others that he has scheduled."

"Here, let me help you get back in bed before I leave."

He climbed back into the bed and reached toward the nightstand for his reading glasses. Pain shot through his broken rib, causing him to lower his arm.

"Let me get those for you." Cintia grabbed the glasses and placed them in Chance's hand. She also handed him the remote.

"Thanks. Now you get out of here, and enjoy the rest of your day. It's too nice for you to be cooped up in the house."

"Thank you, Chance. Here's your newspaper. I'll be back in time to make dinner. If you get hungry, I made some sandwiches for you. They're in the refrigerator."

"Thanks, Cintia. You're the best. By the way, how did your nephew make out with those gang members who were bothering him?"

"Nobody's seen the ones around who were trying to force him to join. They said that the leader has been missing, too. Whoever you talked to really did the trick."

"That's great. You tell him that I said to keep those grades up 'cause those college recruiters will be looking at them closely. I'm looking forward to some free game tickets."

"Thank you so much for everything that you do for me, and I will let him know." She nodded her head, laughing. "So do you know what really happened to those gang members?"

"Yeah, I do," Chance said with a cold look, warning her not to ask any more. Cintia forced a smile and headed to the door. "Ok, I get it."

"Ok. Now get out of here and have some fun."

Chance rarely missed the news. When he wasn't able to watch it live, he recorded the programs and watched them later. He was constantly amused at how SPIN manipulated events that the average viewer considered to be factual, and so he was curious to see how his recent mission-turned-fiasco would be fed to the public. Chance positioned himself so that he could see the television screen mounted on the wall across the room. He laid one of the ice packs on his thigh and propped the other against his badly bruised side using two of the many pillows from the bed. After turning the television on, he selected the date and then the 11:00 o'clock local news which was airing live images of chaos outside a subway station. There were fire trucks, heavy rescue vehicles, and police hustling throughout the area. A female reporter was on the scene:

"I'm here live at the entrance to the 14th street subway station, where several people were injured last night when a train full of passengers derailed causing extensive damage to the subway tunnel, and sporadic power outages in the area. Some riders said there was an explosion, and many claim to have seen a tall mysterious man dressed in all black running through the train carrying a knife. Transportation officials refute any claims of an explosion, saying that a large flash might have occurred when the third rail was ripped apart by the train when it derailed while rounding a curve. Police officials are still investigating the claim of an armed man being in the train. A representative from the Federal Transportation Safety Board stated that, while the investigation is ongoing, the accident already appears to be the result of mechanical failure. This was definitely not an act of terrorism. Service has resumed with major delays. Subway officials ask that you give yourself plenty of extra time, as trains are running with up to 45-minute delays. Now back to the studio with Dan and Sandra."

Chance burst out laughing, struggling to find the position that caused the least amount of pain while the television image changed from the train station to the studio where a male and a female anchor were seated behind a large glass desk. The female anchor read the next report from the teleprompter.

"In a separate incident, a fugitive who was wanted by the FBI in connection with a drug trafficking ring that spanned several states, was shot and killed by police when he took a 21 year-old college student hostage on a subway platform at knife point. The suspect was apparently on the subway when the accident occurred, and may in fact be the armed man seen by several riders. He tried to hide in the escaping crowd to elude police, but was cornered before he could get out of the subway. The hostage, Kathy Wells, sustained minor injuries, but praised the efforts of police during the ordeal. The felon had been on the run and was known to have been in the area, and to be extremely violent. Police are not releasing the name of the kidnapper. Chalk up another one for our guys and girls in blue. Over to you Dan..."

"Police are looking for leads in the mysterious disappearance of Dr. Benson Kimble, a popular university physics professor and his daughter Megan who were reported missing from their Philadelphia home for more than a month. Police say that there is evidence at the scene of foul play. Sources say that the professor is an expert in nuclear cleanup and decontamination. The police are asking if anyone has information..."

Fatigue eventually took control and Chance found himself haunted once more by the dream, where he screamed and struggled violently as he was carried away. He watched himself crying helplessly and reaching out for help as his body disappeared. The sound of his crying voice eventually faded away as an angel carried him out into the darkness. Chance felt that this was the moment that his very soul had been taken from him, leaving the cold shell of a person that he was.

His dream was interrupted by the ringing of the telephone. He groped around on the bed for his glasses that had fallen off while he was asleep. Once he found them, he grabbed the telephone on the nightstand and looked at it the LCD screen to see it was blank. But a voice on the other end spoke to him before he could press any of the keys. The familiar voice on the other end was comforting and melodic. It reminded him of his mother's voice, whom he missed dearly.

"Good morning, Chance."

"Hi, Marge."

"How do you feel?"

"A few bumps and bruises, but other than that I feel good as new."

"Good. I guess it looked a lot worse than it was. We got worried when you went off line. Then when we looked at the videos we thought the worse. I spoke with Cintia and she said that you were home resting. Needless to say we were very concerned."

"Thanks. I'm fine. Got a few bumps and bruises but other than that, just a little sore."

Chance understood that the HSA had nothing to do with his rescue, or his medical attention. He avoided any further discussion by quickly changing the subject.

"In fact my doctor has cleared me to come back to work."

"Excellent. The director would like to see you in his office when you feel up to it."

"How about today?"

"Great. How does four o'clock sound?"

"I'll be there."

Chance showered, then dressed in his black military fatigues. After closing the French doors, he picked up the weapons that had been placed beside his bed on the previous night, and approached a closed door that led from his bedroom.

"Open," he commanded.

The door clicked. He pushed it open and stepped into a circular staircase that spiraled down three flights to a small subterranean concrete room. There, Chance sat down in a high back leather chair facing a console that sported several HD monitors. One monitor supplied the weather map—nothing in sight except for warm temperatures and clear skies. The remaining monitors were part of an elaborate home-security system that scanned the entire neighborhood allowing Chance to not only keep an eye on his home, but to secretly watch over the entire neighborhood, including the surrounding woods, the beach on Long

Island Sound, and several miles out into the ocean. Even as he slept, his perimeter was protected by the watchful eyes of his Sentinel System.

After logging off, Chance rose from his chair and turned to face the wall behind him.

"Open locker."

The wall clicked, then slowly opened exposing a well-stocked weapons locker. A counter ran the length of the storage space, with dividing drawers at the bottom and racks on top that held a large cache of assorted weapons. He removed the guns from his holsters, and methodically disassembled and cleaned each one before positioning it back on the rack. He then opened a top drawer that was neatly lined with full clips of various capacities and separated by make and model.

Chance removed two nine millimeter cartridges and placed them neatly on the counter. Each one contained cartridges that held platinum bullets. On each bullet was the microscopic image of an American flag that had been laser etched into the surface of the shell casing. He then removed a set of Sig P226 HSP handguns and inserted a clip in each. He smiled as he looked at the American flag engraved into the stock, then put them in the holsters he had strapped to his shoulders. The weapons were extremely rare limited edition hand guns and he only carried them for symbolic reasons. Each one was tested at the manufacturer, packaged and never fired again.

In the garage, Chance had the perfect blend of speed and power. In one bay sat a heavily muscled 1984 Trailblazer. The black SUV sported tinted high-impact windows, and inside the doors and surrounding the sides and rear of the gas tank was heavy-duty armored plating. The entire vehicle sat above a set of all-terrain tires that, like military transports, were designed to resist small arms fire and even to run flat at relatively high speeds depending on the scope of the damage they sustained. The tires raised the height of the vehicle to well above Chance's six-foot- five-inch frame. High-intensity discharge lights on the customized black grill had replaced the usual headlights, and black tube bumpers were attached where stock front and rear bumpers had been. Dual oversized tail pipes peered out from the rear of the beast to vent exhaust from the supercharged high performance engine that Chance had installed to handle the extra weight.

The second bay held a custom Ducati sport motorcycle with flat black flames airbrushed over a glossy black paint job. A small United States flag was painted on the top of the gas tank so that it was always visible to the rider. Chance had recently purchased it, and had a friend modify it by replacing all of the stock components with racing equipment, which exempted it from being street legal.

After mounting his bike, Chance put on his PTM and a helmet that had been custom-finished to match the motorcycle. He started the engine, which automatically opened the garage door, then slipped on his black riding gloves. Chance rode slowly out of his driveway and turned right onto the remote roadway that was unlined and barely wide enough for two cars to pass.

His twelve-room house, situated on several acres of land on Long Island's north shore was the last one on a long winding, private road that ended at a bluff leading down to the beach. Chance owned the smallest house in the exclusive community where the houses of each neighbor were separated by dense woods and a sharp curve in the road that obscured each domicile from the next. The wealthy inhabitants enjoyed both privacy and obscurity. It was a neighborhood where neighbors rarely saw each other except in passing, perfect for a man in Chance's line of work. A secret society of neighbors, all of whom honored an unspoken "mind-your-own-business" code, included investment bankers, an actor, a hedge fund manager, a Federal judge, and even a reputed mob boss. Neighborhood communication was typically done via email between executive assistants, but several days before each New Year's, a bottle of champagne as well as several expensive gifts were exchanged and delivered to each residence anonymously by courier. The yearly ritual allowed each inhabitant to thank their neighbors for protecting their precious obscurity.

Chance rode slowly and quietly along the road, preserving the serenity he enjoyed, as it wound past the neighbors' homes and eventually met up with the main road. The only indication marking the neighborhood's entrance was a black sign with orange type that read 'Private Property. No Trespassing. Violators Will Be Prosecuted' and a few mailboxes, lined up side by side. From the entrance, the main road made its way past several developments, shops, and a gas station before reaching the service road heading onto the Long Island Expressway.

Chance turned into the entrance to the Calverton Naval Proving Grounds, rode to the scanner and waved his badge in front of it. The gate in front of the motorcycle began to beep as it slid open. He revved the engine before slowly proceeding through the gate to a guard house twenty-five feet ahead. A guard wearing military fatigues and carrying an M16 approached Chance and recognized him immediately. His young, stern face lightened to a friendly smile.

"Good afternoon, sir."

"Good afternoon." Chance surrendered his badge, as the guard inspected it.

"Are you armed, Mr. Barnette?" The guard who barely looked 19 years old seemed to be more interested in Chance's motorcycle once he had inspected the ID.

Chance opened his leather riding jacket and revealed his weapons.

"I'll have to ask you to come inside and sign them in."

Chance dismounted his bike and walked into the guard house. His escort turned to look back at Chance's bike once, then turned to him.

"Step inside please and show your weapons to the Chief." He handed the badge to a soldier standing behind the counter at the sign-in sheet.

The guard inside the shack appeared to be older and never rose from his stool. "You are authorized to carry weapons on the base, but we just have to check them in."

Chance removed a Sig P226 HSP 9mm from each holster, the saif from its sheath, and placed them all on the counter. The Chief stared at the two guns which Chance had laid down with the American flag etched into their frames facing up.

"The last time that I saw one of these, a four-star general was wearing it. How did you manage to get two of them?"

"Safety's on. Knock yourself out." At the invitation, the older guard picked up each weapon, fondling them carefully with awe.

Chance turned to see the younger guard looking out the window at his motorcycle.

"It's a Ducati. But I added a twelve hundred cc engine," Chance affirmed.

"Wow. Talk about overkill."

Chance smiled. *"Overkill, yup, that's my style,"* he thought.

"That's mine over there," the younger guard said, pointing to a covered motorcycle in the parking space. "You from around here?"

"Yeah."

"Some of us here on base get together with some of the local cops every Saturday to ride. I think a couple of your guys ride, too. We meet right here at eleven. You're welcome to ride with us if you'd like. We open 'em up when we get out on the Long Island Expressway."

"Thanks. I might just do that."

"The Chief rides a hog," the soldier said, nodding toward the sergeant. "But the old guy doesn't ride with us. His rig can't keep up."

The Chief laughed, rose to his feet, and walked over to the window. "Damn little boys and your toys." He handed Chance back his weapons. "Look at those three bikes. Note the difference?"

All three men stared out the window at their motorcycles.

The sergeant turned back to the group. "I got a place for a chick to sit, so when you're out playing grab-ass with the other little boys, I'll be cruising with my lady." They all laughed and the Chief returned to his post behind the counter. "The safety is on, Mr. Barnette."

Chance bid the guards farewell and returned to his motorcycle. With his guns secure, he put on his PTM and helmet, then drove slowly through the base thinking about what it would be like to have friends like normal people. Any friend of his would be in constant danger and he could never tell them about his work. His entire friendship would be built on secrets and lies.

He turned right at the Provost's office and continued past a row of brick barracks. He veered into what seemed to be an unremarkable alleyway, just past the last row of brick buildings. The road, about a half mile long, was straight and narrow, edged with thick trees on either side. As he rode away, the buildings of the base were no longer visible, and he gunned the engine and sped to the entrance to the HSA compound. There, an outer gate slowly opened as Chance approached, and he drove into the holding area stopping directly between the outer gate that was closing and an inner gate that remained closed. The executive guards here kept a watchful eye on the visitor from the opposite side of the inner gate. He turned to his right and looked directly through the tinted glass. The structure to his right had a metal door and a large heavily tinted window, while several cameras were mounted inside the holding area.

A female guard exited the guardhouse through the metal door. She held up a portable retinal scanner that uploaded the image to a computer inside the guardhouse. Chance removed his PTM to the delight of the guard. She gave him a lusty smile and mouthed his name. She raised the scanner and pressed the button. When she finished, she stood speechless, staring deeply into his black eyes. For her, the scanner was simply a formality. She had seen the videos of Chance in action, and not only admired his toughness, but had also idolized his good looks. Though he didn't realize it, nor did he care, Chance was very quickly reaching the status of legend within the agency. He looked back into her eyes, and unlike his enemies, he was unable to maintain eye contact as he put his PTM back on. A chain jingled and the gate in front of him opened, as he slowly passed through, acknowledging the standing guards inside the gate with a wave of his hand.

They in turn relaxed, shouldered their weapons, and greeted Chance as he rode by slowly. The second gate closed behind him and he continued around a curve to the parking lot. His trip ended in a parking space marked 'Reserved' located in front of the metal building. Chance dismounted from his motorcycle, walked to the door and stared into another retinal scanner. The door buzzed, and Chance entered inside. He quickly perused the vestibule from left to right, where he spotted a guard behind a thick glass window. He gave Chance a casual salute and pointed to a set of elevator doors to the left. Chance acknowledged the instruction with a two-finger wave. Before going down though, Chance saw that straight ahead was a double set of closed doors with windows with wire-reinforced glass. Looking through the windows,

Chance could see that other than the foyer, the back portion of the building was a small gymnasium.

The floor inside the gym was covered with wrestling mats, and a group of people were inside sparring. He listened to their voices wondering if they were controllers but, for security purposes, the controllers' voices were synthesized and encrypted before being transmitted. This process distorted the voices, giving them a deeper richer tone. However, after watching them, Chance recognized by their lack of hand-to-hand combat skills that they were not agents, and so he assumed they were office personnel.

He slowly opened the door and stepped inside. Thinking that the door would close silently, he let it go, but instead it slammed loudly behind him. The clang echoed throughout the gym, and the entire room suddenly fell silent and motionless. All attention turned to Chance, prompting a whisper in the air, "It's Chance."

The instructor, a slightly petite woman who had well-toned arms and legs, rounded hips, and a small waist, stood solidly in the center of the room. Although she had a frown on her face, she was stunning. Her facial features were soft, yet powerful and her large brown eyes were separated by a near-perfect nose. Her lip gloss made her pout glisten, while holding her own against three men. She appeared to be in charge when she stopped fighting and turned to Chance.

"May we help you?"

Less than impressed by her squeaky hi-pitched voice, Chance hesitated and looked back at the door, as if looking for his escape route. He was, however, stunned by both her beauty and toughness. She wore black tights that revealed both a feminine figure and her lethal toned muscles.

"No, I just always seem to be attracted to a good fight," Chance teased.

"Well, Mr. Barnette, since you've interrupted our session, why don't you come in and show us how it's done?" one of the men responded to him.

"No, I'm sorry. Carry on." Chance waved them off.

"You are an agent, right?"

Chance remained silent.

"Why don't you come in and show us how tough you really are," came the voice of another. Now from the voices, Chance knew that these were indeed a group of controllers.

"No. I've got some things that I have to do. Maybe I can play later." Chance turned to walk out of the gym.

"I thought that was Chance Barnette. Must be some guy interviewing for a controller position," another controller teased sarcastically.

The agents like Chance viewed the male controllers as something other than masculine. Too soft to be agents, too smart to be civilians, the only possible purpose for them would be to serve as controllers. The female controllers were considered unattractive geeks, even though the agents rarely saw them.

Insulted, Chance slowly turned around, unbuttoned his jacket and opened it revealing his weapons. There was a sudden hush, and a startled look appeared on all of their faces. He proceeded to remove his equipment slowly, ceremoniously laying it on the mat by the wall. He stripped down to his black fatigues, and stood there, an imposing figure facing the group. Several of the male, and all but one female controller, walked off of the mat. Chance smiled and started walking toward the remaining five controllers.

"Hey!" the woman yelled, "Take your freakin' shoes off on our mats. Who do you think you are?"

Chance looked from face to face and realizing that he had nothing to gain by disobeying the command, he sat down and removed his boots. One of the men charged at him just as he was getting up. With a quick leg whip, Chance flipped his feet out from under him. His legs continued to rotate around until they came to rest under his body. The controller shrieked with pain as he fell to the floor.

"My ankle. He broke my ankle," the controller began to cry, and all but the woman in black ran to his aid. A very slight smile came across Chance's lips, knowing that in one move, he had ended any desire to see if he was as tough as his legend. He looked at the lone female controller standing before him. She had fire in her eyes, and no fear of the agent.

"You didn't have to break his leg, you animal."

Chance didn't bother to defend himself. Instead he turned and walked back toward his gear, further infuriating the woman who stood before him.

"Don't you walk away from me!"

To his surprise, he was met with a roundhouse kick to the side of his head, causing a ringing in his ear. Instinctively he turned to face her and received a straight judo punch to his solar plexus. She rolled backwards and then did a back flip, landing on her feet in the offensive position. She immediately ran back to him in a flurry of punches and kicks, some of which found their mark, sending a sharp pain throughout his healing body.

Agents were conditioned to respond to aggression with immediate and fierce aggression, whether it was at the hands of a man, woman, or even a child. Because of his admiration for this woman and her bravery, his wrath was swift but non-lethal. After grabbing her arm in full swing, he twisted it around her back, wrapped his arm around her neck and gradually tightened his grip until she began to lose consciousness. She gasped for air as he gently lowered her to the mat. After laying her down, he looked into her fading eyes, then got up, donned his gear and left the gym amidst the jeers from the other controllers.

Chance looked over to the guard station where he had entered. The guard, who had watched the altercation through a second window facing the gym, was laughing hysterically. Chance knew that the guard behind the glass would have made a much better competitor than the entire group in the gym. He wondered how long it would have taken for him to dispose of the guard who pointed again at the elevators on Chance's right. The door opened as he approached. He turned, winked at the guard and the doors slid shut.

The elevator descended for a few seconds, the doors opened and Chance stepped out into a dark hallway that was immediately illuminated. On his right was a men's room. He went in to look at his new injuries in the mirror. His left cheek was beginning to swell around the cut under his eye. Blood from his injured leg once again seeped through his pants. He smiled in the mirror, thinking about the woman who fought with such aggression. Then he got some wet paper towels and applied pressure to the opened wounds on his leg until they stopped bleeding.

Chance left the restroom and tried not to limp as he walked down the hall toward the director's office. He read the name tags on each door as the motion sensors turned the lights on. He stopped at a set of doors on his left labeled "SPIN." This was where the stories he heard on the news had been fabricated. The exact events would remain classified so as not to cause a panic or to call attention to what needed to be done to protect an unaware public from the truth that terrorists were here and seeking to create mayhem on a regular basis. He held his face up to the one-way glass in the door, but was unable to see inside. The SPIN area was classified even to field agents.

Chance continued walking down the long hallway, wondering how many eyes were trained on him. To the right were a set of doors labeled 'Control.' He held his face up to the retinal scanner and the door automatically slid open. He stepped into another well-lit hallway that appeared to be empty till a short, portly figure rushed to meet him. Chance immediately recognized this voice from his first mission, which took place before the voice encryption initiative.

"Great to see you, Barnette." He extended his hand and Chance did likewise. "Welcome to headquarters."

"Well if it isn't Mack Hackett from Yemen. I was wondering what happened to you."

"Your first mission was my last as a controller. They promoted me to shift supervisor and soon after I became the Department head."

Chance would never have pictured "Hack" to be this short, stocky balding man who smelled like cheap cologne. The buttons on his dress shirt were stressed to the limit, covered by a gaudy, unattractive tie. He wore wing tip shoes, suit pants, and on his left hand was a wedding band.

"You've been making quite a name for yourself in the field. The controllers constantly argue about who's the toughest agent. You get a bigger percentage of votes with every mission. You're sure to be the number two vote-getter after that last mission," Hackett laughed.

"Who's number one?"

"Hardaway. Well, he has been ever since Pendleton was killed."

Hackett and Chance both hung their heads. The details of an agent's death were never revealed to anyone other than the on-duty controllers and the administrative staff so it was customary to respect a deceased agent with a moment of silence. Chance did, however, feel honored to be in the running with Hardaway. He admired Hardaway, and often when in a bind, he'd ask himself, *'What would Hardaway do now?'*

"Come on. Let me show you around."

Chance followed Mack down the subterranean hallway that measured just short of a quarter-mile long. Doors appeared on the left side of the hallway about every fifty feet, but the duo didn't reach a door on the right for two hundred feet.

"What's with the lights, Mack?"

"Security. Our cameras can watch the hallway just as if it were lit. We'd be able to catch any intruders before they could get anywhere."

"What if they used night vision?"

"That's the funny part, Chance. The hallway appears to have the complete absence of light but in fact it's flooded with light just above and below our visible spectrum. Our cameras use the light but it's so bright that it completely washes out night vision systems."

Mack waved his hand and an automatic sliding door opened. They stepped into a large lounge complete with a widescreen television covering a good portion of the wall facing the entry. Colorful matching sofas and chairs were placed throughout the space, forming small intimate areas for conversation and socialization. On either side of the room were ramps, leading up to glass sliding doors. In the far right hand corner were vending machines, a large sink, two refrigerators, and two microwaves. The machines were separated from the lounge area by several round tables.

Two people sat at one table drinking sodas, while another table contained a lone person reading. Two other figures sat in chairs that had been positioned to face the television while they watched a sports talk show.

A younger, tall slender man came through the sliding doors behind them. He wore sharply creased khaki pants and a black polo style shirt.

Mack turned to him. "This is Kevin Scott, our director of information technology. This is Chance Barnette." Everyone in the lounge turned and looked.

"Chance Barnette. Pleasure to meet you." He shook Chance's hand. "Come this way I'll show you around."

He led them up the ramp to the left. The sliding doors opened and they entered a large, well-lit room which resembled the NASA control center. Six rows of workstations faced the wall to the left, which contained three eight-by-ten foot monitors that stretched across the entire front of the room. Each workstation was manned and several technicians and supervisors moved about the room. Floor to ceiling bullet- and heat-proof windows stretched across the entire length of the rear wall. Through the windows was a massive room that was completely dark except for millions of LED lights. Some were blue, some green and others red but amber lights dominated the array of colors. As he looked closely, he could see pockets of fluorescent lights in the distance.

"This is our data center. It's manned 24/7/365. These are the operators who monitor the hardware and call the system administrators if there's a problem."

"This is impressive. How many computers are there?"

"This data center is relatively small, but we have over a hundred thousand file servers within our various facilities. The largest is called the Farm—an underground facility in North Dakota. It runs at ninety-five percent capacity from September to May. That gives us time in the winter to lighten the load at each of the other centers for maintenance and upgrades. We get a five-year service life on each server and when one is replaced, it's always with something more powerful."

"Why September to May?" Chance asked.

"Economics. It's the only time that it's financially feasible to cool the facility when it's in full operation. The hot air that is drawn out of our data center is used to heat the office building we have there. The hot air that gets sucked out is replaced by that nice brisk North Dakota air."

"Also, we get communication intelligence, such as telephone, cell phone, and email from the NSA but remember, we monitor satellites, public cameras, web cams, and listening devices. Pretty much anything that the NSA can't monitor, we do. In return we give them information that they can't legally obtain so they can get the search warrants necessary for their Intel."

Chance stared at the glass window at the rear of the room.

"Those are the servers out there beyond that window. Four hundred feet wide and a mile long. They don't need light so only the sections where we are working are lit. There are work crews in the areas where you see fluorescent lights. They work in teams of at least four and are driven on trolleys to the work site. It would be impossible to find any particular server out there without being guided by the Server Locator System. The teams go out in four-hour shifts. Any equipment they say they need, once they get out there to inspect a problem, is sent to them by trolley."

Chance stood staring into the room until Mack touched his shoulder. He looked at Mack who nodded his head toward the door. They followed Kevin out the sliding doors and down the ramp to the lounge that had more people than before.

"Here's one of the work crews now." Kevin said before yelling across the room. "Hey Skip."

A young man walked up to them. He wore a white jump suit with booties and a hood.

"Can you tell Mr. Barnette here what it's like to work in the barn?"

His face remained expressionless. "Hot, dark, and loud. The suits keep us from contaminating the room with stray dust particles. We wear headbands with lights and ear protection. We can't hear each other so each one of us is required to be able to do sign language."

"Thank you, Skip. This way gentleman." Kevin led Hack and Chance up the ramp on the opposite side of the lounge. "This side here is just like the other control room but it takes less people to man."

Chance looked around the room that was a mirror image of the room they previously visited, but there were only ten operators.

"Welcome to Warehouse One. Out past the glass on this side are all memory storage consoles. Processing of data is done over there and then all of that data is stored in warehouses like this one. There is one crew out there whose sole job is to add hard drives and cabinets to hold the memory storage. All of our data warehouses operate like this. This warehouse goes out for three miles. We have twelve throughout the U.S."

"Why do you need this much hard drive space?" Chance asked.

"First of all, I have no idea how much space we even have because a drive is added system-wide about every fifteen seconds. But remember, we keep records of almost everything, including pictures of eighty percent of every man and woman on Earth for our facial recognition protocol. We know their relatives and acquaintances. We even know where they stand politically. There are people for whom their only known record of existence is here."

Chance stared out into the void beyond the windows and wondered what records existed about him. He tapped the glass with his knuckle and could feel the thickness.

"Keeps the heat and noise on that side, and unauthorized people on this side. Also we use halon to fight fires and we don't want that on this side."

"Halon absorbs oxygen right? What about any workers who happen to be in there if there's a fire?"

"All crews carry oxygen tanks in case of emergencies."

"Thanks, Kevin. Come along, Chance. Let me show you the mission control area."

Chance followed Mack out through the lounge area back to the main hallway. Directly across the hall was another door that automatically opened as soon as Mack approached. Inside was a lounge similar to the one in the data center but two times larger. Three corners of the lounge were configured into pleasant alcoves, complete with their own televisions. The fourth corner was set up as a snack room with vending machines, tables and microwave ovens. They walked to the center of the room and turned right through a set of sliding doors. On either side behind glass walls was a room with a ten-foot video screen in the front and four rows of computer workstations along the floor. Both rooms were dark. As they walked up the hallway they reached two similar rooms on either side. Two of the rooms were lit and controllers sat at each workstation.

"These are our tactical control modules." He pointed to one of the lit rooms. "These controllers are looking for that missing nuclear professor in Philadelphia. The FBI wasn't having any luck, so they asked us to give them a hand."

Chance looked up at the screen at the front of the room. On it was a world map covered with lines representing satellite trajectories. Some controllers were working together in small groups. The drone of human interaction reverberated throughout the large workspace. He looked at the screen in the other room and could see the image that originated on the team leader's PTM. The team was in an active firefight with the inhabitants of a campsite.

"This is Tac 6. They're working an active mission in Afghanistan."

"Zulu Team?"

Mack smiled, "Zulu three."

Zulu teams were small covert HSA military teams that did the HSA's bidding outside of the United States. They lived and slept in the field until their next mission. The team members were comprised of former Special Forces, Navy Seals, and Marines who could not readjust to civilian life. Damaged by the horrors of war, many had violent criminal records and were given the choice to return to the field where they would live and fight in exile or spend years doing long prison bids or execution. Zulu members never returned from the field alive unless they were too old to fight, or sustained permanent disabilities that rendered them harmless to society. They lived the remainder of their lives in facilities for disabled and homeless veterans. Families of Zulu members were informed of their deaths within ninety days of their entry into the program so that they could begin immediately collecting their death benefits and have closure.

Chance watched the screen for a few minutes and saw that the shooting had stopped. He watched the image on the screen that came from the team leader's PTM as he ran to three of his troops huddled over the body of one of their fellow fighters. He lay motionless with his eyes open. Chance saw the team leaders hand reach down and feel his neck for a pulse. Chance turned from the screen and looked at Mack.

"This way," Mack immediately said. Neither man mentioned what they had just watched.

Mack was breathing hard as a result of his lack of fitness, but he still moved at a quick pace to the next set of sliding doors that led to a large space filled with cubicles. Only half of them were being used, though the occupants in place seemed to be working very intensely, not even looking up as they walked down the aisle.

"These are our analysts. When the computer gets a hit, it's immediately sent to an analyst who investigates further and figures out if it's harmless or not. If they decide that it may be harmful, it's sent to the situation room where a group of senior controllers called the Council decides on the next course of action." Hackett beckoned Chance to follow with the wave of his hand. "This way," he extolled Chance as they exited through the sliding doors and turned down another long corridor.

"If there is a job to do, it is given to the tactical officer whose team plans the mission down to which tactical pod, controller team and individual agents will be assigned. I'm sure that you wouldn't be surprised at how often your name comes up in these sessions," Mack laughed. "Then it's handed over to the control team lead. Each team is structured differently depending on the team lead's preference. The team then moves into the Tac pod and goes to work. Some missions take days and the controllers work in shifts, but I've seen an event go from analyst to completion in just forty-five minutes. Some very large missions may use multiple controller groups, or they draw junior controllers from our junior pool. We also have a specialist controller pool, who are the veterans that are in demand. They get promoted from being controllers into a pool of their own."

"Like Jasmine?"

"Yes, exactly."

Hackett stopped before entering the next door. "Controllers from that pool work in here."

Hackett pushed the door open and they walked into a dimly lit room containing only a few workstations. The majority of the light in the room initiated from a large flat screen monitor in front. The screen itself was completely blue. They approached a group of controllers huddled around one of the workstations engrossed in conversation. The lone female controller noticed the duo as they approached.

"Hey, it's Chance Barnette," she announced.

"Wow, you're right." They all rose to their feet.

"Umm, I'd notice him anywhere," she added, lustfully scanning Chance's muscled body from top to bottom.

One of her male companions leaned over and spoke loud enough for the group to hear. "See I told you that you needed a man, but what does Chance have that I don't?"

"For starters, how about hair." She smiled as Chance approached and extended her hand to him. "Hi Chance, you look even more delicious, I mean, better in person."

The unattractive, poorly groomed woman looked him up and down as he shook her hand. He could see patches of scalp under her thinning brown hair that was gray at the roots. It looked as if she hadn't combed it in weeks. She had bags under her eyes on a pockmarked face, and the area above her upper lip was covered by a thin layer of peach fuzz. She wore a baggy gray sweat suit and the print on the shirt read "Kiss a Geek." She had worn out fuzzy bedroom slippers on her feet. The smell of old cigarette smoke was not hidden by the scent of her cheap perfume. Chance studied her voice, but was unable to tell who she was.

"And you are?" He asked politely. In his heart, Chance hoped that she was not Jasmine as his fantasy would have been destroyed.

"Oh, I'm sorry," Hackett interrupted. "This is Nina."

"Nice to meet you, Nina." Relief set in as he confirmed she was not Jasmine, causing the crime fighter to break a smile.

Hackett continued to introduce Chance to the male controllers. He greeted each one, shaking hands in the usual way but they each squeezed extra hard, trying to impress the agent by reinforcing their masculinity. "I really appreciate you guys for keeping me alive out there."

"You'd survive without us dude. How many times have you been blown up?"

"Too many."

"That's why you win our survivor pool more than any other agent."

"Survival pool?"

One of the controllers pointed to a dry-erase board hanging on the wall. "At the start of each month, we bet on who's going to get the most injuries. We used to bet on the kills but you won so much that we had to make the rookies bet on the other agents. This is better 'cause you don't even have to survive for us to win the pot." He realized the implication of what he had said. "Uh... sorry, didn't mean to say that." He hung his head and slowly returned to his cubicle

"Ok, folks back to work." Hackett jumped in. "If I recall correctly, nobody's been able to locate that missing scientist yet."

"I've heard so much about this professor. What's his significance?" Chance asked.

"He's a retired government scientist. His specialty was nuclear radiation decontamination. That also qualifies him as an expert in the area of nuclear radiation contamination."

"Do they suspect that he's working for one of the terrorist organizations?"

"Not likely. He's a patriarch. Besides the government set him up with a great job teaching physics at the University of Penn, and they still use him for advice when they need him. We spoke with his sponsor who said that he was very content with his life. Why don't you come over to my office where we can talk privately?"

They turned and walked back toward the door. Suddenly the name tag on an empty cubicle caught Chance's eye. He stopped and turned to Hackett. "Where is Jasmine? I thought I'd get to meet her."

"I made her take the day off."

Hackett looked around to see if any other controller was within listening range. He spoke in a low tone.

"She's the cream of the crop, but she only likes doing mission control, and she can be a bitch on wheels when she's not happy. I've been using her to trace $12 million that was smuggled into the states six months ago by a carrier. The carrier showed up dead, and the money disappeared."

"Think they're related?"

"Judging from the groups involved, I believe so." He paused. "Jazzy pays a lot of attention to details and if she can't find it, I don't know what these other clowns will be able to do. I don't know what I'm going to do when she's gone."

"Gone? She's leaving?" Chance pondered the possibility that he may never get to meet Jasmine.

"Some special mission that the director is working on. He's even kept it secret from me. You know, all the other controllers look up to her. She'll be difficult to replace."

"I'm sorry to see her go, too. She really improvises and adapts well, 'cause it can get ugly pretty quickly." Chance shook his head.

A brief silence filled the air. Hackett looked into Chance's eyes "Chance, can I ask you something?"

Chance instinctively looked away. "Sure, Hack."

"Talk to me about Yemen. What happened to you while you were off the radar?"

Hackett's cell phone rang just then. "Excuse me." He answered the telephone, looking away and cupping his hand over his mouth. "Yes sir, he's right here." Hackett looked at Chance and held up a finger, signaling Chance to wait a second. His voice almost became a whisper. "I just heard. He's one of our best, too. How can I replace him and Jasmine at the same time?" He paused and looked back at his controllers. "Ok, I'll send him down."

Hackett terminated his call, and took a moment to look into Chance's dark intimidating eyes.

"The director is waiting for you now." Hackett pointed to the door. "Go back out to the main hallway, turn left and it's the last door at the end."

Marge met Chance with a smile at the entrance to the director's office suite. Although she was much older than Chance, he found her to be extremely attractive. He loved the sensual quality in the tone of her voice and her naturally green eyes. Her ample cleavage revealing a small mole on her left breast and the floral smell of her perfume combined to arouse his senses, causing him to begin sweating. He quickly and instinctively regained control.

"Mmm, I see why all of the girls are so crazy about you. Look at those eyes. Come in, Mr. Barnette. I'm Marge."

"Good morning ma'am."

She smiled, and extended her freshly manicured hand to Chance.

Her hand was warm and soft and melted into his. He could feel the heat radiating from her body as she pulled him through the doorway.

"Welcome to my office. This is where I sit." She released his hand, allowing him to look around the room. The carpet was plush, the walls freshly painted and the bottom half of the wall was made of mahogany panels that matched the office furniture throughout the entire suite.

"Nice office."

"Thank you." She paused, staring into his eyes and gently shaking her head, causing Chance to feel uncomfortable.

"Come this way; the director is waiting for you."

He followed her down a short hallway while admiring her tight shapely body, and how she moved so gracefully in her four-inch heels that sank into the carpet, leaving an impression with every step. She walked to the end of the hallway and knocked at a closed door. A deep male voice answered from inside.

"Come in."

Marge winked at Chance who opened the door and entered. The director, who had been leaning against the edge of his desk reading a folder, stood up respectfully to greet Chance.

"Chance Barnette. It's good to see you again." He extended his hand and said nothing about the swelling or the cut. "Can I get you coffee?"

"No thanks, but I could use some ice." He pointed to his pant leg.

The director laughed. "Come on in and have a seat." He nodded in the direction of the two chairs in front of his desk, then politely beckoned his secretary. "Excuse me, Marge. Would you mind getting Mister Barnette an ice pack?" He glanced over at Chance. "Better get two." He sat down in one of the chairs in front of his desk.

"Looks like we're one controller short thanks to your little scrimmage today." His face tightened.

"Sorry, my instincts got the best of me."

"No, Chance, no need to apologize. Sharp instincts. That's why you're here." He gritted his teeth and clenched his fist. "What you do, you do naturally and that's a good thing."

"Well, I still didn't mean to hurt him. We are on the same team, after all."

"I always tell the controllers not to engage the agents when you guys come in, especially not in hand-to-hand. You guys are like super heroes to the controllers. Remember they watch what you do in the field all of the time, but often the reality and finality escapes them. Grady knew better."

"Who was that woman?"

"Couldn't recognize the voice, huh?" The director laughed. "I guess the digital voice encryption must be doing its job."

"It's impossible. They all sound alike. So who is she?"

The director motioned to Chance to look over at the door. Chance turned to see the woman whom he had almost rendered unconscious enter the office with the ice packs.

"How's Grady?" the director asked.

"On his way to the hospital, thanks to your barbarian over here. And my neck is killing me, thank you." She punched Chance in the arm, then dropped the ice packs in his lap. The punch was hard enough to cause pain to radiate from his sore ribs, up and down his spine, but he tried not to show how much it hurt.

"I believe you two have met? Jasmine, have a seat."

Chance turned and looked into her eyes, stunned at the revelation. She returned his gaze with coldness.

"Don't even think about looking at me," she snapped and looked away.

"This is Jasmine?" Chance had fantasized about the beauty behind the brain. And now she had turned out to exceed his expectations, right down to her toughness.

"The one and only," the director answered.

"Great job on the subway, Jazzy. A little too high a profile, but at least only the terrorist died." Chance was staring at her without realizing it.

"Thanks. You too," she snapped "You were pretty good yourself."

"Uh... number two, remember?"

"Number two? What's that?"

"The toughness pole."

"Oh please I'm far too busy to play those little games."

She turned back to Chance, secretly admiring the black eyes that she had appreciated so many times before, both on video and from a distance. In person, they seemed even more direct and intimidating, forcing her to look away. She was relieved to see a box of tissues on the director's desk, and she removed one from the box and dabbed a trickle of blood from his cheek.

"Sorry about your eye," she said calmly.

Chance felt a strange new sensation that seemed to emanate from Jasmine's fingertips. "That's ok. It'll heal. Sorry about the choke hold. I didn't mean to hurt you."

Jasmine suddenly became irritated and in her anger, she was now able to hold the eye to eye contact. "Hurt me? You could have killed me!" she retorted angrily.

"You weren't doing too bad yourself..."

The director cleared his throat, causing them both to turn their attention to him. The smile on his face reflected his amusement.

"Ok, kids. Here's why I needed to talk to both of you."

He reached under his desk and pulled out a tabloid and laid it in front of Chance. He picked it up and read the headline. *'Mysterious Man In Black Blows Up Subway.'* He laid the paper back down on the desk without reading the article or responding.

"As you know, SPIN has a lot of control over what's printed in the mainstream press, but we have very little control over the tabloids, and this is what's coming out in the next printing."

"But who reads this? As long as we can control the stories in the legitimate press, who cares?" Jasmine asked.

"Rumors. This causes rumors. One of the stories talks about the black army, a secret military group used by the government to control the citizens." He then turned to Chance. "As you know, your last few assignments have been a little less than discreet. The authorities are looking for the suspicious man in a long black coat, too. Some say he's a hero and some say he's a criminal, or even worse, some claim he was the terrorist. They're even talking about this secret army on the talk shows. Nobody's sure, but everybody's talking."

Chance hung his head. "I've tried to . . . "

"No. No need for an apology. It's impossible to save as many people as you have in the last two weeks without being noticed. It's unfortunate that the citizens of this nation can't know that there are people, heroes like you two, who protect them on a daily basis, but if the citizens know it, then so do our enemies. You'd also have every well-meaning group complaining about our tactics. We can't have that, now can we?"

He reached into his drawer, took out two large brown envelopes and laid one in front of each of them. They opened the envelopes, slid the contents out and quietly read the contents. Then they both looked up at the director.

"The most important thing that we've tried to do is to keep you out of the attention of the H.A.A.D.N."

"The H.A.A.D.N.?"

"Yes. The Humanitarian Aid Alliance for Developing Nations, a group with alleged ties to the Middle East. They've been accused of recruiting and deploying several terrorist organizations, but we can't pin it to them. They wield influence in Washington for their humanitarian ventures while secretly pumping millions of dollars into various terrorist operations as well as financing governments that support terror. They are officially recognized as a food relief organization."

"So you want to move Chance for protection, but what does that have to do with me?"

"We've decided to get you both out of town."

"No disrespect, sir, but I think I can make more of an impact here with the rest of the controllers," Jasmine protested.

"They have been known to target controllers as well. That's why we had to disguise your voices. You and Chance will operate out of a field office in Philadelphia. You'll still work with the other controllers, just not from here."

He leaned forward in his seat, braced his forearms on the cushioned chair arms, and clasped his hands. He stared into each of their eyes amidst the silence.

"I'm sure that you've both heard about the missing professor in Philadelphia, right?"

"He's the nuclear contamination cleanup expert that we've been looking for, isn't he?" Jasmine asked, regaining her serious composure.

"Yes. Both he and his daughter are missing, leading us to think that something major, a strike or a bomb of some kind, is about to happen to Philadelphia."

Jasmine sighed in exasperation and slumped in her seat. "But why us?" she moaned.

"That answer is twofold. First of all I wanted to get you two out of the limelight for a while, and then our Philadelphia agent Dylan Rice blew his knee out last week. I need a good agent in Philadelphia to disrupt any possible terrorist plot and to find Dr. Kimble. The government wants him back safe and sound. Your primary focus will be on finding the professor and making sure that national security hasn't been compromised."

"Has there been any word from his colleagues?" Chance asked.

"His assistant came to work but she said that she hadn't heard from him, and that it's not like him to not call if he is going to be gone from the office. We're taking this one very seriously."

"What about the local police? What are they doing about it?"

"Don't worry about them. The F.B.I. has asked us to jump in and give them a hand in finding him because, quite frankly, we don't need warrants and we are free to interrogate in any way that we need to. Your job," the director said as he handed Chance a police detective badge, "is to work out of the 25th precinct, on loan from an outside agency. The Philadelphia Police Commissioner has promised that the department will cooperate fully with the investigation, and will supply you with any resources you need to find Dr. Kimble."

"How does being a police officer help me? I'm an agent."

"You'll be a police detective to be exact. That will give you freedom to snoop around without looking suspicious. It's in your line of duty to ask questions."

The director relaxed back into his executive chair and handed them two thicker envelopes. Chance and Jasmine responded by slitting open their packages finding that each contained a booklet, a passport, a Pennsylvania driver's license, house keys and credit cards.

Jasmine inspected the driver's license. "Uh... what's this?" She inquired in a confused tone; her driver's license read *Jasmine S. Barnette*.

The director laughed, "Oh, yes, I forgot. I now pronounce you man and wife." He placed a marriage certificate on the desk between them. "It's perfectly legitimate."

"I'm not doing that," she reported stubbornly before leaping from her seat. She walked toward the door, but instead of exiting, began to angrily pace back and forth.

The director turned to Chance. "Do you have any problems with this scenario?"

Chance glanced over at Jasmine and smiled at the director. "Yeah, can we stop off at some Caribbean island for a honeymoon on our way to Philadelphia?" He laughed. "Where would you like to go, honey?" he mocked.

Jasmine mumbled as she paced. "I'm *not* working in a field office. *Not with him.*"

"Jasmine, if you don't like it, I'll option you out later, but I really need you to do this. Have a seat, there's something else."

Jasmine returned to her seat and sat down crossing her legs under her body in the chair. The director removed a small box from his desk. He opened it and sat it in front of Jasmine. To her delight, the box contained his and hers wedding bands and a 2-karat engagement ring. Jasmine glowed as she removed the diamond ring from the box. The director smiled, thinking that the issue was now closed.

"Not exactly how I expected this to happen, but it definitely makes me feel a little better. But do I really have to be his wife?" Jasmine protested.

"You'll get used to it," the director said sternly. "Time to move on. SPIN is getting the house ready. Jasmine, you'll have to let them know what equipment you need, and use the credit cards for personal stuff. As usual there's no limit. Contact control for any operational gear that you need."

"Are you sure that this is all a good idea?" asked a slightly amused Chance.

"A good idea and a necessity." The director was all business now. "I want both of you to report to SPIN tomorrow morning for wedding and college pictures. They'll start to brief you on your background lives."

"I am still not happy with this, sir. We need to talk," Jasmine protested.

"You know my door is always open, so stop by whenever you want." The director stared at her.

Jasmine got his message. She stood up and stormed out of the room, slamming the door behind her.

The director looked at Chance and smiled. "Wow, she really likes you."

"Funny, I didn't get the same feeling."

"She's got a bit of a temper but she'll get used to the idea. You've got to admit, she's a hell of a controller. Don't worry I'll talk to her. She's been like a daughter to me. She'll listen and see the importance of the mission."

"I just don't want any friction. I have to be able to trust my mission controller one hundred percent."

"Chance, you know that won't be a problem with Jasmine. She takes her job seriously; besides she's a very nice young lady, a little high strung, but you'll enjoy her company. You two will make quite a team on this case—and we need results fast."

Chance took the envelope. "What do I have to lose?"

"Looking at the mission recap video, I thought that you'd be in really bad shape, then when you went missing for a couple of days, I thought the worse. I'm just glad to see that you're ok, but I want you to take a couple of days off to recuperate while SPIN gets the house ready."

"What do I do for a couple of days?"

"Do what everybody else does on days off."

Chance shrugged.

"Thank you sir, but I don't think I need any time to recoup."

"Listen, Barnette," the director said, placing both forearms on the desk and leaning forward. "An injured agent is not much good to me, besides you need to give the construction crew time to do their job preparing your house."

Chance hung his head. "Whatever you say, sir."

"Now get out of here. Get your stuff packed."

Chance and the director both rose to their feet and shook hands.

"And stop by the infirmary and see the doctor about that leg."

Chance looked at his leg and was surprised to see a large wet spot. His wound was re-injured when he sparred with the controllers.

Throughout his adolescence, Chance had excelled as a student and athlete, while remaining relatively isolated with respect to his peers. He found solace in the company of some of his teammates on the football and wrestling teams, especially among those who appeared to have a penchant for sadistic or aggressive behavior. He compared himself to the "big lion" that roams the plains, hunting in solitude. And as he grew older, he felt a constant need to measure up to the other lions.

On the day before he was scheduled to go to Philadelphia, Chance got up early and polished his motorcycle until he could see his reflection in the paint as well as the chrome. He slowly poured the additive given to him by his mechanic into the fuel tank, being careful not to spill any on the paint. After dressing in his matching leathers, he breathed life into the engine and sat for a moment listening to it purr. He backed the machine out into the driveway. Once the door closed, he rode slowly down his street, being careful not to disturb the tranquility of the neighborhood.

Several riders were already at the gate with David, waiting for others to arrive. He introduced Chance to the waiting group and to each of those who arrived after him. The final rider arrived on a custom built sport motorcycle. Chance doubted it was even street legal, but then neither was his Ducati.

"Sorry to keep you guys waiting but we had a big drug raid this morning. A lot of guys getting arrested means a lot of paperwork," said Rob McNeil, who happened to be a Captain on the state trooper force.

David interrupted. "This is Chance. He works here at the base."

"Nice to meet you Chance. You a cop?"

"No."

"Well about half of us are, but like I tell all the other non-officers, if the troopers chase you, just keep riding to River Head. The first gas station you get to on the right after the expressway ends, I'll be there waiting and I'll vouch for you. Ok, let's roll fellas."

"Rob's a trooper captain," David informed Chance. "He's crazy and his bike isn't even street legal."

"I figured that. Let's go."

Within less than a mile, the group was clipping along in the express lanes of the L.I.E. traveling at 80 mph. David was the first rider to break away from the pack. With a car in the left lane, passing a car in the center lane, David broke from the left all the way over to far right lane and powered past the two cars before returning to the outer lane. The remaining riders including Chance followed suit. The guys took turns upping the speed, challenging each other. The further they traveled the fewer cars they had to share the road with. With each increase in speed, riders who couldn't handle it fell behind. Some were defeated by fear, while others were held back by the capabilities of their machines. The pattern continued until the lead riders were Rob and David, with Chance following closely behind.

The two riders had gained Chance's respect, and he knew that the remaining guys would lose capability before they lost heart. Rob upped the ante and began to pull away from David, forcing Chance, who had yet to make a break away, to pass him. His tachometer red lined while Rob continued to increase his speed. Chance had no limits to his nerve and had not yet exceeded his machine's capability. He shifted to a higher gear and powered his thoroughbred past Rob. He continued to accelerate until he could see only Rob in his rear view mirror. The cars on the highway seemed to be parked as Chance weaved his way around them.

His ride ended fifteen seconds ahead of Rob, who finished about twenty seconds ahead of David, as they pulled in to the gas station lot. Chance once more felt like the alpha of alphas.

His Bronco rumbled into Philadelphia with his motorcycle in tow. Chance turned right at a large abandoned house, at one time the family home of a wealthy shipping merchant. It was abandoned during the Great Depression, and after World War II converted to a multi-family dwelling. As the neighborhood declined, so did its desirability, and the house eventually became a boarding home for the aged. A few years later, it was abandoned entirely. It now served as the self-proclaimed headquarters of a local bunch of hooligans who called themselves the 52nd Street gang who used it without fear for their open air drug trade.

He drove to his new home in the middle of the block, scanning the exterior for any telltale signs of surveillance equipment. The large detached, formerly abandoned house stood in the middle of the block as a testament to the urban blight that had overtaken the neighborhood years before. HSA engineers, disguised as contractors, had converted the one-family home into a high tech fortress. The house had been completely gutted and reinforced with steel beams. Metal armor plates were installed between the beams, then the inside walls were covered with a layer of Kevlar before the interior walling was finished. The windows were all replaced with a high-tech bulletproof polymer. Surveillance and communications equipment, including a satellite up-link dish, rested in a recess built into the roof. Small cameras were strategically placed inside various exterior decorative ornaments at the front and rear of the house, while larger more powerful cameras were installed on the roof and on the tops of several utility poles in the area.

Satisfied that no surveillance equipment could be seen on the house, Chance turned his SUV into the narrow driveway that passed between his home and the neighbor. The driveway ended at a large new detached two-car garage at the rear of the backyard, which bordered an alleyway. Chance parked and entered a gate into the back yard, then bounded up the steps through the opened back door. Just inside, Jasmine was talking to an older woman who stopped talking and stared at him as he came through the doorway. Jasmine turned and leaped up onto Chance, wrapping her arms around his neck and her legs around his waist, squeezing his hidden guns against his sore ribs between her thighs. Chance winced in pain, so he retaliated by grabbing her rear with both hands.

"Honey, not in front of the company," she whispered, lowering herself back to her feet and removing his hands to push him away gently.

"But I missed you sooo much, sweetheart," Chance teased. He smiled at Jasmine who now had her back to the elderly woman and responded by sticking out her tongue and crossing her eyes.

She took him by the hand and pulled him toward their guest.

"Mrs. Johnson. This is my husband, Chance. Mrs. Johnson lives next door."

"Wow, our first guest. Nice to meet you." He took the woman's hand and gently shook it.

Mrs. Johnson's eyes lit up. "It's a pleasure," she said turning to Jasmine. "He's a big cute one, honey."

"Yep, he's my big ole crime fighting hunk."

"Jasmine told me that you were a police officer," Mrs. Johnson said, nodding her head in approval. "Well let me leave you two alone. Maybe sometime soon I'll hear little footsteps over here. That would be so nice."

"We'll start working on it right away," Jasmine laughed. She ushered Mrs. Johnson out the back door and down the steps.

Chance watched as the elderly lady walked out of the gate across the driveway, where she disappeared behind a tall wooden fence. Chance went out and met Jasmine in the yard.

"Did they give you a key to the garage?"

"Yep," she grinned, teasing him.

"Well, can I have it I need to put my bike in?"

Jasmine reached into her pocket, pulled out a small automatic door remote control and handed it to him. "There's no more room, though."

"No more room?" Chance pressed the green open button.

"Nope."

The door opened to reveal a 60's-era yellow Volkswagen Beetle, with a large flower decal on the back. Next to it was a tarp covering a second car.

"What's that?" Chance said, pointing at the Beetle.

"My car, of course."

"No. What's that on it?"

"A flower," she laughed, looking at Chance's sarcastic frown.

"You actually drive this?"

"Yeah, silly. It's a classic."

"Classic? This belongs in a museum."

Chance turned and pointed at the gray tarp covering the second car. He looked back at Jasmine, who was stifling her giggles, then back to the tarp. He slowly removed the tarp, revealing a 1969 Shelby Cobra. Its black metal flake paint glistened with every shift of position, even in the shade of the garage. Red and black leather seats looked as if no one had ever had the privilege of sitting on them. Behind each seat, a chrome roll bar extended upwards. Chance ceremoniously folded the tarp and laid it on a shelf at the rear of the garage, all the while admiring the esthetics of this classic beauty.

"This is my other car. You like it?"

"This is a kit right?"

Jasmine was beaming, as she walked over to the driver's side door, got on it and swiftly swung her legs into the cockpit, gracefully lowering herself into the seat. For a moment, Chance's attention was drawn away from the car to Jasmine's bronzed legs, exposed by the short summer skirt that she was wearing. His spell was immediately broken when she started the engine. The entire structure of the garage shook as the beast rumbled inside it, and at that moment Chance knew that this car, like its owner, was an original.

"Nah. It's authentic." Jasmine climbed out of the running car and gazed at Chance, her eyes glowing with sexual tension. "Nothing turns a girl on like a big powerful snake." She sashayed out the garage door, leaving Chance next to the running Cobra.

Once outside, Jasmine turned back to business. "The Beetle keys are on the ring. You can park it in the driveway. C'mon and look at what they did in the house." Chance stood for a moment admiring the curves that make the Shelby Cobra unique. The flawless black paint job made the vehicle's surfaces glisten, while its curves were accented by chrome trim. Chance reached into the car and turned off the ignition, then exited the garage, closed it, and followed Jasmine through a gate in the chain link fence that led into a small landscaped back yard. Freshly planted flowers lined the walkway that crossed the yard and led to the steps that climbed up to the back door and into the kitchen. The space was spotless and sterile. Brand new cabinets and granite counters adorned one side of the kitchen, while a teakwood table and solid teak chairs were on the opposite side under a window overlooking the driveway. A stainless steel oven, refrigerator, microwave and flat-top electric range were matched to an assortment of stainless steel small appliances and utensils on the counter tops. The room looked as if it were ripped from the pages of a classy home design magazine.

"Looks like a real chef's dream. Too bad you can't cook."

Jasmine laughed, then squared off with him and punched Chance lightly in the belly. "Funny, you."

Chance could suddenly feel his heart pounding in his chest as he faced her. He had felt this sensation before, but it was usually when he was trying to dispose of a bomb or when he had a gun pointed at his head. He found himself staring deeply into Jasmine's eyes, her dark eyes staring back in a moment of awkward silence which caused him to look away.

"Um, yeah," Jasmine said after quite a few seconds seemed to tick by, breaking the spell. "Come on, I'll show you the rest of the house."

"Yeah, good idea."

Along with a hutch filled with expensive china and a huge pedestal mahogany table with a place settings for six, the dining room had several original paintings, in various stages of completeness, hanging on the walls.

"Are these yours?" Chance asked.

"Helps me to relax. Maybe you should try it sometime. You need something to balance with the death and destruction."

The living room was completely furnished with a sofa, two plush chairs and a large coffee table covered with Home and Garden and Architectural Digest magazines. On the wall hung an 84-inch HD television. They continued over to the staircase and climbed to the second floor. The top landing was a large open space on which stood an easel and a table full of art supplies. From there, they walked down the hallway to the left and Jasmine opened the first door on the right.

"This is our control room."

On the right-hand wall was a console stretching the entire length of the room. Several keyboards and track balls were visible along the length of the console, and a row of 20-inch flat screen monitors sat on the console. Each one was angled so that it could be viewed from the center of the console, right where Jasmine had seated herself in a high-back leather chair. A second row of monitors was positioned above the first row, with a 42-inch screen directly in the middle. The wall to the left was entirely covered by racks of computer equipment. On the far wall stood a vent-free air conditioning unit.

Chance looked over the monitors, each screen showing a different image, and on the one directly in front of Jasmine, there was a flow of constantly changing textual information. Some screens displayed images from the cameras installed throughout the neighborhood. One view showed the Shelby Cobra in the garage. Two screens were filled completely with messenger sessions.

Chance pointed to one of the message screens. "You don't get out too much, do you?"

Jasmine looked down at the floor, clearly annoyed.

"Hey. Sorry. I didn't mean to . . . "

"Don't worry about it. You're probably right. I'll never meet a nice guy sitting in front of this computer screen all the time. In fact, the only people that I hang out with are the other controllers. Maybe one day I'll get rescued by a man that I could love."

"I kind of know how you feel. I spend my whole life running and gunning. Sometimes I watch couples . . . I mean people, and I wonder what it would be like to live a normal life."

Jasmine spun around in her chair with a smile. "Yeah me too, with two children and a dog."

They looked into each other's eyes and it quickly became an awkward stare, forcing Jasmine to spin back around in her chair.

Chance had been taught by his high school coaches, Take a deep breath, exhale slowly, It calms the nerves.

"Uh . . . Who are all of those messages from anyway?"

"Ok . . . Umm . . . " she giggled nervously "Those are the other controllers. If there were on a mission right now most of them would be doing surveillance work and supporting us primary controllers. They watch our backs while we watch yours."

She pointed to the screens that showed images of the neighborhood. "For instance, if there were a mission going on, we'd see all of the images related to the mission on these, and this one . . . " She pointed at a screen that had a split image of the front and rear of the house.

"This one watches our backs in the house." Jasmine slid her finger across the screen, making the image pan. "Here, you can move it around to check the perimeter."

Chance moved the camera around until he saw a teenage boy dribbling a basketball. Suddenly the image on the screen blanked out. He held his hands up.

"I didn't do it."

Jasmine giggled. "It's not your fault. It's a bad connector on the wire. They didn't have one long enough so they had to splice it. Didn't do a good job though, but they'll fix it. Trust me. If you had broken it, I would have broken your hand."

"So beautiful, yet so violent." Chance shook his head.

"Come on." She grabbed a key fob from the desk in front of the center monitor, and led Chance out of the control room.

"This is your room."

She opened the door directly across the hallway from the control room. A window overlooking the driveway was on the facing wall. On the left was a bed and nightstand while on the right, a set of double doors flanked by a desk on one side and a large chest of drawers on the other. Jasmine flung open the double doors to reveal a walk-in closet where a metal bar spanning the entire length of the closet held Chance's wardrobe.

"Now. Repeat after me. 'Simon says Open.'"

"Simon says Open?" The entire rack of clothes and the rear wall of the closet to rise into the ceiling, revealing Chance's cache of weapons and ammo. "Nice, but Simon says Open?" he inquired.

"Guess how you close it."

"Simon says Close?" The weapons locker closed. Chance shook his head, "We have to change that."

"I sleep in the bedroom next to yours, and the bathroom is right across the hall from my room. I hope you don't mind looking at a bathroom full of girlie stuff every day," Jasmine warned, as Chance pondered the idea of sharing his space and decided that, if he had to, he could always retreat to his Long Island hideout.

"Any word on that professor yet?"

"No. The others are still looking, but now it looks like his assistant is missing too. Now nobody's heard from her either."

The darkness was suddenly disturbed when the metal door was flung open. Doctor Kimble and his daughter shielded their eyes. Though the brightness of the sunshine had been dimmed by the structure's high dirty windows, after being in complete darkness, any light was blinding. Before their eyes had even begun to adjust, they were both forcefully pulled from the confines of the damp side room into the expansive warehouse room, where they stood with their eyes squinting and their heads down.

One at a time, they were escorted to a lavatory that included a sink and a toilet. The professor went first and when he came out, Hodges led him up a flight of metal stairs to a metal catwalk that stretched across the entire side of the building. They approached another metal door, which he opened and then pushed the professor into a laboratory, filled with scientific equipment on metal shelving. Through the shelving units, he could see a woman sitting at a workbench with her back to the door.

His captor allowed him to walk freely along a shelf until he reached an opening between units. He turned toward the woman in the chair, and walked slowly toward her. Tess turned to face the professor, smiling warmly as he approached.

"Hello Dr. Kimble." Her smile departed as she noted the professor's confused expression. "Surprised to see me here?"

"Tess. What are you doing here? What's going on?"

"I told you I wasn't as innocent as you thought."

"But what are you doing here?"

"I'm struggling. That's why we needed you."

"But for what?"

"Stick around and you'll find out."

"Are you in trouble, Tess?"

"No not at all. In fact, it's sort of my idea," she laughed to herself. "Well actually, it's your idea. I'm just bringing it to fruition."

She paused for a moment, staring coldly into his eyes, then rose to her feet. "What about your career? Your future?"

"What future? You think my future looks good? As it stands, I'll be paying my student loan till I retire. Sorry, I'll take my chances working for the highest bidder and do what I can to help my people."

"But how could you betray me like this? I trusted you. I gave you access to my personal research." His eyes began to fill up.

"How touching," Stryker said clapping as he entered the room with Hodges and Megan. "And who have you betrayed doc? I'm sure you screwed a lot of people along the way."

"I've always been a fair man. Obviously, a little too trusting."

"Like with that pretty little wife. You left her alone for months at a time, then questioned whether your only child was really yours. Then you left her for years to die from a broken heart."

Megan charged at Stryker, but he connected a backhand with the side of her face, knocking her to the ground. Dr. Kimble lunged toward Stryker who quickly took out a Colt .45 and pointed it at his head, stopping his advance. He quickly turned the weapon on Megan who was struggling to get to her feet.

Suddenly a sinister chuckle emanated from a dark corner of the room just before another familiar character stepped into the light and toward the professor. "Dr. Kimble." He smiled as he approached. "Maybe I can shed a little light onto the subject."

"Gaylord Poole?"

"Don't look so surprised."

Gaylord Poole was a very tall thin man who stood 6' 8" though he only weighed 200 pounds. He was a well-known history professor at the university who constantly challenged popular history facts. The chairman of the history department had given him bad reviews and tried to terminate his employment, but each time his job was saved by a powerful, yet mysterious unknown supporter.

"You've known for a long time how I feel about the government. It's time for a change and that change has to start with the US Constitution."

"Come on Poole. You can't be serious. What are you and your little band of rebels here going to do? Overthrow the government of the United States?" He turned and glanced at Stryker.

"Don't look at me. I'm just a hired hand. You wouldn't be able to find enough fighters to overthrow the government. I've been in the military and trust me on that one."

"You took an oath to defend this nation."

"Oh you mean this nation that kicks you to the curb when you can't serve any more? Look at the homeless vets, or go visit a veterans rehab facility, or better yet . . . ask Mr. Hodges here how you treat your faithful." Stryker shook his head. "No I'm not going out like that. I offer my services for money placed in an off-shore account."

"Kimble. You're such an idealist. I represent U.S.A.L.A. That's the United States of America Liberation Army. We plan to take back America and start all over again with a new congress and a new constitution. We don't want slaves, we don't want the tired, we don't want the poor, or the huddled masses. We want to preserve America for those of us who started it, those of us who can afford to live here. We want to send everybody else home. If they want freedom, let them fight for it themselves, just like my ancestors did," Poole said.

"But you yourself said that your ancestors were Irish immigrants who moved here to make a better life for themselves."

Poole laughed. "You're absolutely right and we did. That's one of the tenets to be included in the new constitution. It's not that your family was here from the beginning but if your family has been here for hundreds of years and you haven't picked yourself up by the bootstraps and made something of yourselves, then we have no place for you here."

"Come on. Everybody hasn't had the same chances or opportunities."

"For crying out loud Kimble. Your family made it as well as mine. Nobody was able to stymy our determination. If the chances or opportunities weren't there then your ancestors should have created them."

Dr. Kimble shook his head.

"Don't you dare look down on me or my ideas," Poole said angrily.

"What do you want from us?"

"That's much better," Poole nodded. "We want to render The Independence Mall uninhabitable along with the copy of the Constitution that they keep there."

"Do you really think that they would store an authentic copy there?"

"It's purely symbolic Dr. Kimble. Besides you know and I know that the average citizen is asinine enough to believe that it's the real one."

"I thought it was the original one," Brandon blurted out.

"Shut up, you idiot," Megan responded.

Stryker looked at him and shook his head while Hodges slapped him on the back of his head.

"Dumb-ass," he added.

"Sounds like you already have a plan. So what do you need us for?"

"We originally wanted to get our hands on some decent quality weapon's grade plutonium. Unfortunately most of the countries where we could find the good stuff keep it well out of reach. That left us with two choices. Russia still has some old depleted stores of cold war plutonium and Iran, who just sucks at enriching plutonium. We opted for the Iranian weapons grade garbage because we got an excellent price for it," Poole reported.

"We need to use the low grade supply, and get the same results as better quality plutonium," Tess added.

"There seem to be plenty of easier ways to destroy Independence Hall than a nuclear detonation."

"We don't want to destroy it," Poole laughed. "We want to leave it just as it is as a reminder of the old United States."

"So what do you plan to do?"

"Create a nuclear cloud with Independence Hall at the epicenter. Our government take- over has already begun and we'll eventually introduce our New Constitution for a newly built Independence Hall."

"Let Megan go and I'll help you."

"As soon as we let her go, your government cronies will put her in hiding and you'll do something stupid and we'll end up killing you."

Tess stood up from her chair, and walked to within inches of the professor allowing her breasts to touch him slightly and engage in a lusty stare.

"Get away from my father or I'll kick your ugly ass... bitch."

Hodges grabbed her before she could charge at Tess.

"You've got to finish the job or they'll kill you. Then they'll kill Megan. Trust me," Tess pleaded.

"I did at one time."

Poole walked over and stood next to Tess. "She's absolutely right. We've been given a green light to do whatever it takes to get you to cooperate. I'm not a man that you want to mess with. Now the sooner that you and miss cutie pie here get finished, the sooner that you can go home."

Poole stroked Tess' hair but she immediately grabbed his thumb and forearm and drove him to his knees before letting go. Stryker, Hodges and Brandon all laughed and Kimble shook his head. Poole leaped to his feet as did Tess who then shoved him. He looked at Stryker angrily.

"So you'll just sit there and let this happen? What am I paying you for?"

Poole's eyes widened and his bottom jaw dropped as Tess stepped back and Stryker walked to Poole who retreated until he backed into a table which was already against the wall. He removed a gun from its holster and pressed it tightly against Poole's forehead.

"Don't forget, men like you always need men like me." Stryker holstered his weapon and walked away.

"I'll have you know that I'm more than capable of taking care of myself. I possess a black belt in Kung Fu."

Stryker turned to Tess. "Are you afraid of him?"

"Hell no," she replied with a smile.

"Ok. I'm on the clock. Hodges and Brandon take that little bitch downstairs so the Doc can get to work."

"Good idea," Poole agreed.

"Let Megan go now. I'll finish the job," Dr. Kimble yelled out.

"No, professor. The job first, then I'll let you both go."

Chance opened the front door, stepped out onto the stoop and walked down three steps to the sidewalk where his SUV was parked on the street. The morning air was crisp and an orange glow could be seen rising over the rooftops, through the thin fog. Next door, Mrs. Johnson was sweeping the curb in front of her house. She was still wearing her robe and slippers. Up and down the street, the pavement was strewn with litter from the night before.

"Nice morning." Chance smiled.

"Good morning. On your way to work?"

"Sure am. Are we the only ones up this early?" Mrs. Johnson shuffled over to Chance. "There are a lot of seniors who live here and nobody will come out till the drug dealers go in for the day."

Chance looked toward the corner at the vacant house being used by the local gang. There were about ten of them on the corner, still drinking and selling drugs.

"I see what you mean."

"We've been trying to get the city to tear down that old house but they said they don't have the money to get rid of it. Also it's a historically registered building. You're a policeman. Do you think that you can do something about it?"

Chance nodded a yes to Mrs. Johnson and climbed up into his truck. After starting it, he made a U-turn and slowly drove to the corner, coming to a full stop. Three runners came over to the truck. They weren't even teenagers yet, but they already wore the gang symbols tattooed on their hands and arms.

"You guys are on your way to school, right?"

"Yeah, we goin' to school."

"Good. Who owns this corner?"

"We ain't tellin' you shit, man. Who you, the cops?"

Chance reached out the window, grabbed the top of one of the kid's t-shirt, and twisted it tight. He lifted him off his feet and pulled him up until his head was in the truck. The kid was gagging and choking, but Chance never changed his expression. The other two ran to the safety of the house.

"Tell him that business is closed from now on and that the house is off limits. Tell him that I'm his worst nightmare. You've seen the movies where the monster goes after you and he always finds you, and you can't even kill him, huh? The only thing that stops the monster from eating you is that you wake up. Well, I'm that monster."

Gang members watching this stood frozen in front of the house. Chance pushed the kid out into the middle of the street, where he lay, holding his neck. Some of the older gang members gave Chance the finger as he pulled away. Others showed their guns tucked into their belts. Chance formed his hand to simulate a gun, then pointed his finger at them, pretending to shoot, then continued up the street.

Chance entered the police station and walked over to the information officer stationed behind the safety of thick bulletproof glass. On the shoulders of his blue uniform were three stripes. Chance showed his badge and the sergeant pointed to a door to the right of the booth that buzzed as Chance approached. Passing through, he was met by a young officer, a rookie in his early twenties. His uniform was pressed and neat, but he wore a plain white shirt with the same navy blue pants with a yellow stripe, and a navy blue tie. His gun shone as if it was just out of the box, and his holster showed no signs of wear whatsoever.

"Officer Barnette?" he extended his hand. "I'm Officer Greg Hunter."

Chance ignored the gesture and thought about how young and innocent the rookie looked.

"The Chief sent me down to meet you. You're pretty late, and he doesn't like that. Come on, I'll take you in."

Chance was led up a flight of stairs to the administrative suite. At the top of the stairs was an electronic entry keypad. Greg positioned himself between Chance and the keypad while he entered his code. The door buzzed and they passed through.

"They keep the door locked 'cause they don't like the uniformed guys coming up here without an invitation. I just got out of the Academy, and the guy that I'm supposed to ride with is having back surgery." He turned to Chance and whispered, "I carry this gun pretty much for show. I just run errands all damn day. Only way I'd get to make an arrest is if somebody robs the sandwich shop while I'm picking up lunch."

Chance laughed as they approached an older lady sitting behind her desk working a crossword puzzle. The room was in a well-lit open space, with metal file cabinets along each wall. The air was chilly so Rose wore a sweater draped over her shoulders. She didn't bother to lift her head to acknowledge their presence, but Chance could still see her wrinkled, frowned face.

"Mr. Barnette. You're late and the Chief doesn't like it when his appointment is late. He's waiting. Go ahead in." She looked up from her puzzle over her glasses and pointed with her ink pen at Greg. "Hey, you."

"Yes Ma'am?"

"Go down and take everybody's lunch order so I can call it in."

Chance stopped in the doorway. Precinct Chief Dalton Halowell didn't look up, but continued to read his morning report. He was a veteran officer who had been eligible to retire seven years earlier, but he was a cop's cop. His father had been a cop and his son was a cop. It was in his blood so retiring probably would have killed him. His hair was gray and balding, and the scowl on his face was set permanently, from years of forcing it on his men. He was an old-fashioned cop who believed in loyalty, favors, and the precious chain of command.

"Take a seat, officer," he grunted, finally taking a brief look up at Chance. He slowly straightened out the pages of the report that he had been reading, placed it in a folder, and laid it perfectly on his desk. He took a few more seconds in an attempt to humble Chance by staring him down. But then, he figured that if Chance was going to apologize and look away, he would have done it already, so he began to give him 'the speech.'"

"Officer Barnette, is it? From H.Q.?"

Chance shook his head yes.

"I don't know what you expect to find here, but we run a tight ship. Nothing happens without my knowledge or my approval. See this? This is my daily report. I read it like some people read the Bible. Even on Saturdays and Sundays, the Captain hands it to a patrolman and he personally delivers it to my house, knocks on the door, and hands it to my wife. She brings it to me just like it was the morning paper. Then I read it front to back. I highlight it, I get a pen and I calculate the times. This is information. This is the information age, but I can't seem to find any information about you. What do you say to that?"

He opened his drawer and took out a folder and laid it on his desk. The tab read 'Chance Barnette.' When he opened the folder it was empty.

"When the Commissioner sent you over, he told me he would send your file. But it never got here. Think maybe it got held up in the mail room? I've been around long enough to make a few personal friends at HQ. I asked them to check up on you. You know what they found?"

"Nothing?" Chance chimed in.

"That's right, Officer Barnette. Nothing." He pounded his fist on the desk. "I don't even know if you are a real officer. I called around to some of my friends in the other precincts and do you know what I found? Nobody knows anything about you."

The Chief stood up and walked over to the window and gazed out. Without turning around, he mused, "In fact, Mr. Barnette. I can't find any record of your existence, so I thought, hmmm, maybe we got a Federal Agent? So why are you in my department, Mr. Barnette? Who do you work for? Internal Affairs? The FBI? What are you looking for? My men do everything by the book."

"I'm just a crime fighter like you sir. I'm not investigating you or your department."

The Chief turned and once more stared silently into Chance's highly-trained cold black eyes. Again, Chance sat silent and expressionless. He didn't expect a retort, but got one anyway.

"They told me to give you all the latitude you need and not to interfere. The truth of the matter is that we're stuck with each other, so let's make the best of it."

"I appreciate it Chief. I'll make sure to stay out of your way."

The Chief finally gave a pained-looking smile. "I'm sure you will. I called in a favor with the Commissioner. He agreed to let me have a man work with you."

He walked over to his desk and pressed the intercom button "Roe. Is that kid out there? Send him in."

"He's taking lunch orders."

"Lunch orders? Get his useless ass up here right now."

"Right away, Chief."

"You're kidding me, right?" Chance turned to face the captain. "That's not part of the deal."

"I didn't make any deals with you. Out of the blue the Commissioner shows up in my office, telling me that you'd be working in my precinct. I told him that the only way you'd get my cooperation would be to let me have a guy keep an eye on you."

Greg entered the office and his voice trembled, "Yes sir."

"You're gonna be working with Officer Barnette here. Stay out of his way and report back to me every day for a debriefing. Take Officer

Barnette out in your car and show him the district. Mr. Barnette, I trust that you will use proper judgment in the field."

Chance rose to his feet and reached for the Chief's hand. "You have my word. This has nothing to do with you or your department."

Chance followed Greg out the door and into a large parking lot where the squad cars were lined up. The Philadelphia police cars were white, with gold and blue trim, and a police shield decal on the front doors. They were each in their respective parking spaces, waiting to be retrieved that morning by the squadron of Philly officers.

"There's my car over there." Greg pointed to an older model car painted black and white. The shield decal had been removed from the door, leaving a permanent dark outline where it once resided.

"This car was supposed to be auctioned off last month, but they kept it out just for me so I'd have something when I graduated from the Academy. They encourage all the officers who live in the city to drive their squad cars home when they get off. I took it home the first day and my landlord said, "Hell no, don't park that piece of crap here." They both laughed. "Wait till you see what's left for you if you need one," Greg joked.

Greg got in the car, inserted its key and turned it. No response. He began to violently pump the gas pedal. "You gotta do this to get it started. They said the float sticks." He turned the key again and again, but the only sound it made was that of the starter. He stopped and once again pumped the pedal. This time it sputtered and started.

"How old is that car?" Chance remained expressionless "Let's take my truck."

As soon as they entered the SUV, Greg noticed the LCD screen built into the dashboard.

"GPS?"

"No." Chance turned to Greg "Listen, if we're going to be partners, there's something that we've gotta talk about. When there are things you need to know, I'll fill you in, but until then you'll have to trust me and not ask a lot of questions. Like tomorrow, wear your civilian clothes. We have a special thing to go do. And uh ... let's not discuss what we're up to with the Chief just yet."

"What do I tell him every day?"

"You look pretty smart. Make something up."

"He'll see right through me."

Chance turned and stared directly into Greg's eyes. "Trust me. It's better to piss *him* off than to piss *me* off."

Chance then took a call coming in on his cell phone. He turned to Greg. "Show me how to get to Franklin Park."

At the park, Chance and Hunter sat on a bench in the shade. Hunter sat on the seat while Chance boosted himself onto the back of the bench so that he could get a better view of the park. Hunter overlooked the area with his sense of preserving law and order. He noticed a group of four young men on the other end of the square drinking from bottles wrapped in paper bags. Chance perceived the park as being small and insignificant and the four young men even less significant.

"Those guys over there are drinking. That's illegal. Are we gonna go over and say something?" Greg rose to his feet and took a step toward the group.

The largest kid looked across the park at Greg and stuck his middle finger up. One of the others pointed to the finger. They all laughed, and as he lowered his left hand with the middle finger up, his right hand lifted a brown paper bag with a bottle in it up to his lips and he took a long sip. He passed it on to the next kid who took the bottle completely out of the bag, balled the sack up and threw it in Greg's direction. The gesture was purely symbolic, as Greg was a hundred yards across the park.

"That's it. Let's go get them." He turned and looked at Chance who continued to look straight ahead not moving from his perch.

"Go ahead."

"What are you going to do?"

"Wait"

"What are we waiting for?"

"My controller . . . I mean my wife."

Greg laughed. "What did you do, forget your lunch? Did she make some lunch for me too?" He took his seat back on the bench.

"She's a scientist. We're going to check out Dr. Kimble's house."

"That's that missing scientist right?"

"Yes it is. What do you know about it?"

"Just what I hear on the news. Nobody in the department really talks about it." He turned, glanced at Chance, and then turned to see what Chance was looking at.

Jasmine entered the park from the corner next to the four young men and walked confidently past them. Chance had spotted her about a block earlier. She was wearing a tank top, a short pleated shirt, sandals and a backpack.

"Hey Chance, check her out. She's hot." Hunter turned to Chance whose expression still didn't change.

"That's my wife." Chance replied calmly. Though he didn't show any expression, his heart started to race and his palms were already sweating.

"Damn! She's hot. I mean no disrespect but . . . "

"Better not let her hear you say that." Chance said, thinking *"Hope those jerks don't say anything to her."*

Jasmine had seen Chance long before she entered the park. She saw the four young men but didn't feel threatened and so paid them little attention.

"Good morning guys," she said with a smile to the young men.

"Damn! You made my morning much better. Just look at that ass on you, bitch!" one of the young men quipped as Jasmine walked by.

"Excuse me?" She stopped and turned sharply toward them, looking them squarely in the eyes. They all laughed and pointed to the only guy who wasn't paying attention. He was drinking from a bottle that had been wrapped in a brown paper bag and the sleeves on his sweatshirt had been cut off, revealing a pair of well-developed biceps covered with tattoos. They caught him off guard, but their laughter egged him on.

When he looked up, his eyes were slivers. "Huh?" After turning to one of the others, he lowered his voice to a whisper. "What did I do?"

They all laughed, including Jasmine.

"You were talking about her ass. Ass."

Jasmine frowned as she looked at the young man who was talking.

"Oh yeah! I did say it. No disrespect, but you just a fine bitch." The others laughed and he rose to his feet, switching hands holding the bottle.

"What's going on?" Hunter jumped to his feet but Chance didn't move.

"Have a seat." He patted Hunter twice on his shoulder and chuckled.

The drinker taunted Jasmine. "You got a man? Cause I bet he can't give it to you like I'm getting ready to do."

Jasmine laughed sarcastically, shook her head and turned to walk away but he ran over and grabbed her shoulder.

"Where you going, baby? You think that cop over there can help you? We run this park."

Chance had been trained to read lips.

"OH SHIT!" Chance winced. "He called her baby."

Hunter was completely confused and worried, until he saw Jasmine turn, grab the guy's right thumb, forcing it back against his wrist and twisting it, causing the bone in his wrist to snap. She then took the bottle, and smashed it over her attacker's head, as it exploded into light brown foam. She dropped the broken bottle just as two of his friends jumped to their feet and rushed toward her. She took a step back and kicked one punk under his chin. The other took a swing at her as his unconscious friend fell to the ground. She grabbed his wrist and elbow mid-swing and spun him around, forcing his feet to fly up into the air. He landed on his stomach with her knee in his shoulder, one arm pinning down the bend of his arm and the other holding his wrist. She then twisted and separated his shoulder. The fourth one, a large muscular young man with a long scar down the side of his face, stood to his feet and raised his hands in the air and shook his head.

"Sorry about these low lives, miss."

Jasmine walked over to him and without warning, kneed him in the groin. He grabbed himself and fell to his knees.

He groaned in pain. "What was that for?"

"You need to be more selective about who you hang out with," Jasmine replied. She turned and started walking away.

"You bitch," he grunted.

Jasmine turned and kicked him in the side of his head rendering him unconscious. She then turned and marched toward Chance's bench.

Hunter stood up, but Chance remained seated. "Shouldn't we arrest those guys?"

"Go ahead, but what are you going to write in your report? About how we sat and watched a woman get accosted in the park?"

"Guess you got a point. But what if she files a complaint?"

"The only complaining that she's going to do will be to us."

Jasmine was about half way across the square. She was furious and even though Hunter didn't know her, it wasn't hard for him to read her expression.

Chance who wasn't accustomed to not being in control, secretly struggled to gain control of his heart rate and sweaty palms.

"Hunt. Listen to me. She's a really a nice girl but she has a temper, and right now she's really pissed, so if I were you I wouldn't say too much to her yet." Chance released a light chuckle, "And whatever you do, don't make any sudden moves with your hands."

As Jasmine approached, she began yelling, "A little help from you two would have been nice. A lady shouldn't have to fight when she's wearing a skirt."

Hunter stood in awe. She was more beautiful up close than from the distance. On the other hand, she was dangerous. He doubted that even the hand-to-hand combat training he received in the police academy would have been able to slow her down. *This lady breaks bones, kicks people in the head and knocks them out,* he thought. As much as he wanted to introduce himself, he decided it best to take Chance's advice. Still angry she turned directly to him.

"Well, what about you? Where were you, Hunter? Were you going to stand there and let me get my ass kicked, too?" She looked at Chance. "I would expect that from him, but not you."

Hunter was surprised when she called him by name. He stood motionless and silent, as she removed her backpack and dropped it on the bench. Something heavy and metal made a thud when it hit the bench.

Chance rescued the defenseless Hunter. "I figured that you don't get out too much, and you wanted to have a little fun. You ok?"

Jasmine took a series of deep breaths. "Yeah, I'll be fine."

"Jasmine, I guess you already know this is Greg Hunter."

Jasmine extended her hand toward Hunter who was staring and responded by saying, "You're so beautiful."

Chance hung his head and covered his eyes expecting that Greg was going to get punched.

"Why thank you, Mr. Hunter," she responded politely.

Chance immediately jumped in. "Greg, this is my forensics expert, and oh, my wife, Jasmine."

"Don't be getting all jealous," she said to Chance, as she poked him in the mid-section and laughed.

"Your wife? Whoa, she's beautiful."

"Sorry if I scared you. Stuff like that gets me ticked. Then your buddy Chance here makes me so, mad . . ." She sighed. "Good thing I was wearing panties today."

Sensing retribution, both men let the comment alone.

"Are you ok?" Greg asked.

"I'm fine." Jasmine looked at Hunter. "He grabbed my arm and called me baby. Can you believe that asshole?"

"Those bastards," he scowled as they all began to laugh.

They watched across the park as the thugs got up one by one and limped away. One continued to sit on the ground with his head slumped over. He rolled over onto his elbow but couldn't get up to his feet, and fell over onto his side. He wasn't able to sit back up.

"Ok let's get going out to the Kimble place," Chance said as he jumped from the bench.

"Wait. How do I look?"

Hunter tried not to stare as Jasmine stopped and twirled.

"Well, what do you think?"

Chance waited for the right words to come to him. But since none came, he just nodded and smiled to show his approval.

On the way to the Kimble house, Chance followed each command from the GPS navigator. Greg listened to their conversation. Jasmine, riding in the passenger seat of Chance's SUV, turned to Chance.

"I'm sorry for the way that I acted in the director's office. But I was still angry about Grady."

"That's ok, I got a little carried away, too." He turned and glimpsed her reaction. "I must admit, I was a little bit out of my element."

"And Grady knew that he was way out of his class, but that's how you boys are. Trying to prove yourselves, no matter how foolish."

"So what were you doing? Protecting your cubs?"

"You made me mad. They look up to you, respect you. They always have these debates about who's the toughest, you or Hardaway. Then you come by and pummel them without cause."

"It was reflexes."

"And that's what makes you dangerous to be around." She looked out the window, reflecting a moment. "Personally I think that he is."

"What?"

"That Hardaway is tougher than you."

"Who's Hardaway?" Greg asked.

Jasmine immediately removed a nine millimeter handgun from her backpack, reached around and pressed it against Greg's forehead. He froze and panic struck his face.

She smiled. "If I tell you, I'll have to kill you."

"Remember when I said that I would tell you the things that you need to know? This is not one of those things," Chance stated without any expression as he drove.

Jasmine's smile then turned to laughter, and she put her weapon back in her bag. Greg relaxed and slumped in his seat.

"I'm honored just to be compared to him."

"Well, he's only like that when he's on a mission."

"Yeah, right, I bet," Chance said sarcastically.

"No. Seriously. He's married with three kids. He even coaches his daughter's soccer team."

Chance gave Jasmine a surprised look. "He coaches kids?"

"Yup, ten year-old girls. He's just the sweetest guy. His wife is so lucky."

Jasmine stared out the window for a moment, wondering what it would be like to be Mrs. Hardaway. There was a man who would come home after a day of saving the world, feed and change the baby while she cooked dinner. Chance remained silent, now feeling even more envious of the man whom he had secretly and apparently incorrectly, patterned his life after. She turned back to Chance and gave him a disarming smile.

"You know, you can let your guard down sometimes."

"Why would I do that?"

"So you don't kill me by accident."

"Point taken."

Chance turned from the street and drove a short distance up the driveway to the house. In his mind, Jasmine was becoming a predator unlike any that he had ever faced. This woman disarmed Chance in ways he didn't understand. He parked at the foot of the brick steps that led up to the double front doors.

Hunter finally broke the silence in the car as he climbed from the vehicle. "Does the Chief know that we're here?"

Chance ignored him and walked slowly up the steps.

Hunter caught up to him as he stopped at the door and took the knob in his hand. "Chance, we can't just break in. The Chief will have a fit."

"Don't worry, sweetie. It's all covered," Jasmine said as she removed her cell phone from her purse and looked at Chance who nodded back.

Jasmine entered a number on the screen and the automatic door lock clicked.

Chance motioned for Jasmine and Hunter to wait outside. He removed one of his .45s while Jasmine took her gun from her purse. Greg got his 9mm from his holster. Chance turned the door knob and pushed the door open.

Jasmine touched her earpiece. "We're ready to enter the residence. Any thermals?" She listened to the reply. *"Nobody's home. At least nobody who's been alive within the last 24 hours."*

Chance stepped into the dark house and turned on the light switch to illuminate the foyer. In the distance, he could see areas of the living room brightly illuminated by the sunlight shining through the windows. He motioned for the others to enter.

"Seems like no one is here," Jasmine concluded.

Chance turned to Hunter, "Give Jasmine a hand while I check the house."

Chance holstered his weapon, adjusted his glasses, and walked up the steps. Jasmine holstered hers, and she and Hunter made their way through the foyer into the family room. The television was off and one chair had its back turned to it. She began to spray and photograph the light switches, door knobs, and other surfaces for prints.

"What is that stuff?"

"This is UV sensitive and sticks to residual body oils. When the UV flash hits it, we have an instant fingerprint photo that gets sent right to AFS for analysis."

"Right through the cell phone?"

"This cell phone is really a file server that I can also use to make phone calls," she laughed.

"Upstairs is clear," Chance said entering the room. "Nothing seems to be disturbed at all."

"I have lots of prints, but they all come back to only the doc and his daughter."

Chance scanned the room with the aid of his PTM as Jasmine walked over to a sun room behind the kitchen. The backyard ended at the woods connected to the park. The grounds in the rear were a full story below the main level of the house. Jasmine used her cell phone to scan the wood line. Nothing unusual.

"This is a nice house. I didn't realize this section of the city even existed," Hunter said as he looked out over the lawn.

"Over here, guys. I've got some blood on the door," Chance yelled.

Jasmine removed a different spray can from her bag and sprayed the area. She pointed her phone at it and clicked the shutter. Several spots on the floor illuminated, though the glow faded quickly. Jasmine knelt down, scraped up each drop and put them into separate test tubes. Chance then made his way down the hallway leading to the back door where he reached for the knob.

"Don't touch it," Jasmine snapped.

Once again, she sprayed the knob and took a snapshot. They opened the door and stepped out onto the large wooden deck. Chance walked down the steps leading to the plush lawn. He studied the grass carefully as he walked across the green carpet until he came to a halt. Though the lawn had recently been cut, Chance saw what he had expected. Tire tracks leading out into the woods.

He followed the tracks disappearing into a thicket while Jasmine studied the area next to the house where the vehicle had been parked. She removed a small cylinder from her purse and pointed it skyward.

"What is that thing?"

"I'm looking for a satellite."

She traced the tracks toward the woods as Chance was coming back into the yard.

"Anything?"

"No, just looks like the trail goes out through the park. They didn't spend any idle time out there."

"No, they parked next to the house out of view of our satellite. You know the worse part?"

"What's that?"

"They must know the satellite's crossing times."

Chance looked out toward the woods. "This crew, they were professionals."

"How do you know that?" Hunter inquired.

"They left us nothing to trace them by," Jasmine said as she took pictures of the tire tracks.

"Let's get out of here," Chance advised.

Chance started the car and backed down the driveway to the street, stopping at the mailbox. Jasmine got out and retrieved the mail that had been accumulating. She climbed back in and put it into a plastic bag. Chance began driving off, but spotted a landscaper at the neighbor's house. He looked over to Jasmine.

"Sit tight."

Chance turned back to Jasmine and winked. He removed his holster, laid it on the seat and exited the SUV. He walked slowly over to a short, stocky man who was loading his gardening equipment onto a trailer hooked to his truck.

"Excuse me .... Hi, how are you?" The landscaper looked up. "Do you take care of the Kimble property?"

"Yes. What can I do for you?"

"Well, it's for sale and I'm thinking about buying it. I saw you here and I figured I'd see if you're the one who maintains it."

"Yeah, he's been my customer for years. I didn't know he was selling his house. I hate to see him leave."

The man took out his wallet and handed Chance a business card. "I just did his lawn on Wednesday."

"Great, it looks beautiful." Chance raised his brow. "How often do you work on it?"

"Once a week."

"Guess the professor is pretty picky, huh?"

"I've never met him personally. All of my instructions come through a company called Regional Property Management that handles the properties around here."

"Regional Property Management?"

"Yes. R.P.M. They manage the maintenance on most of the estates around here. That's who contracts me to do the lawns."

"Thank you. If I decide to purchase the property, I would like to keep your company on as the landscaper."

"Sure I would appreciate it. You have my card and that's the number to R.P.M."

Chance returned to the SUV and climbed in. He handed the business card to Jasmine. "Maybe you should start with these people."

"As soon as I get back to the house."

Chance dropped Jasmine off at her car, and Hunter off at the police station, and then slowly navigated his way home while familiarizing himself with the city. While turning onto his street he slowed to a crawl in front of the gang house, and studied the young men on the front porch. They cursed at him and gave him the middle finger while others threw up their gang signs. One even pointed his finger at chance simulating a hand gun.

Chance parked in front of the porch steps and entered his house. He went directly upstairs and found Jasmine in her chair searching for whatever information she could find on the professor. She spun around in the chair, greeted him then spun back around.

"Did you make that call?"

"Yeah. Somebody's supposed to call me back."

"Do me a favor? See what you can dig up on that house on the corner. Looks like they have the whole neighborhood on edge."

She turned back around in her chair. "I was kind of thinking the same thing. Guess great minds think alike huh?" She turned back around in her chair.

Chance turned and headed out the door then paused and turned back to Jasmine. "And see if you can find any information on Greg Hunter."

Jasmine turned and smiled while motioning Chance closer with her finger. She spun back around in her chair and pointed to a monitor on her right. The latest police academy graduate group picture appeared on the screen.

"He graduated from the academy a month ago. There he is right there."

"He looks like he's twelve."

Jasmine laughed. "Apparently he was a pretty solid cadet. He finished top in the class and even got an award for helping some of the weakest classmates." She advanced the picture on the screen showing a document. "Highest shooting range scores, Top hand to hand combat scores. He was already a black belt in Aikido. Highest test scores ever. And guess what?" She showed a picture of the police commissioner "This is his uncle."

"No wonder they treat him like crap."

"Graduated first in his high school class. A junior ROTC member. The list goes on and on."

"Well. I'm kind of stuck with him. We'll make the best of it."

Chance went downstairs and turned his attention on the Simulator 750 where a smoked-glass front dimmed the flashing lights inside the unit.

"Simulator on."

"Simulator 750" in black letters faded onto the 84-inch television screen.

"Load Sanctuary."

"Sanctuary loaded," the system responded.

"On screen," Chance commanded.

A map with driving directions appeared on the large television.

"Drive to Sanctuary."

The map disappeared and a street-level image of his house appeared. The image then rotated and began moving up the street, simulating a running video of the street-by-street drive to Sanctuary.

Jasmine ran down the steps with a big grin on her face. "Come!" she said excitedly.

"What? Why?" Chance turned from the television to Jasmine.

"We've got company," she whispered.

Chance reached behind the cushion and took out his gun. Jasmine grabbed his arm, pushing the gun down.

"No. Not that kind of company," she whispered.

"What?"

She touched his lips with her finger, causing a foreign sensation to travel throughout his body. Jasmine was grinning as she pointed to the door. The doorbell rang and they looked at each other and simultaneously counted silently to ten. Jasmine calmly walked to the door.

"Who is it?"

"Estelle Johnson," came the voice on the other side.

Jasmine opened the door and was greeted by Mrs. Johnson who was holding a foil-covered plate in her right hand.

"Hi, Jasmine, dear. Did I disturb you two kids?"

"No, not at all. Please come in."

"You remember my husband, Chance?" She turned to Chance and beckoned him to come over.

Chance stood beside Jasmine, smiled broadly and put his arm around her shoulder.

"Yes, the policeman. You two are such a nice looking couple. Are you newlyweds?"

"Yes, ma'am," Chance replied as he slid his hand down Jasmine's back, letting it come to rest on her rear.

"As a matter of fact," Jasmine said as she elbowed Chance in the ribs and forced a smile at him, "we just got married a few weeks ago."

Chance removed his hand from her backside and rubbed his head, nodding and smiling to affirm what she said.

"The house looks so nice now. I saw men working on it the past few weeks. It was abandoned for so long and really was awful, so awful."

"Yeah, we really like the remodel our contractors did."

She handed Jasmine the foil-covered plate. "Sweetie, I baked some cookies for you."

"Oh, good, something homemade for once," Chance mumbled to Jasmine.

Jasmine elbowed him in the ribs again.

"Oh honey, give her some time. I'm sure she'll get better at cooking with practice. Do you work, Jasmine?"

"Well, I'm an artist and I'll be working from home for a while." She pointed to some of the paintings that decorated the walls. "So you'll see me around during the day."

Mrs. Johnson grinned. "A police officer and an artist." She clasped her hands together and looked skyward. "Must be a match made in heaven, dear Lord."

"Oh, we're just your average couple, Mrs. Johnson," Chance jumped in to say. He sidled up to Jasmine, and putting his hand around her, he reached under the foil on the plate and began to snatch a cookie. Jasmine yanked the plate away.

"Now remember your weight problem, my little puppy. Do come on into the living room, Mrs. Johnson."

Jasmine walked her neighbor around, pointing out all her original artwork, and the elderly lady was impressed. Chance eyed Jasmine as she waltzed through the kitchen and living room, her hips swaying so gracefully. He thought to himself about how lucky he was to be able to look at her every day. Not only because Jasmine was beautiful, but because most of the controllers were guys.

Jasmine turned and caught Chance staring at her butt. She let Mrs. Johnson come back through the kitchen doors first, then turned around and shook her fist at Chance who was left standing in the living room.

"He's a handsome guy," Mrs. Johnson whispered, winking her eye.

"I know. I hope I make him a good wife."

"Just make sure that you have his dinner ready when he gets home. And when he does little affectionate things, don't elbow him in the ribs like I saw you do, honey," she laughed.

"I didn't want to make you feel uncomfortable."

"I know, but it's ok with me. Men do that. My Ted could hardly keep his hands off me right up until he died," she smiled.

"Aww that must have been so sweet." Jasmine smiled. She paused and leaned into Mrs. Johnson, confiding, "You know, I'm really not a very good cook."

Chance went back to watching the TV, looking for coded messages.

"Well, don't worry. I'll have you cooking in no time, dear. Feel free to come over any time and we'll practice."

When he saw the kitchen door open again, and the two ladies coming back, Chance pressed the mute button on the remote. He stood up and walked with Jasmine and Mrs. Johnson to the front door.

"She's a nice girl, Chance. Gee, you two make such a nice couple."

"She's great, Mrs. Johnson." He leaned over and kissed Jasmine right on the lips, trying to make it seem as natural as day. Jasmine pulled back, ever so slightly, then forced a smile. "Honey, not in front of our guest." Jasmine turned back to her neighbor.

"Good night, Mrs. Johnson, and thanks again for the cookies. Chance, walk with her please and make sure that she gets in her door. I'll be upstairs. Waiting..." Jasmine winked.

When he returned from walking Mrs. Johnson home, he went upstairs. Jasmine was sitting at her console, her window to the entire world.

"That was sexual harassment," she yelled.

"You can't sexually harass your wife, and legally we are married. Besides you enjoyed that kiss."

"You enjoyed it more than I did," Jasmine laughed.

"Nope, cause you closed your eyes."

"I did not," she insisted, her laughter now gone.

"Yes you did."

"I did not."

"Well, this arguing is not going to settle it. I'm going to bed now. I'll leave the door unlocked, *honey*," Chance winked.

Jasmine sat silent for a moment and wondered if she had shown him any signs of pleasure. Surely she didn't close her eyes. She turned back to the console and began to type on the keyboard.

Chance checked the monitor in the control room prior to going to the police station. The street was empty, except for two older teenage gang members leaning on his SUV. He chuckled to himself, went over to Jasmine's bedroom and knocked on her door. Getting no answer, he jiggled the knob a little.

"Go away," yelled the voice on the other side.

"You know it's my duty to inform my controller when I'm going to have a dangerous encounter."

"You're just going to the police station, Chance. Go away."

"What about the dangers I encounter on my way to work?"

"Leave me alone. Besides, I don't have any clothes on."

"I've seen naked women before."

"Not this one. Besides I need my sleep. Leave me alone."

"Don't I get a kiss before I leave?"

Chance heard angry footsteps in the room headed for the door. The door suddenly opened and there she stood in her T-shirt and panties. Her hair was a mess, but she was beautiful. Chance started to sweat and his heart pounded.

"Ok. Come on in," she challenged him.

"Huh?" Chance was caught completely off guard, panicked and turned away. "Listen, I've got some company outside. You might want to check them out for me."

Jasmine understood and went into the control room. She studied what she saw on the magnetic imaging system, then came out of the room.

"The big guy has a gun in the back of his belt, and the other one has a knife in his right pocket and a gun in the front of his pants." She headed back into her bedroom.

"Where you going?"

"I'm going back to bed."

"How 'bout a little help?"

"I hardly think that you need me to help you handle two little boys."

"Little boys? That big one has to weigh 250 pounds," Chance teased. "Besides, they have guns."

"You've handled men with guns before so why not these two little boys."

Jasmine went into her bedroom and slammed the door. Chance went down the steps and out the front door. When he exited the house, the two thugs were still leaning on his SUV.

"Hey cop! You better mind your business. You just got here, but we been here a long time."

"And we ain't scared of you either, mother fucker." The little guy opened the front of his jacket, revealing the gun that was tucked into the belt.

"I hope you have a license to carry that," Chance said, staring straight at the larger counterpart, then he laughed.

The kid looked back at Chance. "Yeah, cop. I got a license. Show him my license, Slugs." The young man made a gang sign with his fingers.

The bigger man started to go for the gun in the belt behind his back. In one motion, Chance closed his distance between the two young men, grabbed the .45 from the front of the smaller man's belt and hit the larger youth, who stood about 6'6" in the front of the head with the butt, causing an immediate gush of blood. As the kid fell, Chance turned and shoved the barrel into the other youth's mouth, knocking out one of his front teeth. He removed the butterfly knife from the young man's pocket, opened it and stuck it into the side of his thigh, causing him to fall to the ground.

"Stay off my block, punks. Understand?"

"Uh-huh," the youth managed to say through his choking and tears.

"I will shoot you. You and your little punk friend laying there, bleeding all over my sidewalk." Chance removed the .357 Magnum from the belt of the other youth who by now was struggling to get to his feet.

"Now you help him up and get out of here. Oh, by the way, I wouldn't take that knife out of his leg right now; it's the only thing keeping the blood in."

As Chance turned around, he saw a small crowd had gathered. He sheepishly waved and smiled to everyone.

"Good morning, everybody. Looks like it's gonna be a nice day."

The neighbors clapped as Chance climbed into his SUV, laid the guns on the front seat and turned on the ignition.

"That was police brutality," Jasmine reported in his ear piece.

Chance shook his head no. "Can you follow them?"

"Yeah, of course. I can see them on the neighborhood watch cam. I'll let you know what they do."

"And I'll turn these in at the station and see what our boys have been up to."

Chance returned to his SUV and drove up the street past the young men who were stumbling and struggling to get back to the gang's club house. The smaller kid was sitting on the sidewalk, writhing in pain. Other gang members had gathered around him trying to help him to his feet. Chance slowed his vehicle and opened the window.

"Be gone when I get home."

One of the teens gave Chance the finger and opened his jacket to reveal a handgun that was tucked in the front of his pants. Chance removed a submachine gun from the seat and pointed it out the window. Everyone except the two injured gang members saw it and scurried out of the way, retreating to their headquarters. Chance turned the corner and continued his journey to the police station.

Hunter met Chance in the lobby of the police station.

"Hey there Chance. You're late again. The chief just ripped me a new one."

"Here give him a peace offering." He handed the guns that he had just taken from the gang bangers in front of his house. "See if they match any open crimes."

"Ok. You coming with me?"

"I'm gonna go back to Dr. Kimble's neighborhood and take a look around and see if anybody has a surveillance camera facing the street. Let's meet back here tomorrow and compare notes."

Chance rode slowly thru the neighborhood studying the homes on both sides of the street in search of a street facing camera. He saw none but spied a young couple walking along the sidewalk hand in hand. Out of nowhere a scruffy looking man approached the couple and began to rant. The young man stepped completely between his girlfriend and the man. They exchanged words and the man staggered by and continued down the sidewalk. Chance thought about his own altercation with the gang and sped home to make sure that Jasmine was safe.

"Jazzy?" He yelled as he entered the front door.

Getting no answer he ran up the stairs and straight to an empty control room. The bathroom door was open and empty when he looked inside. He frantically knocked on her bedroom door and when there was no answer he opened it and looked inside, but it also was empty. He ran down the stairs and back to the kitchen where he noticed that the back door was ajar. He exited the house and ran down the concrete rear steps just in time to see Jasmine standing at the foot of Mrs. Johnson's back steps. He jumped over the fence, ran to her and hugged her.

He breathed a sigh of relief while still holding her. "I thought you were . . . Uh. Hi Mrs. Johnson."

"Hi Chance. Home mighty early. You missed that young bride didn't you?"

She smiled. "Sorry I scared you. Hold on." She walked up the steps and took a foil covered serving dish from Mrs. Johnson and handed it to Chance. "Thanks Mrs. Johnson." she replied handing the dish to Chance as they walked toward their house.

"I didn't see you. And the back door was open."

"I know. I was standing right there. I could see the door. Besides, I'm armed."

Chance stopped and looked as Jasmine continued to walk with a smile. She was wearing yoga pants and a sweat shirt. She exaggerated her walk switching her hips widely. Once inside she took the platter from Chance and took him by the hand.

"You were really worried about me, weren't you?" she said without smiling.

"Well you know what happened this morning. Yes I was concerned. But I knew that you could take care of yourself."

Jasmine looked him in the eyes and shook her head. "You looked so sexy jumping over that fence. Like my knight."

Jasmine put her arms around Chance and held him so tight that he could feel the gun which was tucked into the side waistband of her yoga pants. She sighed and released her grip and they shared a silent awkward moment.

"Uh. Hunter took those guns to the crime lab. We may know something in a few days. Any luck with Dr. Kimble."

"Not yet but I'm running out of ideas. Mrs. Johnson made us some spaghetti. Let's eat before it gets cold."

After dinner Chance sat in front of the television watching the breaking news.

"Howard Neal was found in his Northern Virginia condominium this afternoon by a friend. He had apparently died from a single bullet wound to the head. A gun registered to him was lying next to his body. Police believe that this was a case of suicide and have ruled out foul play."

Chance yelled up to Jasmine. "Hey, Jazzy? Don't we know Howard Neal?"

"Yeah. He's a creeper," she yelled from upstairs.

"A creeper?"

"Yeah, a bona fide A-hole who's up to no good. He was the Assistant to the Prez for National Security."

Chance suddenly heard the rumble of a motorcycle come to an end in front of the house. He pressed the remote button to turn off the news, and the TV switched to show the view outside his front door. Hunter was dismounting his bike and walking up the steps to the front door. As the bell rang, Chance opened the door and looked confused.

"Hunter, what are you doing here?"

"I figured that you didn't know anybody in town, and I wasn't doing anything, so I came over to hang out with you."

"Hi, Greggers," Jasmine yelled out as she reached the bottom of the stairs. "Come on in." She grabbed Hunter by the hand and pulled him in past Chance.

Chance closed the door and gave her a frown. Jasmine frowned back.

"Have a seat, Greg. Can I get you some dinner? We had spaghetti."

"Uh. No thanks I had a couple of hot dogs and a soft pretzel." He turned to Chance. "Guess what. Those guns had two robberies, a police shooting from last year, and two murders on them."

"How'd you get them done so fast?"

"Well once I told the Chief that you gave me the guns, he called in a favor and they dropped what they were doing and did the ballistics checks and voilà. He thinks you work for the FBI ... Do you?" Hunter's eyes lit up as he suddenly became distracted. "Whoa, look at the size of that TV."

"Chips and soda okay?" Jasmine yelled from the kitchen.

"That's cool," Hunter yelled back to her. "Where did you get those guns? He wants to pick the guys who had them up."

"Got them from the gang house up the street."

"This isn't our precinct but hey ... He'll have them picked up tomorrow."

He noticed the simulator console. "Simulator 750? What's that?"

Chance smiled. "You play video games?"

Hunter laughed. "It's what I do dude."

Chance jumped to his feet and walked to the locker that matched the Simulator 750 front. *"Simulator seven fifty. Open Locker."*

The door opened and Chance removed two booties made of a shiny stretch nylon-type material and tossed them across the room to Hunter.

"What are these for?"

"Slip them over your shoes."

Chance removed a second pair and tossed them to the chair where he had been seated. He then removed two PTMs, a 9mm handgun, and a 45mm. He approached Hunter and handed him the 9mm.

"This is as heavy as a real gun," Hunter commented, weighing the gun in his hand.

"This is more than a video game, man. It's a simulator. Put these on." He handed him the PTM. "Load simulation twenty."

"Whoa. This shit looks real." Greg turned completely around and marveled at the 360° image of the room where he was standing.

"Alternate the balls of your feet and you'll move forward."

Greg quickly learned to make the image turn wherever he faced. He eventually raised his weapon and took a shot. The weapon in his hand was silent but it simulated the recoil of a 9mm handgun.

"Hey, I even feel the recoil."

"Look to your right."

Hunter turned quickly to his right and Chance was standing right there looking at him, holding his gun down by his side.

"Follow me." Chance turned to his right and began to walk, opened the door and stepped outside the house.

"This looks so real," Hunter gasped, watching the image on his PTM.

"That's the idea. Shoot somebody."

"What?"

"Shoot somebody." Chance raised his weapon and shot a man in a suit who was walking toward them amidst a crowd of people. No one else responded to the shot as they continued to walk past them while the man in the suit fell to the ground." Go ahead. Don't be shy."

Hunter raised his weapon and shot a truck driver who had gotten out of his truck to make a delivery. The weapon in his hand kicked backwards. He then shot the store keeper who was waiting in the doorway for his delivery. Hunter removed his PTM for a reality check. "This is too real. The recoil is crazy, and these people that I'm shooting, what a sense of power, huh?"

Chance laughed while Hunter put back on his PTM. Now he began to shoot random people until his gun would only click.

"You have to reload. Remove the clip and put it back in."

"Damn. This is too, too real."

"Tell you what. Study this building layout on TV and memorize the layout. I'll be back in a minute. Load simulation fifty three."

Greg removed his PTM and studied the layout of the four-story structure displayed on the TV He opened the soda that Jasmine had put on a coaster on the coffee table and took a sip. Chance returned with two pairs of gloves.

"Put these on. It'll give you the use of your hands to climb, open doors or even take hostages. Now, you've got ten seconds before I put my glasses on and blast your ass."

"What do I do?" Hunter asked excitedly, putting the gloves and his PTM on.

"Run, dope." Chance replied calmly. "Nine seconds."

In his vision, Hunter ran up a set of marble steps leading up to a glass door. He pulled the door open, then briefly turned and looked back at the door, then ran straight toward the back of the building. He took cover behind a concrete pillar. He heard the shot from Chance's gun and immediately heard the projectile hit the pillar. He reached his weapon around the pole and fired several shots back, then ran down a set of steps at the rear of the building. He heard another shot behind him and then a bullet whizzed past his ear.

He pushed through a metal door, now finding himself outside the building in an alley. He turned and leveled his weapon at the metal door that closed behind him. Seconds later, he pulled the handle on the windowless steel door but it had locked behind him. Looking down the alley from one corner of the building to the other, he saw a fire escape going up the side of a four-story tenement He pulled the ladder down and climbed three flights up, pausing for a breath. He pointed his weapon at the door and then at the ground below.

After a pause he ran up the metal steps to the top floor, where a window appeared. He pulled on the window, but it did not open. He hit the glass with his gun, then cleared the broken glass from the pane with the barrel before climbing through. Inside were two children who immediately ran out the front door of the apartment. Hunter followed them to the door and peeked out into the hallway. He leaped out of the door, stood still and considered pushing the button on an elevator. Then, deciding not to use the elevator, he ran to the stairway at the end of the hallway. He carefully entered the stairwell behind his raised weapon. He quickly looked down it to inspect for other signs of life, then slowly turned and made his way up the stairs to a door that led out to the roof. He kicked the door open and quickly exited out onto the roof where he walked the perimeter, looking down at the street, amazed at how real the traffic and people looked below him. Even the sounds were genuine. He returned to the door that led to the steps down through the building. Hunter opened the door, only to find the barrel of a .45mm pointed right at his face. He immediately received a shock and his screen went blank.

"Shit. That hurt." He removed his PTM and looked at Chance who was removing his.

"Incentive not to get shot. You lose," Chance chuckled.

"Let's go again," Hunter demanded as he put on his PTM.

"Reset simulation fifty three," Chance commanded.

"Ok. Now you run," Hunter demanded angrily.

Chance smiled. "Ok." He turned and ran up to the top of the step into the building. Well. What are you waiting for?" he yelled back to Greg.

Hunter bounded up the staircase and entered the door just in time to see Chance disappear behind a wall to the left and up a set of stairs. Hunter went to the right side of the foyer and pushed his back against the wall as he climbed up the eight steps sideways, keeping his gun pointed out. At the top, he stayed low and kneeled as he turned in the direction in which Chance had run. Through an open doorway was a hallway directly in front of him. He could see another opening to his left and he immediately jumped to his feet and positioned his back to the wall. He turned and pointed his weapon up the hallway and quickly peeked around the corner leading down the hallway to his left. He glimpsed Chance standing at the far end, then saw the flash and a bullet hit the wall right next to him. Instinctively Hunter dropped to his knee while returning several shots up the hallway, but Chance had already vanished through a doorway to his left.

Hunter got up and carefully approached the door that Chance had exited. He felt defenseless in the hallway but resolutely followed his prey. The door that Chance had gone in led to another stairwell. Hunter went in and listened for footsteps. He could now feel sweat dripping down his face as he started up the first flight of stairs, then strategically turned the corner to the next flight. He froze when he heard several footsteps running down the steps toward him. Three children rounded the corner that led to the next flight. The last child who was the oldest stopped and looked into Hunter's eyes. He pointed up the steps and held three fingers up. Hunter nodded thanks, and the three children vanished down the steps.

Hunter entered a door that led out to the second-floor hallway and raced to the stairwell at the opposite end. As soon as he entered it, shots rang out from behind him. He kneeled behind the wall and held the door open with his foot while returning fire. He reloaded and continued to answer the gunfire from the opposite end of the hallway till it eventually subsided. He peered around the wall just in time to see that Chance had run up the stairs.

Hunter then ran up the stairs at his end of the hallway to reach the fourth floor. He kneeled and fired several rounds down that hallway, then raced down it to the opposite end. He leveled his weapon and quietly made his way up the steps that led out to the roof. He breathed heavily as he eased his way through the roof-top door, checking both directions. He let the door close while backing away and looked over at the roof of the stairway enclosure. He walked around the structure then relaxed confident that Chance didn't come to the roof. He walked back to the door leading to the stairwell. When he opened it, he was immediately shocked and the screen in his PTM went blank.

"Reset simulation fifty three," Hunter commanded with no results.

Chance laughed and repeated the command. Hunter immediately ran inside and to the pillar that had given him cover in the first round. This time he immediately began to shoot at the front door using the pillar for cover. Chance took cover in the foyer at the bottom of the marble stairs where he began to return fire. Hunter alternated sides of the beam and when he had emptied his clip, he reloaded and continued to fire.

Hunter had run and lost his life twice already, and he didn't want the same result again. This time he decided his strategy would simply be reckless abandonment; he'd just go for it full steam. He alternated shooting from each side of the pole non-stop. It was working. Although he was trapped behind the beam, he had managed to pin Chance down in the foyer at the bottom of the stairs.

"Run for it, Hunt," Chance taunted him.

"Maybe it's time for you to run from me."

"Been there, done that. Either way you don't stand a chance." He laughed sarcastically.

"No? Well how about this?"

Hunter unloaded his weapon around the left side of the pole, then reloaded. He fired two shots around the right side, turned left and ran toward the foyer while releasing a barrage of bullets, pinning Chance in the stairwell. He even managed to reload before reaching the top of the steps, where he leaped into the air, diving toward the glass entry doors. He saw the small crimson splash in the front of Chance's head, just as he received his own shock. Chance and Hunter both ripped their PTM's from their heads in response to the shock. Chance looked at Hunter and laughed.

"That's what I'm talking about!" Hunter said excitedly.

"Just how I would have done it," Chance said, giving Hunter a high five.

"Jasmine didn't hear Hunter leave but when she checked the outside monitor. Hunter's motorcycle was gone. When she stepped out into the hall she could hear the water running in the bathroom and the door was ajar.

She tapped lightly at the door, hoping Chance didn't hear her knocking. After slowly opening it, she walked in. Through the steam and the opaque shower doors, she could barely see Chance's outline. She admired his figure as she walked over to the sink and cleared her throat loud enough for Chance to hear her. The shower door opened just enough for Chance to stick his head out.

"Can't a guy get a shower in private?"

"Sorry, I had to brush my teeth." Jasmine glanced over at Chance, smiled innocently and put toothpaste on her toothbrush. Chance slid the door closed.

Not wanting to leave, she propped herself against the edge of the sink facing the shower and slowly brushed her teeth, admiring the image through the shower doors. To her delight, the door slid open and Chance stepped out, his muscular, naked, wet body approaching her in the misty air. He wrapped his strong arms around her, soaking her nightshirt with his hug. He glided her off the sink so they were standing face to face, his nude body pressed against hers while her hands squeezed his buttocks. He loosened his grip and let her turn to the sink and spit out the toothpaste and rinse her mouth.

Jasmine raised her hands when she felt Chance pull the bottom of her T-shirt up past her waist, then up over her head, exposing her firm bare breasts in the steamy mirror. Her breathing got shallow as he wrapped his arms around her, cupping her breasts and gently kneading them, causing a surge of excitement to radiate throughout her body, which was now soaked. He slid her panties down past her hips and allowed them to fall to the bathroom floor, exposing her sculpted smooth butt cheeks to his rising erection.

Jasmine turned to face Chance and he lifted her effortlessly onto the sink. He leaned in and parted her lips with his finger, causing her jaws to go limp and her mouth to open. She grabbed Chance by the back of his head and forced her tongue against his. He pressed his body against her hard and she responded by wrapping her legs around his body and locking her ankles together. Jasmine tilted her head back submitting her slender neck to him. Chance in return placed his left hand behind her head and began to slide his tongue up and down her neck. She offered her body to him, and he took it, thrusting gently until her body became relaxed. Their thrusts intensified in frequency and force, as Jasmine moaned softly with each one.

Jasmine exhaled and moaned louder with each thrust that she had imagined, then looked at the figure behind the steamy shower doors hoping that Chance hadn't heard her.

"Are you finished brushing yet?" Chance snapped.

"Uh, yeah."

"Well then, I'd like to get out of the shower."

"I've seen you naked, anyway," Jasmine said. "And it's my job to watch you, right?"

Chance opened the door and stuck his head out once more. "I assume that what you saw satisfied you, huh?" Chance winked, then smiled before sliding the door shut.

Jasmine was caught off guard, wondering if he had in fact heard her. She looked away, then flushed the toilet and rushed out of the bathroom, forcing a loud yelp from Chance.

After drying off, Chance wrapped himself in a towel and exited the bathroom. He walked down the hallway, going past the control room. He looked in and could see the back of Jasmine's head as she studied her monitor. She raised her finger in the air without turning around.

"You're going to owe me after this one. Come check this out." She turned to see Chance wearing only a towel. She immediately felt flush with warmth and quickly turned back to the screen, trying not to show any interest. His image was in her head and she took a deep breath before continuing.

"Look at this. They knew when there would be a satellite blackout over the area where Kimble's house is located. What they didn't know is that twelve degrees to the south was an NSA Audio Receptor Satellite. It appears that NSA didn't trust Kimble or somebody in that area, so I filtered through the conversations that NSA was picking up on the satellite. Listen to this."

Jasmine started to play a muffled, barely audible conversation.

"Megan are you awake... Megan. Are you ok? What's wrong with the light?"

"Good evening Dr. Kimble."

"Who are you?"

"My name is Stryker."

"It's been a long time, and they assured me that as long as I never discussed the project that they would leave me alone."

"Sorry to disappoint you but I'm not with the government."

"Who are you? Get out of my house."

"Don't you hurt him!"

"Ouch! You little..."

"Please don't hurt my daughter. She's innocent. She doesn't know a thing."

"Innocent? Hardly. But it is true she doesn't know anything about your research. In fact she doesn't know too much about anything. But I suspect that you kept her that way for this very reason."

"Please let her go. It's me that you want."

"Now you're a very bright man Doc. You know we can't do that."

"Let him up Mr. Hodges."

"Be careful with him. If he's dead or too injured to work, we don't get paid. Let's get them out to the truck. We only have thirteen minutes. Let's go."

"Who are Stryker and Hodges?"

"Don't know, but I'm sending the recording to the researchers now."

"So we know the 'who' part. Now we gotta get to the 'why' and the 'where.'"

Jasmine looked into Chance's eyes, and smiled broadly, being careful not to let her eyes wander down to his naked chest. "I already got that covered. I figured out where they took them."

"How?"

"Every engine has its own distinct sound, even though we usually can't differentiate them with our brains. My computer can though. I followed the sound of their Ford Econoline van for thirteen minutes and then I was able to track it on our surveillance satellite. In fact, at that point I was able to follow it on street cams. Here it is."

Chance and Jasmine watched the van in silence as it made its way to the northwest section of Philadelphia, then parked.

"What are they doing?"

"I don't know."

The van then pulled out of the parking space and made its way to an abandoned warehouse.

"They waited for the next satellite blackout," Jasmine said, turning back to Chance.

"Call the Dean and have a crew meet me there. No, call Hunter and have him meet me at that corner." Chance pointed to the screen.

"Ok."

"I'm going to gear up, then you can guide me there."

Hunter was already waiting on the corner when Chance arrived. He approached the SUV and Chance signaled him to jump in.

"Here, put these on." He handed Hunter a PTM and he put it on.

"Hi, Greggers."

Hunter was surprised and beamed. "Jasmine?"

"Yup, it's me," she laughed.

"Ok you two, let's get to business," Chance barked.

"Ok, guys, listen up. The lights are on but nobody's home. I already did a thermal scan."

"Let's go Hunt. Jasmine, when we breach, give us night vision."

"Roger that."

They drove to the warehouse Jasmine had spotted and silently got out of the SUV. Walking over to its steel, locked entry door, Chance removed a tool from his belt and used it to unlock the door. He pushed it open and Hunter immediately entered the dark warehouse with his weapon drawn, checking to the left of the door. Chance followed and turned to the right. They stood back to back as they lowered their weapons and looked around the massive room. Along a far wall was a white Ford Econoline. Raising their weapons once more, they slowly approached the vehicle.

Both men stared into the unoccupied vehicle through the windshield. Chance inspected the right side while Hunter checked the left. They met at the rear of the vehicle and opened the rear doors. Hunter continued to visually survey the warehouse interior, while Chance inspected the van in which he found a set of unused tie wraps.

"Ok, let's check over there." Chance pointed to the opposite end of the warehouse. They approached a steel door with an empty circular hole drilled into it for where its lock used to be. Chance eased the door open and they were immediately hit by the stench of human waste. Chance scanned the room and saw it had two chairs and a bucket in the corner.

"Looks like this is where they were held. Let's move upstairs."

They walked up a flight of metal stairs that led to a metal catwalk along a wall. A metal rail was on one side while the cinderblock wall with a double door in it was on the other. They could see a light shining through a window in the metal doors. They entered the room; a large metal table dominated its center space. The table and the surrounding chairs had only a light coating of dust on them, compared to the other furniture that was covered with a thick layer of dust from years of abandonment.

"Give me an element spectrum scan, quick," Chance said.

"*Roger.*"

Chance looked at the table and confirmed his thinking. "They were definitely here. Let's go, Hunt."

They exited the room and walked down the steps and across the expansive warehouse floor.

"What makes you think they were there?"

"Kimble used his finger and wrote his name in body oil. Jazzy, did you find any vehicles leaving?"

"*Negative. They used a blackout and there was no audio satellite to give us a starting point. We did some research on those names though. We could find no reference to a Stryker. Hodges is a different story and it's not good.*"

"What is it?"

"One of our zombies went missing about a year ago and his name is Jason Hodges."

"I thought that everyone on the Zulu teams had transponders implanted."

"Not all of them. Apparently Hodges is one that didn't."

"Ok, guys. What's a zombie and a Zulu team?" Hunter asked, thinking this was something he needed to know.

"To put it simply, Hunt, a zombie is a member of a Zulu team. A Zulu team is sort of a militarized, private, covert assassination team."

"Bad, huh?"

"Even worse than it sounds." Chance paused. "Jasmine, can you get me some info on Jason Hodges?"

"Ten four."

Chance was awakened by the sound of his ringing phone. When he opened his eyes he could see the sunlight shining in from around his blinds.

"Hello."

"Where are you bud? You're late and the chief wants to see you."

"Ah man. I overslept. What time is it anyway?"

"It's nine o'clock."

"Oh shit! Is the chief mad?"

"No he's actually excited. Look up the street and you should see them raiding that gang house," he laughed.

"Ok. I'll be there in a little while."

Chance got up and walked down the hall toward the bathroom. He looked in the control room and could see Jasmine's chair swiveling back and forth.

"Why didn't you wake me?"

"Am I your mother now?" She said without looking around. "Look at this."

Chance smiled as he watched the police escorting the gang members to the prisoner transport vehicle.

The Chief smiled when Chance entered his office with Greg. "Officer Barnette. Been waiting for you. Good job with those guns. They went in and arrested most of the 52nd this morning. They actually tied those weapons to quite a few robberies and two murders."

"That's what I was hoping when I wrestled the guns from them."

"And Greg here tells me that you guys found out where they were keeping the professor."

Chance turned and looked at Hunter. "Had to give him something," Greg mumbled to him.

"We have a CSI team on the way there right now."

Chance sought Sanctuary and was pretty sure he was approaching it, as he slowly rolled in his SUV along a mostly abandoned side street. The block was rife with drug dealers selling their product in the open-air market. He stopped at a street sign and his truck was immediately swarmed by the industrious children of the night. They looked into the truck and immediately knew that Chance was much more dangerous than they. They whistled and waved the others away. Chance despised the dealers and thought about how he had dismantled the 52nd, but this was not his turf and he knew he had to respect it. These dealers were petty criminals, while the work of the terrorists was a real danger to the US with serious potential consequences.

He continued driving up the street until he reached another corner, no different from any other one along this street. He made a left turn onto a dark, deserted, dead-end alley, then drove slowly to a set of large garage doors at the end of the block. Both sides of the alley contained cars in various stages of repair. Some looked as if they could be driven away; some were stripped down to the frames, while others sat in stages in between. Directly outside the garage entrance were several small cars with expensive paint jobs. As Chance pulled up to the garage door, it opened automatically. He had found Sanctuary.

There was a Sanctuary in every city where field agents went to bond with their only peers—other agents in the area. Sanctuary was a place of understanding and bonding, a place where everyone inside was aware of what had to be done and what had already been done. It was a sacred area where an agent could talk about his first kill, his last or his most disturbing, and everyone understood. Everyone at

Sanctuary was a killer with a common goal, a common code and even a common symbol—two parallel straight lines, both the same length but one of them placed one-quarter higher than the other, symbolizing the World Trade Center towers in New York.

Sanctuary was different in every city. New York was a gym with offices and living quarters, but about half, including Philadelphia, were garages. The agents loved fast cars and one was usually an expert mechanic who could use that as his cover.

As Chance drove his truck into the dark garage, his headlights were absorbed by the dingy wall and workbenches facing him. Several custom cars were parked inside the garage. Chance could sense eyes trained on him from the shadows in the garage. Seeing no one, he turned off the engine and reached into his jacket for his guns.

Then there were two sharp slaps on the hood, and a figure emerged from the darkness. He was a middle-aged African American who stood only stood about 5'10", with muscles bulging out from a clean white T-shirt. He was the garage owner, Agent John Walker. John was in his fifties, old for an agent but his toughness was legendary. He had been with Special Forces in Afghanistan, hunting terrorists long before coming to the agency. He was also one of the only agents who survived the pre-controller days. That was a time when they operated in small groups, similar to their counter-part terrorists cells, but they operated without the technology advantage that today's agents currently enjoyed.

"Hold on cowboy," he said as he walked around the front of the truck. "Don't shoot anybody. We're all brothers here." He continued around the SUV to the door, opened it and Chance stepped out.

"Dean. It's been a long time." Neither man smiled.

Walker wrapped his massive arms around Chance and patted his back.

"Been taking care of yourself, kid?"

"Trying to."

"I've been watching you, and no you haven't." The Dean smiled, as another agent approached. "I know you know this guy." Chance's old friend Charles Peak grabbed him and squeezed the air from his lungs. Peak was short and stocky, but his massive muscles dwarfed the Dean's. He had a reddish beard half as long as Santa Claus'. Chance tensed his body to avoid injury from the crushing.

"Blown anything up lately, Junior?" he laughed. "Oh, I forgot. That subway."

"That was an accident."

All three men laughed, visualizing the explosion.

"Hey Charlie, every time I see you, that red thing on your face gets more gray in it."

"Wisdom, my boy. See, now I get to stay inside until my expertise is needed."

Peak put his arm around Chance's shoulder as they began walking.

"I still remember your first mission. You sitting there on the plane, trembling like a little bitch," he laughed. "Come on in and meet the crew."

The Dean led them through the garage past the row of seven small street racing cars, each worth a fortune and only driven when there was money was on the line. The agents slowed as they passed the sport motorcycles, stopping at a gold pearled one.

"How's the bike working for you?"

The Dean was the man responsible for working on both Chance's motorcycle and his SUV. He had turned Chance's motorcycle into nothing less than a pro racer, disguised with a paint job that you would only see on the street. It was capable of top speeds of well over 200 miles per hour.

"It's running like a champ," Chance proudly reported.

They walked through the stockroom. At the back was a loose sheet of plywood leaning against the wall. Dean slid it over to reveal a narrow stairway heading down. At the bottom was a steel door. Dean placed his hand on the doorknob.

"Enter."

The door buzzed and clicked as Dean pulled it open, condensing the space in the already cramped stairway where the men stood. They went in one by one. Inside was a large room, complete with well decorated living area. A blank white wall was on one side of the room. Off to the side, there was a kitchen with a fully stocked refrigerator and two fully stocked freezers. It also had a full bathroom and three bedrooms down the hallway.

A short, younger man met them just inside the door. "Hey Chance. How have you been?"

"Good, Brock."

"Welcome to Philadelphia." He extended his hand to Chance. "Uh, not too hard buddy. That's my trigger hand, don't forget."

Chance laughed, but he knew that Brock was serious. He hadn't seen him since they worked together in Afghanistan, saving that group of British hostages.

"That's a sweet deal that you got. Who do I have to kill to get my own personal controller in my house?"

"You gotta get from behind that rifle and get your hands dirty, buddy."

Peak laughed but Brock couldn't wait to add his next comment. "But out of all of those controllers, you get that hot little Jasmine."

"Well, let me say. I didn't have to kill anybody at all. It's just my natural good looks and magnetic personality. We were a match. Besides you look old enough to be her dad."

"Hey, Brock. Throw a couple of those pizzas in the oven," the Dean commanded.

His orders were followed without question.

A hulking figure limped down the hallway and stepped up to Chance. Though he was built like Chance, Dylan Rice stood at least two inches taller. Except for a pronounced limp, he was an imposing figure, even for Chance. He had comparable good looks, and similar dark eyes but a permanent smirk on his face that never changed, and it went along with his stoic personality. Like Chance, Rice was a field agent.

Chance hugged Rice, then stepped back. "Sorry about the knee man. How's the rehab coming?"

"Too slow. I need to get back out there. I'm bored to death."

"Take your time, I'll hold down the fort."

Rice shook his head. "This is the only fun that I have right now." He turned on the Simulator 750 which was attached to a projection

TV spanning the entire wall. The others grabbed their peripherals and crowded around choosing sides and situations. The game characters shown on the wall were life size.

"Chance, I've got something for you." The Dean reached into the entertainment center and took out a backgammon set. "Have you forgotten how to play?"

"Never."

"All these knuckleheads play is video games. Nobody knows how to play a real man's game, one that's all about strategy and memory, and not just reflexes and vision."

"Hey, Dean, you're just too old to understand," one of the agents on a sofa yelled out.

"Sit over here at the table and set up the board. I'll grab us something to drink from the fridge."

Chance took a chair at the table as Dean sat the case in front of him, then headed to the kitchen. He returned with a pitcher of brown beverage and two glasses of ice.

"I take it that you still don't drink alcohol, so I made a pitcher of iced tea just for you."

"Thanks. You're right."

The Dean sat at the table across from Chance and poured the refreshing liquid into each glass. He lifted the dice and rolled them on the board. The two played a few throws of dice, then Chance suddenly broke their concentration.

"Dean, I gotta ask you a question. Have you ever been married?"

"Our lives are not compatible with marriage, son," Dean replied without lifting his head up. "Maybe when I retire."

"Don't you ever wonder what it would be like coming home to a wife and family every day? Raising some kids? You know, things like that."

"Well, I guess you're one of only a few active field agents who even gets to take marriage out for a test drive with your situation there. Anyway agents who decide to slow down and get married get put on one of the inside teams. It's less dangerous."

"Sometimes I feel like I couldn't be happy without the danger," Chance attested.

"In our line of work, it's all about the danger so you don't want to ever get too comfortable."

"Yeah, I guess you're right."

"Who could understand all of this anyway?" The Dean held his hand up and motioned it from side to side, honoring the Sanctuary.

"Jasmine understands."

"Oh. Is that what this conversation is all about?" Dean leaned forward to make the dialogue more private. His posture invited Chance to speak.

"My life is crazy, and Jasmine understands," Chance whispered.

"Uh huh. And she's attractive, too." Dean winked.

"No, it's not just that... Sometimes I feel like we can read each other's minds."

"Don't get confused, Chance. This is an assignment and you're on a mission. Don't get distracted and get yourself killed."

Chance looked up at his mentor and felt the moment of recognition. "As usual. You're right."

"But she does have a tight little ass," the Dean laughed.

"And those legs... yumm."

The Dean rolled the dice one last time and made his move. "Looks like you just lost again little brother. See what *distracted* does for you?"

"Yeah, I get it." Chance's mind wandered for a moment. "And she has the cutest temper, you know?"

"Boom, you're dead," the Dean laughed, pointing a finger gun at Chance. He leaned in again to say something privately to Chance. "That temper. That's her self-defense mechanism. It protects her from being concerned with the other life."

"Other life?"

"Civilian life. Get up in the morning. Take the kids to school, go to work. End your day cuddled up on the sofa watching a movie with your lover. If she thinks too much about what we do, our lives won't make much sense to her, so she resorts to using her anger, you know?"

Chance pondered what he had just heard. He looked over at his fellow agents who were deeply involved in their video game. "What if I get onto one of the inside teams and work my way up like Hardaway did."

"You're not like Hardaway. Hardaway is a soldier. He carries out orders and follows the rules. We're killers, Chance. We get to be judge, jury, and executioner. We make snap decisions on whether to kill a person or not. It's completely up to us. At the end of the day, we have to go home and see their faces, and realize that some of them are carrying out their assignment under duress," the Dean reminded him.

"Like the guy that I killed outside the FBI field office," Chance said. "The cartel was holding his wife and children hostage to make sure he would blow himself up at the entrance to the building and take as many agents with him as he could."

The Dean looked into Chance's eyes. "And what you may not know is that intelligence verified that they had executed his wife and children long before you shot him."

Chance shook his head. "In cold blood."

"We have to fight fire with fire," the Dean asserted. "That's too much for the average American to fathom. They all think that if you just rattle the biggest saber, your enemies will leave you alone. Nobody wants to think that you have to shed blood to be safe."

"I guess that's why there is a need for guys like us, huh?"

"Hell, yes. We get blood on our hands so the average guy doesn't have to. And if we get caught, we do time because nobody can think there are assassins working for our government." Dean paused once more. "So can you turn the switch off every day and go home and make love to your wife while thinking about the people you killed?"

Chance shook his head and replied sternly, "They're terrorists so I don't have a problem."

"Why is that? You are still killing someone, and for me, that's not very compatible with lovemaking."

"I respectfully disagree. They are all terrorists. I look at it this way. I've never killed an innocent man, woman, or child."

"Let me tell you a story," the Dean said and he launched into it without waiting. *"John Walker sped to his girlfriend's Cathy's apartment. A half hour before, he had been watching a football game when he got the call. She phoned to tell him that she was taking a bubble bath by candle light. She vividly described every inch of her entire nude body."*

"Ok honey. I'll be over after the game and a shower," he told her.

"You'd better hurry because I'm also drinking wine and you know what happens when I get a little tipsy," she replied.

John Walker smiled and said, "Tell you what. I'll be right over."

She replied again, "Better hurry 'cause the water is not the only thing wet over here."

John Walker rang the bell and was greeted at the door by his Cathy, who was completely nude.

"Your wife let you come out to play?" she asked.

"I told you that I'm not married," he assured her.

"Uh, huh," she replied, grabbing him by the collar. 'Then come on big boy, you've got work to do."

John Walker and Cathy shook the bed until both were completely satisfied.

"Listen, Cathy, I'm not married," he assured her.

Cathy protested, "All that I know is that I can never come over to your place. I call you and you always whisper you can't talk, and then there's the phone call that always interrupts us."

"It's just business baby," John Walker told her, ever so promising.

"I know there's always a woman on the other line because you go out of the room and whisper. Then you get dressed and leave." Cathy was starting to cry.

"It's not like that," John Walker swore up and down. Suddenly the phone rings.

Cathy looked at John Walker, sighed and folded her arms. Her eyes became glassy and a tear rolled out from a corner down her cheek. John Walker ignored the ring until it stopped. But within seconds, the phone started ringing again.

"Sorry babe, I gotta take this. It's business."

Well, he climbed out of bed and went out into the hallway. Cathy immediately jumped up and started to put her clothes on. John Walker came back into the room and saw Cathy getting dressed.

"What are you doing?"

"Look, John Walker. If you're not married, take me with you."

"I can't do that babe. Just wait here I'll be back." He started to unbutton her pant.

"That's what you always say," she replied, buttoning it again. "What kind of business are you in anyway?"

"It's complicated," he stuttered.

Cathy looked to the left and ran to grab John Walker's keys from the nightstand where he always placed them. She put them in the pocket of her pants. In a struggle to retrieve his keys he ripped the pocket off and the keys fell to the floor. Cathy slapped him.

"I'm sorry but I have to go. When I come back I'll explain everything."

"When's that gonna be this time, tomorrow or the next day? Maybe next week?"

"I'm sorry, Cathy, I have to go." He got dressed as fast as he could and went to the door to leave.

"I'm going with you," she insisted.

"No you can't. Not this time, babe."

John Walker opened the door and started to step out. Cathy pushed her foot into the doorway so that he couldn't close it. John Walker got angry and pushed her back inside, causing her to fall back into her apartment. He ran out the main door of the building, jumped into his car and headed down the street. He looked in his rear view mirror and saw Cathy's car in pursuit.

He continued driving as he had to. He spotted an old model Crown Victoria stop in the middle of the street, just one block from a carnival. The driver, a young man, exited the car and began to walk quickly toward the carnival. John Walker stopped his car next to the kid, who began running away. He jumped out of the car and chased the kid for half a block before diving and tackling him. He leaped up to his feet and immediately shot the young man in the head just as he reached for a switch hanging from his sleeve. John Walker ripped open the kid's shirt to reveal a vest filled with explosives and shrapnel.

A van pulled up, two men got out of the rear doors and ran over to them. They grabbed the body and threw it into the rear of the van, then ran back toward the bomber's car, ignoring Cathy, who stood in horror at the execution she had witnessed.

John Walker ran over to Cathy. She was crying hysterically. "You just killed that man," she screamed at him. "Get away."

"Listen there's an explanation."

"No! I don't want to hear it," she shrieked as she turned and ran back to her car.

John Walker returned to his apartment and picked up a small box from his nightstand and went out to his car. He drove until he reached a bridge over a narrow creek. He stopped his car on the bridge, got out and walked over to the railing. He opened the box and looked at the one-karat diamond engagement ring before throwing it into the fast moving waters...

The Dean paused and locked his fingers on top of his head while walking in two tight circles.

"Then what happened to them?" Chance asked.

"Nothing." The Dean took a deep, deep breath and waited a very long moment, then looked straight into Chance's eyes. "Maybe I was wrong, but for her sake, I let her go. I knew that we'd never be the same after that incident. We're killers, Chance."

"Well, Jasmine has seen me kill," Chance insisted.

"Yes, but that also puts her life in danger. Don't get too close, Chance. For your sake and for hers."

Chance always went to the Dean for answers, but as he sat there pondering the John Walker and Cathy story, he now had more questions than he came with.

Humidity hung in the air and the pavement was still hot from the day, when Chance reached his street. The seniors and families on the block had relinquished their hold of the street to the 52nd who were hiding in the shadows of the old abandoned house. The gang members seemed unphased by the raid, but they kept a very low profile, as he rode past the house and parked his SUV on the street and went inside.

Jasmine was sitting at the dining room table sipping tea. She was wearing nothing more than a large men's button down shirt. Her heel was resting on the edge of the chair and her entire thigh was exposed. She put her foot on the floor and lifted herself from her seat just enough to pull the shirt down covering her upper thighs. Chance stood motionless, trying to figure out what to say.

Jasmine broke the silence. "Sorry. I didn't expect you home so soon."

"It's ok," he said as he plopped himself down onto the sofa. "I had a talk with the Dean this evening and uh..."

She sat her cup down and looked at Chance "And what?"

Chance got nervous and changed the subject. "He just wanted to know how close we were to finding Dr. Kimble."

"No luck," she said as she turned back to her tea. I feel like we'll never find him. "His kidnappers were too prepared."

"We can never give up." Chance wondered if he had actually said that for himself.

"And that's true for here, too," Jasmine added. "I mean look at the house on the corner. I'd love nothing more than to rid the neighbors of that nuisance before the mission ends."

Chance sympathized with her frustration. "Maybe we can do something, I have an idea. Why don't you go up and keep an eye on them."

By 11:00 pm, the open air drug market was at its peak.

Jasmine was in her studio painting while Chance sat on the living room sofa watching the evening news. He heard Jasmine come down the stairs and walk behind him into the kitchen. When she came out, Chance turned and looked directly at her. She stopped just as she entered the living room.

"I was thirsty," she said plainly, a glass of water in her hand.

Chance found that he couldn't remove his eyes from her. Her hair was down and she was still wearing the shirt. This time it was unbuttoned revealing pink lace bra with matching sheer panties. His eyes scanned past her bra and down her smooth yet firm abdomen. A gold piece of jewelry dangled from her navel. He inspected her smooth legs down to her perfect bare feet with painted toenails.

"Chance. I see how you look at me. You are attracted to me, aren't you?"

"No." Chance saw his opportunity slipping away. "I mean, you *are* a beautiful woman."

Jasmine approached him slowly, holding her shirt closed with her left hand. She kneeled on the floor in front of him, her face between his hands. She rose to her knees and moved her right hand up to his head and stroked it. She leaned in and began to kiss him passionately. Chance, like a deer caught in the headlights froze, unable to respond.

She began to rub his bare chest, sliding her fingers over the ripples in his abdomen.

"Show me Chance."

"What?"

"Show me how much you're attracted to me."

"How? What?"

"Come upstairs. Sleep in my room with me tonight."

"Slow down a little."

"I'm tired of waiting for you Chance."

Chance finally mustered enough nerve to put his arms around her twenty-four inch waist and pull her toward him. Her legs straddled him and she gyrated her hips causing him to breathe heavily.

"Let's go."

"Where?"

"Upstairs and finish what we just started."

"We can finish right here," Chance pleaded.

"Come on Chance. Wake up! Come upstairs, you have to get ready. Chance! Chance!"

Chance opened his eyes and saw Jasmine leaning over him, smiling and wearing a paint-smudged white undershirt, baggy sweatpants, and work boots.

"They just got a delivery. Come on, you've got to get ready."

"Ok. Be ready in ten," Chance said, rising to his feet and trying to wake up.

"Make it five, and I'll be in the control room." She turned to him and mouthed, "C'mon lover boy."

Chance thought about his dream. "How long were you standing there?"

Jasmine ignored him and headed up the stairs.

Chance followed Jasmine up the steps and went directly to his room. Within fifteen minutes he entered the control room wearing a full body armor suit, which was made of a black light absorbing material. The torso was molded to the shape of his chest and abs. Each arm protector was in two sections. One section covered his arms between the shoulder and elbow, while another, just below the elbow to his wrists. They were molded to the shape of his arms. His legs were covered similarly with thigh protection and lower leg protection. On his head was a matching SWAT style Kevlar helmet. Under the helmet he wore a stretch mask which covered his entire head and neck, leaving only his eyes exposed, but hidden behind his PTM.

"Ok, here's your pill." She handed a small red capsule over her head.

"Are your hands clean?" Chance swallowed his 'Transponder/Physical Monitor.'

"Nope." She swung the large chair around where she was sitting with her legs crossed in the chair. She eyed his armor. "Damn! What kind of superhero are you?"

"I'm just trying to impress you."

Inside his black Kevlar trench coat, he wore two .48 caliber hand guns in his thigh holsters.

"I do just love a man in tights, with big guns." Jasmine eyed him from head to toe.

"Come on now, did you need to bring the shotgun? They're just kids." Chance smiled as he attached the shotgun to straps inside his trench coat that came all the way down to his calves. Although the trench coat offered some protection from projectiles, Chance mainly wore it for the visual effect.

"The shells I'm using tonight were designed to maim but not kill. The shot will penetrate the skin, but the metal is very soft and will flatten on entry. They'll end up with hundreds of painful little wounds. You sure you don't want to come with?"

"Gee, you've never asked me on a date before, but you know the rules. I only get to come away from this equipment if you're down and no other agents are close by, but thanks for the invite." Jasmine turned and looked back at the monitor. "But I will be watching."

"Okay, you have two armed guards at the rear door." She pointed to the red images on the screen. Then she pointed to another light red area. "That's our entry point."

"What's this one doing?" Chance pointed to a gang member who was staggering back and forth.

"I think he's high." She glanced at another screen and pointed. The images were well illuminated as if it was bright sunshine in the middle of the day. She zoomed in. "Look at his eyes, see. And yes, he is armed. And here, we can see there are two people in the rear room and two in the front room. None of them are armed. Upstairs there are two unarmed smaller kids. The kids are runners. They drop the drugs out the window when the guys on the street make a sale."

"Looks like we're ready. Let's go," Chance said, unable to hide his excitement. He had a chance to do his work, even though he was just using lethal force as a last resort. The thought of a possible gun fight still excited him.

"Lock the door on your way out honey," Jasmine laughed.

Chance stopped in his room, opened his weapons locker and removed a portable hand held rocket launcher. He slung it over his back and strapped it tight before leaving the house through the rear door, holding his tactical shotgun in his hands while hugging the shadows in the narrow alleyway behind the houses. He moved quickly and silently, until he reached the vacant lot next to the abandoned house that was being used by the gang. Though it was cloudy with very little light from the night sky, the view on the LCD screens inside the lenses of Chance's PTM gave him a completely illuminated image of the activities going on in the darkness. The night was on his side.

Jasmine relayed the image of the two standing guards at the rear stoop to Chance's monitor.

"No other activity. You're clear," she advised.

He slithered through the darkness and up on the porch which was being guarded by two gang members. He moved swiftly up on to the porch and rendered the one closest to him unconscious with one blow to the head before they even noticed him. Before he could deliver the same fate to the other, the kid managed to shoot his gun in Chance's direction. Chance immediately returned fire with his shot gun, which was still strapped to his coat, striking his victim in the mid-section. He fell to the ground writhing in pain.

"They heard the shot and you have three targets running around the house," Jasmine relayed.

Chance removed his two holstered handguns before leaping over the porch railing. He dropped to the ground immediately and rolled out from the protection of the building, while firing three shots in the direction of the approaching gang members. All three fell to the ground, with wounds in their lower bodies. As he rose to his feet Chance noticed one of the young men in the house stick his head out the window to see what was going on. He reached up and pulled him from the window, slamming him to the ground below, then delivered a knockout punch to the jaw of the stunned youth.

He leaped back up onto the back porch, and holstered his handguns and unhooked the shotgun from inside his coat before ramming the door open with his shoulder. The remaining guard inside raised his weapon but didn't have a second to get a round off before he was hit with the painful shot. Chance tossed a percussion grenade out the back door onto the porch, scaring off any gangsters that had decided to follow.

Once inside he shot one young man in the kitchen before tossing another percussion grenade into the front room rendering its inhabitants helpless. He turned to the staircase and shot both knees of the person coming down, causing him to tumble to the bottom.

Chance holstered his weapon and ran up the steps and to the front room where two very young boys were huddled against the wall, cowering. One of them had peed in his pants. Chance pulled them to their feet and dragged them by the collars down the steps and threw them out the front door.

He raced back upstairs where there were two large cardboard boxes of carefully packaged white powder on a table against the wall beside the front window. Chance dropped a percussion grenade on the table and dove to the floor beside the far wall. The grenade exploded causing the contents of the table to erupt into a white cloud which quickly settled to the floor.

"Hellcat to base."

"Go Hellcat," Jasmine responded.

"Am I clear?"

"Three confused gang bangers are standing on the front sidewalk staring at the house. They're in shock. Everybody else scattered."

Chance jumped out the window onto the roof of the porch, running right past the stunned youths over to a small neighborhood park on the diagonal corner. After removing the portable rocket launcher from his shoulder, he armed it, flipped up the sight, took aim and fired. The projectile entered the house through a front first-story window. Moments later the house exploded into a ball of fire.

Chance waited for the debris to fall to the ground before making his way back across the street into the alley and back to his place. Going in through the back door, he was met by Jasmine who greeted him with a high five, a hug, and then a kiss on the lips. He quickly put on his blue jeans, a sweatshirt, slippers and a holster containing an unfired gun. He ran back up the street to meet the approaching squad car and showed his badge to an officer who got out.

"What the hell happened here, Detective Barnette?" the young patrolman asked.

"Looks like a gang war to me. What do you think officer...," Chance paused and read the patrolman's badge, "Officer Carr?"

"I don't know, but I've never seen this much devastation. Did you see anything?"

Chance shook his head. "And to think I live right down the street."

Chance turned Jasmine's doorknob and stuck his head into the dark room. Jasmine immediately pulled the covers over her head. He smiled at her and waved, then closed the door quietly and walked down the hallway. He made his way through her studio and down the steps, through the kitchen and out the back door into the crisp early morning air. The garage door opened automatically when he approached it. He went in and mounted his motorcycle, then rolled it quietly out of the garage onto the driveway. Just as he started it up, Hunter pulled up on his cycle.

"5:30 a.m. sharp, like I said. Ready, dude?" Hunter asked. "I see you had some action up at the corner last night."

"Yeah a little chaos."

"You did that shit, didn't you? Don't worry I'll never tell anybody and it's about time they got what they deserved."

"Let's roll." Chance had no need to say any more. They rode slowly for a few miles, taking in the awesome joy of a new day on earth. The sun was barely visible as it rose on the eastern horizon. Both riders stopped at the first red light and high fived each other. It was time to launch. When the light turned green, Greg was the first to respond. His front tire lifted from the ground as he gunned it. Chance started slowly, knowing his machine's capabilities. Building speed, he soon powered past Hunter as they negotiated the first sharp curve, sharing the winding road with only a few early morning commuters. At their backs, the wispy clouds to the east were set against a bright orange morning sky. Ahead of them to the west, stars still dotted a deep blue sky.

This was the reason why Hunter had invited Chance for an early morning ride on one of the nation's most notorious roads. There was very little traffic on the normally busy roadway that winds downward through Fairmount Park to meet Kelly Drive and runs along the Schuylkill River to the art museum. The roadway had been responsible for taking many lives and causing even more injuries as well as destroying scores of vehicles. Early morning was the best time to control the road for speed demons like Chance and Hunter.

At Carpenter Street, the duo turned slowly onto Lincoln, a docile little roadway cutting through a very desirable residential section of Philadelphia. It was lined on both sides with homes made of brick and cut stone with rooftops of red clay tiles or shingles of various earth-tone colors. The lawns were well kept and some were separated from the sidewalk by short garden walls constructed of cut stones, while others hid behind meticulously trimmed hedges. A few cars were parked on the street, but most were parked in the nicely paved driveways.

Hunter took the lead, heading west on Lincoln Drive with its two drive lanes and a turning lane in the middle. They throttled back to a casual pace on the uphill section of roadway that curved slightly to the right, allowing Chance who was unfamiliar with the area to test the road surface. They passed several early morning exercisers, some on bicycles and others jogging, then stopped at the traffic light three blocks further on.

Hunter turned to Chance. "It gets better."

Chance looked at Hunter and sized up the man on the machine next to him. He thought back to the ride in Long Island and how easily he had left the other riders in his wake. He was sure that his machine, built for the track, could far outclass Hunter's stock bike, but he wondered how quickly he could dismantle his nerve. He revved the motor just as another group of riders on sport bikes came to a stop at the light. They all waved in acknowledgment of the fun ahead, having the same romance for this road.

The two men allowed the other riders to pace them through the residential stretch of roadway along a smooth left curve followed by a sudden sharp right, covering the half mile at a brisk pace. While stopped at the red light at Wayne Avenue, Chance could see that the road, which had already taken a slight downward slope, dropped much more steeply as it left the residential area and became tree-lined on its way into the park ahead.

"Map Lincoln Drive south from Wayne."

A map appeared on the PTM built into his helmet face shield. He briefly studied the shape of the road before the light turned green and all of the other riders powered off, white smoke billowing from the tires. Hunter immediately shot out and took the lead while Chance was last to leave the light. The three-lane roadway didn't get any wider but it became divided into four lanes, two narrow ones in each direction barely wide enough for two cars. A double yellow line divided the northbound and southbound lanes.

Chance lagged behind and watched the other five riders from behind as they approached a lone car driving for no reason in the left lane. Three cycles crowded into the right lane, barely missing the tattered guard rail that separated them from the flood plain of the creek below, to pass the car while two others passed the car on the left without caring they were in the oncoming lanes. Chance lurched forward, riding within two feet of the last rider. When they reached the next traffic light, he moved to the far left of the left lane.

The road ahead descended again, dipping into a much steeper downward grade. The north and southbound lanes were now divided by preformed concrete barriers, one after another. Shoulders were nonexistent, as the edges of the road pavement were flush against a steel guardrail that was a mix of newly replaced and badly damaged sections, reminders of past accidents. A sharp left curve was visible less than a quarter mile ahead, while the road grade fell rapidly to meet the altitude of the Wissahickon Creek.

When the light turned green, Chance darted off in a cloud of white smoke. His tires hardly gripped the road and he struggled to keep his front tire on the pavement. He leaned hard into the sharp left turn, keeping just on the right side of the dotted lines. In his left mirror, he could see the other riders lose their wills to ride at his pace. They lagged further and further behind as he threw his machine into a sharp right turn. Just as he downshifted, he saw Hunter on his right about half a motorcycle length behind.

Chance looked ahead and was barely able to pass an SUV slowly moving into the right lane. What he did not see was that Hunter had managed to squeeze through the space between the SUV and the guard rail. He emerged from the right side of the SUV slightly ahead of Chance. He had to rely on the fact that he had superior hardware for the rest of the ride, though he could see that Greg matched his skill as well as his heart.

They passed under a high overpass just as the roadway reached creek level. A colonial style stone bridge arched over the water for pedestrians, as the creek pushed its way around large stones ranging in size from car-sized boulders to pebbles. There was not much time to enjoy the view before reaching a slight dog-leg turn, followed by a looping left curve where several automobiles were unsuspectingly weaving their way along the roadway. Chance zoomed between two cars, then zigged into the right lane ahead of another.

Under another stone arch overpass and around a sharp curve, high rise luxury condominiums were straight ahead, but there was no time to enjoy that view. Chance became airborne when the road suddenly fell below him, then turned sharply where the Wissahickon Creek emptied out into the Schuylkill River. Chance momentarily slowed as he rounded a curve with a concrete wall on his left and on his right, a narrow strip of green grass and a sidewalk where he passed a stream of joggers and people out walking.

Hunter took advantage of Chance's hesitation and shot past him to take a slight lead. The north and southbound lanes came together once more, becoming a narrow four-lane road with a double yellow line between the two directions. Chance saw Hunter's bike go airborne just before his as they negotiated a slight drop in the road. Chance then slowed to a tourist's pace just as he approached several teams rowing crew boats on the river.

The two continued at this slower pace, allowing Chance to enjoy the river. The road curved following the shape of the river and passing under several overpasses, including a place where the roadway cut through a rock arch that made its way to the water's edge. When they reached boathouse row, Chance began to notice couples, some jogging together and some just walking and holding hands.

He pulled into a parking area, got off of his bike and walked toward the water. Greg hadn't seen him stop, so he made a U-turn and joined him at the water's edge.

"What the hell kind of engine do you have on that thing? I thought I was gonna blow my engine."

"Nice ride. Thanks Greg."

"You know if I had equal steel, you wouldn't have been able to keep up."

Chance had never slowed down before to look at the places that he had blasted his way through. For the first time, he wondered what all he had been missing. The morning sun shone on the back of his neck and a light breeze brushed across his face. He watched a young couple walk by. He imagined himself and Jasmine as them. Could this be what romantic attraction feels like?

The smell of mildew filled the air. The basement was vaguely illuminated by the remnants of the setting sun, though that was even further diminished by a thick coat of grime on the window glass. Dr. Kimble sat on the cold damp concrete floor with his back against a steel support post. He had little feeling left in his hands that were bound tightly behind him, and his ankles were shackled together. He looked through the darkness at Megan whose wrists were tied in the same manner to a support post on the opposite side of the basement, with her ankles tied together.

Stryker and Hodges had been gone for hours. Stryker had insisted that Poole hire two paid guns because of his mistrust of Brandon and the U.S.A.L.A. Militia members. The two paid guns were vigilant and professional, motivated only by money. Dr. Kimble and Megan were nothing to them but a means to an end. They harbored no ill feelings toward them and at times treated them kindly while trying to get them to cooperate with as little resistance as possible. The U.S.A.L.A. Militia who were left to guard them on the other hand were uncaring, irresponsible and mean. Their every action was guided by hatred for the U.S. Government and minorities. They viewed Kimble and Megan as prisoners of war. Brandon constantly belittled and argued with them. He considered himself one of the professionals and above the terrorist fighters. Being in their presence made the professor frightened and worried.

The terrorists were also inexperienced and undisciplined and demanded frequent cigarette breaks. They claimed to be true to their mission, but each had his own standard of behavior. Many times Stryker or Hodges and even Brandon had stopped the terrorist guards just short of ripping Megan's clothes off and having their way with her as she often verbally fought them.

Brandon sat in a chair with his pistol in his right hand. His arm dangled carelessly over the arm of the chair with the barrel pointing at the floor. He had fallen asleep and even began to snore. One of the mercenaries stood in front of Brandon while the other smiled and leaned into his ear.

"Wake up dick head," he yelled, laughing.

Startled, Brandon woke up and pointed the gun directly at the man's head who was standing in front of him. The blade of the other man's combat knife quickly came to rest against Brandon's neck.

"Now you don't want to do that," he said, calmly pushing the gun barrel away with his finger.

The other scraped the knife up Brandon's neck and across his chin. He removed the blade from Brandon's face and inspected the hair on the blade. He showed Brandon the hair.

"You need a shave young man." They laughed as he wiped the whiskers on Brandon's shirt.

"Stryker just called. Told us he'd be back with the truck driver in about an hour. He said we can get out of here. You think you can protect little miss sunshine from your hillbilly buddies?"

Brandon rose to his feet. "You guys should know me by now. I've got this under control," he smirked while nodding his head.

The two men looked at each other and laughed. Brandon laughed with them not understanding that they were actually laughing at him.

As soon as the two mercenaries left, the armed terrorist stationed on the steps to watch the hostages got up and disappeared up the stairs to the first floor to be with his comrades, giving the father and daughter the time to maneuver their bodies so that they faced each other. Sensing that the terrorists' mission was almost over, moving their fate even closer, the professor had struggled with his bindings to the point of exhaustion, although Megan continued to struggle to free herself. She felt the fibers of the rope digging into the raw flesh of her wrists. Their eyes adjusted as the light gradually diminished and he could see her struggle come to an end when she finally managed to free her hands. She ignored the pain in her bloody wrists as she waved a victory sign in the direction of her father, and immediately went to work to untie her ankles.

Once she had freed herself, she gingerly rose to her feet taking a moment to regain her balance. Her joints ached from inactivity but she managed to stagger over to the pole where her father was tied.

"Just get out and get help," he whispered.

"No, not without you." She managed to untie the bindings on his hands but soon heard the basement door open and a bit of light began to seep in from the top of the steps.

Megan dropped back down with her back against the pole she had been tied to, crossed her legs and put her hands behind her back. As the door closed, cutting off the light, the steps creaked as someone slowly made their way down into the basement. Their eyes gradually adjusted again to the darkness and Megan could barely detect Brandon coming toward her. He straddled her legs then knelt on his knees in front of her.

"Listen Megan, You know we had some good times, but you have to understand that this is just business. I'll make sure that they let you go when this is over."

"How can I trust you, Brandon?"

"When this is over, you and me can take the money they're giving me, and we can go away so nobody will find us."

Megan wished that she had been able to unshackle the professor's legs before Brandon came down. He moved in closer to kiss her, and in the instant that his lips were just about to touch hers, she leaned forward and bit his lip hard. He pulled away. "Ow, bitch, you're going to pay for that."

He rose to his feet and turned to untie her legs.

"How about having your dad watching me have some fun with you, huh?"

"You leave her alone."

"Don't fool yourself old man. I did it to her before but this time you're gonna watch her get it."

As Brandon looked over at the professor, rubbing his bleeding lip, Megan kicked him hard in the groin, causing him to grab himself and fall to the concrete floor right next to Dr. Kimble. Kimble immediately grabbed him with his untied hands and held on.

"Get out, Megan."

"No, I'm not leaving you." She checked Brandon's pockets as he struggled to get out of Dr. Kimble's grasp. "Where's the key Brandon?"

"Get out and go get help."

"I won't leave you daddy."

"I can't hold him much longer. Go and get help."

"Ok, but I'll be back."

Brandon yelled out for help and one of the guards upstairs ran to the basement door. Megan picked up a brick and hid on the side of the staircase. When the guard, a small man, arrived at the landing, she hit him on the top of his head and he collapsed. Still holding the brick, Megan jolted up the stairs but Brandon, who had managed to kick his way free from the professor, chased Megan up, grabbing her ankle as she reached the top landing. Uncertain for a split second what to do, she finally turned and threw the brick hard at him, striking him right in the head, causing him to tumble to the bottom of the steps, blood spilling from his cranium.

At the top of the stairs, Megan turned and bolted right past two terrorist guards sitting on chairs, unaware of what had gone on down in the basement. She bulleted herself out the back door and down the concrete steps. A warm rain falling hard refreshed her senses as she paused a second to catch her breath. The sound of the rain falling gave her a moment of peace that allowed her to scout the tree line in the distance. Those few seconds of tranquility were quickly interrupted when one of the guards ran out the back door followed by a bleeding Brandon. But the guard suddenly slipped on the wet steps, causing him to fall to the ground below. In his rush, Brandon then tripped over his body and fell face first onto the concrete slab at the bottom of the steps, causing a large gash to open up on his forehead.

Megan could see that Brandon was now bleeding profusely from the two head wounds, the blood dripping over his entire face and blurring his vision. She ran around an abandoned car parked a few feet from the steps, and raced out toward the trees. The guard rose to his feet and helped Brandon pull himself up from the wet ground. Brandon shoved the guard back down to the ground, but the terrorist leaped back to his feet, grabbed Brandon by his collar and drove him forcefully backwards into the abandoned car. Brandon punched the guard in his side, and he retaliated with a punch to Brandon's jaw, causing him to fall back to the ground. Brandon held on and took the guard down with him and the two began to wrestle on the ground both now covered in blood, sweat and rain.

Another guard ran out from the house and fired a shot at Megan in the distance, but it missed. He pointed his gun at the guard, then at Brandon. "Stop it you idiots, she's getting away."

Brandon leaped to his feet and leaned on the car, just in time to see Megan as she reached the trees and vanish into the woods.

"Come back here or I'll kill your father," he screamed out to her at the top of his lungs. His voice was hoarse as he tried to yell again, but he was choking on his blood. They waited for her to comply, but she had vanished into the dark tree line. "Damn. I'm screwed," Brandon mumbled.

He pushed past the two guards and limped back into the house, holding his head, leaving a trail of bloody drops. He was met at the door by a terrorist who had been posted on the front porch.

"Are you alright?" he asked with a drawl.

"Do I look alright to you? Get downstairs and tie that asshole's hands back up," he demanded. "You guys are in trouble now. Wait till Stryker gets back."

The guard with whom Brandon had been wrestling came into the house, holding his side. He slipped in a puddle of water that had formed in the middle of the floor and fell. He struggled to get back on his feet, but was pushed back down to the ground by Brandon. "I'm in charge here. Do I gotta do everything myself." Brandon kicked him several times, but was pulled away by the second guard who had come in from the backyard. "Now get up, get downstairs and do what I said. All of you."

"Idiot," the guard mumbled as he struggled to his feet. Brandon followed him through the house and down the basement steps.

The professor, who had managed to get to his feet, had hopped his way to the foot of the stairs. "She got away, huh?" The professor laughed.

"Yeah, well she won't get far. Tie him to that pole." As soon as the professor's hands were tied, Brandon punched him in the gut several times. "And you won't be so lucky."

"Stryker's gonna kill you, you punk." Dr. Kimble began to laugh hysterically as Brandon became more infuriated.

"Yeah? You think so? Well you won't be around to see it." Brandon turned to the guard. "Shoot him in the chest. We'll tell Stryker that we shot him trying to get away."

The guard raised his hands and stepped back. "I don't know about that."

"What do you mean you don't know? I'm in charge here." He took the guard's gun from his holster. "Gimme that gun."

Brandon pulled the slide, forcing a bullet into the chamber as he walked over to the bottom of the steps. Dr. Kimble closed his eyes and lowered his head. The gun fired and Dr. Kimble felt a warm sensation all over his body.

As he rounded the corner to his street, Chance admired his work when he passed the burned-down gang home and drove toward his driveway. The elder neighbors, including Mrs. Johnson, were out sweeping the street. A neighborhood kid, who was shirtless, was shooting baskets on his basketball court while two teenage girls stood by, doing everything they could to distract the future star. Several younger girls attempted to jump rope while young boys interrupted by running through the rope. The neighborhood was peaceful and the sounds filling the air were the swish of brooms, the thumping of basketballs, the squeals of children playing, and the conversations among neighbors. Many waved as Chance turned into his driveway, knowing that somehow his presence had led to the destruction of the 52nd Street gang headquarters.

As he squeezed past Jasmine's yellow Beetle in the driveway, the automatic garage door opened. He turned the engine off, but sat there a moment, visualizing the road he and Hunter had just taken and the place by the river where he had seen the couples. As he pictured the walking path along the river, he began to smell smoke. He lowered the kickstand and dismounted his motorcycle. He carefully inspected the engine but saw no smoke. Chance paused and sniffed the air, looking back out at the smoky ruins at the burned-out gang headquarters, but then realized that the smell was coming from inside his house.

He darted out of the garage, ran across the small lawn and started up the back steps. He could hear the smoke detector inside screaming out its warning of impending danger, and through the four-pane window, he could see thick smoke curling around the kitchen.

"Unlock door," he said, running up the back steps.

As soon as he opened the door, Chance was hit with a thick burst of eye-burning smoke and the loud shrill of smoke detectors. The stove was turned off, but there were three pots sitting on the burners. When he opened the oven door, it released a thick black plume that billowed out from within. The smoke infiltrated his eyes and mouth, but he felt no heat nor saw any fire. Inside the stove was a pan with something in it that looked like a smoldering burnt log. The contents of the three pots on the stove top were also not recognizable. Chance opened the kitchen windows and door and put the pots out on the back steps.

"Jasmine!" he yelled as he ran through the house and up the steps barely hearing his own voice over the deafening tone. "Jazzy!"

His heart rate continued to elevate as he ran through the living room where the smoke had already begun to clear, due to the fresh air blowing it from the opened windows in the kitchen. He ran upstairs and stood outside of Jasmine's bedroom. Stopping for a moment, he could hear her crying on the other side of the door.

The air upstairs was still relatively clear, but the smell of burnt something filled his nostrils.

"Jasmine. Are you alright?" He tried to turn the doorknob but it was locked.

The voice from inside responded. "Go away."

"Open the door or I'll kick it down."

Footsteps inside the room shuffled toward the door, then the lock clicked. Chance slowly opened the door, but when he stepped into the room, Jasmine had already flopped face down on the bed with her head buried under a pillow.

"Are you ok?" he asked, gently pulling on her shoulder.

"Does it look like I'm ok?"

"Talk to me Jasmine."

"About what?"

"Us. I mean what were you doing?"

"I was trying to impress you," she sobbed from beneath the pillow.

Jasmine turned over, pulling her robe tightly closed, then she sat up on the edge of the bed. Tears ran down her face, streaking her mascara. Chance was surprised to even see her wearing makeup.

"You already impress me. Hey ... you're the best guardian angel that an agent could have."

"No, Chance, you don't understand. I don't want to be your guardian angel, but that's all that I seem to know how to do," she sobbed.

"No. There a lot of things that you can do. So you burned a dinner. We'll order a pizza."

"I don't want pizza. I want a romantic dinner, even if it is pretend." She looked up at Chance with tears streaming from her eyes. "When you first saw me, what did you think?"

"I was impressed by your hand-to-hand combat skills."

She squeezed her eyes shut, made a fist and gently gave Chance a light punch in the chest. "Combat skills? Didn't you even notice I am a woman?"

Chance looked away as his heart skipped a beat. "Yeah, of course, a very attractive woman."

She opened her eyes and stared at Chance, who wasn't able to make eye contact. He suddenly felt weak, helpless and completely out of his realm. "You noticed?"

"Every agent who ever met you said you were beautiful."

"And what about you Chance? I only care about you. The others... they're just business."

"Maybe I should have said something earlier."

"Yes, you should have," she scolded him gently.

"What about me?"

"When I saw you, I thought that you were the most handsome guy that I had ever laid my eyes on. All the female agents... oh and Kyle, too," she chuckled before continuing, "used to fight to be on your missions until you requested me as your lead controller."

"I always thought that we made the perfect team."

"Do you still think we make a perfect team?"

"Absolutely." He paused. "I'm sorry. This is all new to me."

"What's new, Chance?"

"Love, I think." He looked down at his feet and a long uncomfortable silence followed. "Uh, listen. Don't worry about dinner. Nobody has to know about the cooking."

"Chance, did you mean that?" Jasmine asked, stunned at what she thought she had heard.

"Yeah." He looked at her. "If you're uncomfortable in the kitchen, your secret is safe with me."

"No. You said *love*."

"I didn't. I... I guess it just slipped out. Sorry."

Jasmine rose to her feet and stepped between Chance's legs. She put both hands behind his head, bent over and placed her forehead against his. "That's the best thing that you've ever said to me." Sensing his nervousness, she stood up and took his hands. "Let's go on a date."

"A date?"

"Yes." She smiled. "Let's go on a date. Couldn't you use some dinner?"

"I sure could."

"Ok. You go air the house out while I get ready. I know I look a mess."

Chance went downstairs and opened more windows. He turned the exhaust fan on, then called Greg and consulted on where he should take Jasmine. He exited the back door and was met by Mrs. Johnson who had smelled the smoke and was coming over to see what was burning.

"Is everything ok, dearie?"

"Yes," Chance smiled, "just a little accident in the kitchen."

"I see. She'll learn. Is this your motorcycle?"

"Yes it is."

"Pretty slick machine."

His back was facing Mrs. Johnson when Jasmine came out, and he noticed that the elderly woman's face was lighting up. Wondering why, he turned around to catch Jasmine coming towards them, wearing a short, white A-line dress with a halter top and 6-inch heels. Chance and Mrs. Johnson both wore an expression of big surprise on their faces.

"Wow, you look different, Jazzy."

"Different?"

"I mean . . . like hot."

"Yes she does."

Jasmine twirled around to show off her outfit.

"Are you ready to go? We'll ride my bike."

"I'm hardly dressed for a motorcycle ride."

Chance reached into his SUV and handed Jasmine a helmet. "Now you are." He put his on climbed onto the bike and started the engine.

Jasmine waved bye to Mrs. Johnson, then held on tightly around Chance's waist as he sped up the street. He felt the warmth of her body pressed tightly against his. She could feel his chiseled abs through his shirt, lightly sliding her fingers across the ripples. She rested her helmeted head against the back of his head. They rode up the street, eventually finding their way onto the interstate that wound its way toward the Philadelphia skyline.

They eventually found themselves seated at a table in an Old City restaurant.

"This is beautiful, Chance."

"Greg suggested it."

She shook her head. "He's such a player."

"You know, he's a nice guy, but they treat him like crap."

"Are you getting a soft heart, Mr. Barnette?"

Chance reached across the table, but hesitated, grabbing a little flower vase in the middle of the table instead and fiddling with it. Jasmine reached out and took his hand.

"Are you afraid of me?"

"No, I've killed people Jasmine."

"And in killing them, do you know how many innocent men, women and children's lives you've saved. I've watched you Chance. I watched you when you watched the couple with the baby carriage walk by. You're intense, fearless, reckless, strong, and in control. I feel safe."

"I've been wondering what it would be like to be normal. To live a normal life, go to work and come home to someone that I'm in love with." He paused again, looking down at his menu. "Um, what should we have?"

Jasmine stared magnetically at him until he finally looked up from his menu. "Each other?" She smiled and wouldn't back down, causing Chance to look away again. "Do I make you nervous?"

Chance smiled sheepishly. "A little bit."

"I feel like I've conquered the conqueror. Chance, there's no reason to be afraid of me."

"This is all new for me."

"You've never been with a woman?"

"No. Yes but it wasn't like this. We were both alone and scared. It should have never happened."

"That sounds so sad, but I haven't done any better. But I have to admit that I've fantasized about this very moment."

"As beautiful as you are, you must go out on a lot of dates."

Jasmine laughed. "Chance, I work five or six days a week in a bunker five stories beneath a naval base with a bunch of gross nerdy controllers, an hour and a half from civilization. When I get home, I sleep."

"I know the feeling. What about your family?"

"I have no family. What about you?"

"They died."

"Wow! Our lives are so much alike. It's scary."

After dinner, Chance and Jasmine walked until they found themselves at the water front, peering out over the Delaware River. The air by the water was cool and clean. Reflections from the lights on the suspension bridge leading to New Jersey danced on the water, as pleasure boats trolled up and down the river. The lights lining the side of the bridge cycled through red, blue, white, and then back to red. Jasmine wrapped both her arms around Chance's arm and put her head against his shoulder. He was so tall, so strong. For once, she allowed herself to be weak, letting herself slip into a feminine role of feeling unusually docile, soft and protected. Her man was not only the most handsome hunk in the world, but he was practically indestructible.

"Aren't the lights beautiful?" Jasmine whispered, looking up at Chance.

He turned to her and his eyes momentarily brightened. "Sure." He stared at the reflection of the lights in her eyes. "Abso...lute...ly beautiful." The two of them stared at each other for what felt like an eternity. Unable to hold the eye contact any longer, Chance finally turned and looked out over the water.

"What did you think the first time you saw me?" Jasmine asked, trying to draw him back in.

"That you were more beautiful than I expected."

She patted his chest with her left hand. "That was a good answer," she chided.

"No seriously. I couldn't wait to meet you, and you exceeded my expectations."

She turned to face him squarely. "Chance, thank you for rescuing me tonight."

"You would have been ok. You had turned everything on the stove off."

"No Chance. The only thing that made me feel better was you."

"Well..."

"No listen," Jasmine interrupted, "I'm really sorry about the way that I treated you at headquarters. I'm surprised that you don't hate me now."

"I could never hate you, Jasmine."

She leaned in and kissed him tenderly on the cheek, and he didn't turn away this time. They got up and began walking slowly along the waterfront, holding hands. Chance became aware of how the couples he had seen in the morning must have felt. The emotion was new, fresh and exciting for him.

"Chance, are you afraid of anything?"

Chance thought for a while. Was he even capable of fear?

"You know . . . I really can't think of anything. What about you?"

Jasmine laughed.

"That I will never get a chance to make love."

"You've never been with a man?" Chance said with astonishment. He gave out a little laugh.

"No. And it's not funny. I've waited for the perfect guy and I'll keep waiting till I die." Her smile turned into a laugh as she looked up at him, slapping him on the shoulder.

"Well I won't let that happen."

"What, you won't let me die—or you won't let me stay a virgin?" Jasmine stopped, tugging his hand to make him stop and answer. When he didn't, she continued.

"You know, I always wanted to be married and in love. I always pictured my first time to be romantic with incense and candles and a strong man who becomes completely vulnerable in my arms."

Chance finally turned to face her. They looked deeply into each other's eyes, and his mind began to drift. Young Chance held his mother's hand as they walked through the park. The sky was blue, except for an occasional puffy cloud. The birds chirped loudly high above the grass sprinkled with yellow wildflowers. He felt safe in his mother's presence and felt the need to reward her. After pulling his hand from hers he ran out onto the grass and pulled one of the yellow flowers from the earth. He returned to his mother and offered her the flower. She kneeled down, accepted it and cupped both sides of his face between her hands. With a smile, she kissed him on his forehead.

"Thank, you Chance. You are sweet and mommy loves her boy."

He felt the warmth of the sun on his face and wrapped his arms around her neck and hugged her. She in turn took his hand and they continued to walk through the park.

Chance looked into Jasmine's eyes and their faces drew slowly closer together. With both of their eyes closed, their lips lightly touched, then began to press together.

Suddenly they were interrupted by a cry, a desperate scream for help from around the corner of a building. Chance opened his eyes and stared into Jasmine's, as if to plead for another few seconds.

"You gotta help, Chance. It's what you do. I'll wait. I'll always wait for you."

After a sigh of frustration, he ran to the building, stopped and peeked around the edge. An elderly woman was being robbed by thugs. One held a knife to her throat while the other rifled through her purse looking for money. Neither of them noticed him approaching from behind.

Chance struck with the same precision he used to eliminate terrorist threats. He punched the thug who was holding the knife in the kidney. He immediately kicked the other in his groin.

"You guys are messin' up my date," he yelled as if they would understand his meaning.

The knife fell to the ground, along with both men, writhing in pain. Chance kicked the knife under a chain link fence, then turned to the guy he had punched. As the man rose to his feet, Chance dealt a final blow with a kick to the side of his face, rendering him unconscious.

"Are you alright, ma'am?"

"Yes, thanks to you. You saved my life."

"You should be alright now till the police get here," he said as he picked up her purse and handed it to her.

"Thank you so much, young man. Who are you?"

She got a chill when she looked into Chance's eyes. He turned and quickly walked away.

"Wait, who are you?" she inquired once more as he disappeared around the corner.

A thunder clap shook the skies just at that moment that he reached his waiting date. Chance looked up and saw another bolt of lightning sweep through the clouds.

"Let's get out of here before it's too late," he said.

He took Jasmine by the arm and they quickly left the area, passing several police officers running in the direction of the old woman who was now shaking in shock. Jasmine beamed, removed Chance's hand from her arm and placed it in hers as they ran.

"I'm afraid to ask what happened back there."

"It was nothing. Just a little misunderstanding between a couple of guys and an elderly lady."

Jasmine nodded. "Yeah, right, they thought that she was offering them some money from her purse, huh?"

"Yeah. But they understand now." He laughed.

Chance stopped in the drizzle and used Jasmine's hand to pull her closer. Once again he looked into her eyes as their faces slowly drew closer together. Both of their eyes closed, and their lips softly touched once more, moist from the light rain and their own passion.

At that moment, the sky opened up and the rain poured like a spraying faucet on them. They stopped kissing, but continued to look into each other's eyes before breaking out into laughter.

"Damn," Jasmine smiled and shook her head.

Jasmine removed her heels and they took off back to the motorcycle where Chance took a moment to enjoy the shape of Jasmine's body, her wet clothes hugged every inch of her body. . Her hair had already flattened to her head and mascara ran down her eyes.

"My dress is ruined."

"We'll buy you another one."

Chance looked down at Jasmine's feet as she slipped her shoes back on. As his eyes moved upward, he found himself visually peeling off her rain-soaked dress clinging to her, exposing every curve and ripple on her well-toned body in his mind's eye.

"Don't look at me like that," she said. "I know I look a mess." She laughed, welcoming the attention she was getting. He turned and mounted the motorcycle, grabbing her and swinging her on.

"Let's go home and get dry."

He put on his helmet and started it revving the engine. Jasmine put on her helmet and tucked her skirt between her legs. She slid her hands around his waist once more, letting her fingers come to rest inside the ripples of Chance's abdomen, then pressed her body tightly against his. The beast was humbled as the weather forced Chance to drive cautiously and slowly.

Professor Kimble opened his eyes, just in time to see Brandon's lifeless body fall to the floor. Stryker and Hodges ran down the stairs. Stryker holstered his weapon from which a small wisp of smoke emanated from the barrel. The front of the professor's clothing was covered with pieces of flesh and blood.

"Check his bindings." He nodded in the direction of the professor. Hodges followed the order, as Stryker turned to the guard. "What the hell happened here? Where's the girl?"

"Well, I was on the front porch like you said. I heard a commotion inside and when I came in, the girl was gone and Brandon was in the kitchen bleeding. When we came down stairs, Bill was on the floor and Brandon wanted to shoot the professor. He hit me in the head with something and then I don't remember." Hodges checked the professor's bindings.

"Ok. You go check on Bill." He turned to Hodges." You come with me; we have to go out and find her."

The ground in the woods was muddy and slick, even though most of the rain had been caught in the canopy of leaves and branches above. Megan slipped and fell several times as she ran shoeless through the trees. Welts and scratches lined her face from the branches that lashed her as she tore through the brush. She stopped running when she heard a shot in the distance behind her. With tears streaming down her face, she turned and ran back toward the farm house.

Just before clearing the tree line, she stopped and watched a large car, which had been parked in the driveway in front of a semi-trailer truck, back out onto the road. There were lights on in the basement of the farmhouse. She crouched and ran low in the darkness, diving to the ground just as she reached an abandoned car at the rear of the house. She crawled on her hands and knees until she reached a basement window on the side.

The light was on and she looked inside. Her father was still tied to the pole, one guard sat on the steps holding a bloody cloth on his head, while the other stood by holding a rifle. Megan saw a body lying face down on the floor not far from her father. She moved in for a closer look and could see by the clothing that it was Brandon lying in a pool of blood. Megan realized that she had remained at the window too long, when the guard with the rifle looked into her eyes, pointed and ran up the basement steps. Dr. Kimble looked up and yelled. "Run, Megan. Get out of here."

She leaped to her feet and once again ran back out toward the trees. When she reached them, she ran through an opening that led into a thicket, slipping several times in the mud. Though she was cold, wet, and her skin burned from the welts that had begun to bleed, Megan continued to run, not knowing if her captor had chased her into the woods, or if he had given up. At a small clearing she reached, the rain fell directly onto the floor of the forest, forming a puddle in a small indentation in the ground. She stopped, cupped her hands and took a much needed drink while scanning for her captors.

Megan wandered in the dark through the woods until she reached a house on a road parallel to the farmhouse's road where she had been held hostage. The rain was coming down harder, pelting her already saturated clothes as she ran across the clearing and up a set of concrete steps to the back door. Furiously knocking, she continued to look back at the tree line for any sign of her captors. She grabbed the doorknob and tried to turn it, but found the door to be locked. She frantically pushed and pulled the door several times before hearing a car approaching on the road in front of the house. She jumped down the steps two at a time, and raced around to the front of the house, passing an older car parked in the driveway. She followed the driveway out to the street, but by the time she reached the road, the car had passed and was barely visible in the distance. She waved her arms in the air, then dropped them in frustration and ran back to the house.

The wooden porch that spanned the entire front of the house was covered and offered her some protection from the rain. She ran up onto the porch, stood on the welcome mat and knocked hard several times on the locked door. She went from side to side, banging on the windows that flanked both sides of the door and peering into the interior darkness. She tried to open a window but that too was locked.

Megan stood at the top of the steps, contemplating whether she should wait under the shelter until the residents returned or do something else. She thought about her father and realized that he needed immediate salvation. She also thought of the possibility that the guards were still wandering in the woods looking for her. After making one last attempt to pry open the front door, she ran off the porch and around to a car parked in the driveway, where, to her surprise, she found the driver's side door unlocked.

She frantically searched under the floor mat for keys, but finding none, she climbed into the driver's seat and reached over to open the glove compartment. She emptied its contents out onto the passenger side seat. Rifling through these proved fruitless, so she then checked under both seats. Nothing. She reached up and pulled down the driver's side visor, and the keys fell into her lap, causing Megan to burst out laughing.

Her hands were shaking so nervously that only after multiple tries was she finally able to get the key into the ignition switch. Megan paused for a moment and crossed her fingers. She took a deep breath and turned the key. The car started instantly and she approved with a shriek, "Yes!"

Her glee, however, was short lived. Megan had never driven a stick shift. She pressed the brake pedal and used the diagram on the gear shifter to try to shift the car in reverse gear so that she could back it out of the driveway. It made a grinding noise and she was unable to get the car into gear. Trying to force it with two hands made the grinding sound louder but she was not able to shift into reverse.

Megan turned the car off and found she was able to put the shifter into the reverse position. Once again, she started the engine and floored the gas. The car lunged backward, veered into the side of the house, wedged up against it and stalled. Megan jumped out of the car, went to the back and inspected the damage. Other than the rear fender being wedged against the wall, there was little damage, so she returned to the driver's seat.

Looking at the gear diagram on the top of the shifter, Megan shifted into first gear and again turned on the ignition and pressed the gas pedal. The car lunged forward, its two front tires jumping over several railroad ties that formed the border of a flower bed. The tires came to rest in the soft mulch that had been made even softer by the rain. She put the car in reverse and started it once more, but the front tires spun in the mud and the car stalled. She tried once more in vain and finally gave up.

She got out of the car and ran down the driveway to the road, just in time to see headlights approach from around the bend. Megan began toward the lights, but the weight of her wet clothes slowed her down. She was far from the tree line now and when she turned to run across the grass on the side of the road, her feet bogged down in the mud. She stepped back onto the pavement and continued running. The car sped up and skidded to a halt right in front of her. She stopped and bent over from exhaustion, trying to catch her breath, as the car doors swung open. Seeing them, she tried to run again as the two male occupants jumped out of the car, but her legs refused to move and she dropped to her knees.

Chance ran to the linen closet and grabbed two towels and carried them into Jasmine's bedroom. Smiling broadly, he approached the bed where she sat and began to gently dry her hair.

"Let's get undressed, dry off and slip under the covers to warm up." Jasmine suggested.

"Uh, do you think that's a good idea?"

"We are married, remember?" She held up her left hand. "Besides we'll just talk 'cause I want to know everything about you before..." and her voice faded away.

In the dark, they took off their wet clothes, dried themselves off, slid under the covers and lay face to face. Chance stroked Jasmine's hair and they kissed briefly.

"Tell me about your childhood," she asked, stroking Chance's hair.

Chance rolled onto his back and gazed at the ceiling. "I had a very happy life as a child. I couldn't have asked for better parents."

Jasmine wondered, "What were their names?"

"Stan and Tracy Barnette."

"Do you ever visit them?"

"No."

"Why not?"

Chance remained silent.

Jasmine rolled onto her back and pulled the covers up tightly against her neck.

"My life started off good. I lived in a little village in Columbia. My father and the other men were all soldiers. When I was about four years old, they left and went out into the jungle to fight the rebels for the government. While they were gone a group of rebels attacked our village and killed all of the remaining adults, including my mother."

Jasmine began to cry and Chance reached over and took her by the hand. "It's ok. You don't have to talk about it now."

"No, I'm ok, besides talking about it makes me feel better," she said, holding back her crying. "They took us to an orphanage run by the nuns. Then when I was ten years old, the Americans came and brought me here to the United States and I was adopted by Hillary Simon. She was an older lady who had been a librarian."

Jasmine began to laugh through her tears. "I swear we were in the library every day except Sunday. She was really good to me. She died during my senior year of college."

"You don't have any other family?"

"No, just the director. He's been like a father to me and Hackett has been like an uncle."

"That's too bad."

"I'm ok. What about your parents."

"They died when I was nine."

"I guess we're both all alone then. How did they die?"

"In a car accident. One night, while I was asleep my mom came in and got me up. We went out and when we got to the car, dad was already in it waiting for us. We left and I fell asleep on the back seat. I heard a loud sound and then the car crashed. A man who was in another car stopped and got me out of the back seat, then our car exploded."

"That's terrible. Where are they buried?"

"I don't know. I think it's somewhere in New Jersey but every time I look for them, it's like they never existed."

"Who raised you after that?"

"At the burial, an aunt whom I had never seen before took me to live with her. She was rich and she had hired a man to take care of me.

His name was Romeo and he died when I turned twelve. That was in August. She sent me to a military boarding school that September and I never saw her again. They told me later that she had died. On vacations and holidays, I used to go home with teachers. Most of them were retired military guys who never adjusted to civilian life. I went on to the military academy and when I graduated, I worked in Special-Ops until I met Sergeant Major John Walker." Chance began to laugh. "He taught me so much about war. And life."

Chance looked over at Jasmine to see her reaction, but she had fallen asleep. He kissed her on the forehead and turned over to go to sleep himself. That night, he was visited by his recurring dream where he found himself sitting in his crib screaming and struggling violently while his soul was being carried away. Once again Chance could see himself reaching out as his body disappeared from a bright room out the door into the darkness. The dream was vivid but tonight, he did not feel cold and empty, just alone.

As usual, his dream was interrupted but this time, it was by Jasmine who came into the room. She was wearing a silk robe tied at the waist, which clung to her breasts and hip curves just as her wet clothes had the night before. She carried a tray that held two cups of green tea and scones. After placing the tray on the night stand, she sat on the bed next to Chance.

"Were you having a bad dream? You were saying 'No' and you sounded like you were crying when I came in."

Chance looked down at his feet under the bedding. "I have this recurring dream," he began to explain.

"Is it a dream or a memory?" she asked, gently taking his face by the chin and pointing it at hers.

"You know... I never thought about that."

"Sometimes our subconscious mind tries to remind us of something that happened in the past."

Chance seemed to ponder the idea, then looked up and abruptly kissed Jasmine. Leaning towards her, he gently pulled her body back onto the bed and she in turn wrapped her arms around him and they engaged in a passionate kiss. Chance pulled the sash of her robe and it fell open. They continued to kiss, their tongues probing each other's mouth, until they were startled by Jasmine's cell phone.

"Dammit! That's Hackett." She sat up, grabbed her robe and held it closed, then put her finger up to her lips. "This had better be good... hello."

As soon as she spoke the words, Chance's phone, entangled in his wet clothes, buzzed alerting him that he had a text message. He looked at it: *Mission alert. Stand by for further instructions.*

"Good. Chance is there with you. We'll need you both."

"Shit," she mouthed as she looked at Chance.

"Are you guys looking at the information on the screen?"

"Uh, actually, we were just taking a break, sitting down in the kitchen for some tea and scones. But we'll head right back to the screen."

Jasmine used her finger to signal Chance to follow her, then pointed to his clothes lying on the floor. She jumped up from the bed, tied her robe tight and ran to the control room. Chance quickly put on the wet clothes and followed her in to the control room.

"What did you do, Chance, take a shower with your clothes on?" Hackett chuckled.

"A couple of hours ago in Lancaster County, a state trooper picked up a frantic young woman who was running up a road in the rain. Turns out that the woman was Megan Kimble," Hackett informed them.

"That's that doctor's daughter, right?" Jasmine asked.

"Yes it is. Apparently she had been wandering around in the woods for hours. She and her father had been held hostage for weeks, and in the last couple of days they were moved to the basement of a farmhouse somewhere in that area. They're being held by members of USALA."

'That's a domestic terrorist group. Are we sure it's them?"

"She informed us that most of them had 'USALA' patches on their clothes. Apparently they're being led by a couple of former US military types named Stryker and Hodges, her friend Brandon, and the professor's assistant Tess."

"Who are they?"

"We're getting the background on them now."

"Any word on Kimble?"

"The last time his daughter saw him, he was still alive at that farmhouse. She said they were forcing him to work on some type of nuclear device they smuggled out of Iraq. We've taken over the situation and stopped the state troopers from doing a house-to-house search. Jasmine, we need you to work with the controllers to find the house where she was being held. It can't be far from where they found her, but she doesn't know how long she was in the woods or how far she walked. Hopefully we can find the professor still alive. And Chance, gear up and stand by."

"Yes sir." Chance went into military mode, but still cast a lustful eye in Jasmine's direction, as the two smiled at each other.

Chance retreated to his room and flipped the switch, lowering his arsenal from the ceiling. He stripped off his wet clothes and slid into a black cotton jumpsuit. He removed his body armor from the locker and was about to put it on when Jasmine burst into the room and stopped dead, eyeing his body with interest.

"Whoa!"

"What's wrong? Never seen a guy in his underwear?"

Jasmine smiled. "More like a super hero in tights." She admired the view for a moment, then continued, "We found the house."

"So quick? How?"

She looked at him and shook her head. "Still underestimating me?"

"Where?"

"Lancaster County on Rural Route 47."

"How did you find it?"

"Radioactivity levels. It's hot, but not lethal."

They rushed back to the control room, now abuzz with controller chatter and several different images on the various monitors.

"Is it always this noisy?"

"Yeah, I like to hear what's going on in all of the groups so I can stay a step ahead of the council."

"You can keep track of what's goin' on in all that chatter?"

Jasmine turned to Chance and smiled. "That's my gift."

"Well, I'm glad you got it."

Jasmine pointed to one of the monitors where the image of a truck could be seen from a satellite. "The high radiation levels are coming from that truck in the driveway. This image is real time. Hold on. I gotta listen to something from Hackett."

"Two months ago that farmhouse was rented to Gaylord Poole, a former employee of the Humanitarian Aid Alliance for Developing Nations. Mr. Poole hasn't been heard from in a few weeks. Jasmine, review the latest frames with Chance and let's get moving. We're holding back the state police on this one but they're chomping at the bit for the publicity. We can't hold them back forever."

"Yes sir." She turned to Chance. "If we go back past the three months, the people coming and going are the realtors showing the property. Now watch this."

The farm bustled with activity. People and vehicles coming and going. The action went on for several days ending with the delivery of a semi-tractor trailer.

"What happened to all of the action?" He paused. "That sedan. Sometimes it's there and sometimes it isn't but we never see it moving or anyone getting in or out."

"I figured you'd notice it." She used her mouse to move the arrow to the abandoned car in the driveway. "We found a signal coming from the trunk of that car."

Jasmine stripped away the layers of the trunk of the car to reveal a satellite dish.

"They've been tracking our satellite." She looked up at Chance, then back to the screen. "They come and go when the satellite isn't overhead. Then last night, somebody broke their protocol. The images aren't that clear because of the rain but look at this."

The image of a woman ran from the house, around the car and into the woods. Two male figures came out of the house and fell. When they got up, one of them fired a gun. They disappeared back into the house and the woman returned, running then crawling to the side of the house. She jumped up and ran back into the woods. This time one of the men ran out of the house and pursued her into the woods.

"Watch this," Jasmine said.

"What's she doing?"

"Looks like she's drinking some rain water."

"Look, he stopped. She's right there."

"That tree is blocking their view of each other."

"How close is he to her?"

"About twenty feet. And look. He turned around and went back to the house. If she didn't stop for a drink he would have seen her."

They watched the images some more, where back at the farm house, a car with four occupants pulled into the driveway in front of the big rig and all of the occupants went inside. Two of them soon returned to the car, got in and sped off. They drove the car to an intersection and turned right. It continued up the road passing the farm house where Megan was frantically struggling with the back door. She heard the car and ran around the house to flag it down, but it had already passed. Chance and Jasmine watched intently then looked at each other.

"I want her to buy my next lottery ticket," Jasmine confirmed.

"The guy who appears to be the leader never looks up. Not even inside, and he always wears a hat."

Jasmine turned to Chance who was already on his way to his room. She muted the audio output and followed.

"Chance, be careful."

"Why the worried look? It's what I do."

"It's different this time."

"It'll be ok. Just don't try to cook while I'm gone."

"Don't worry, I won't cook alone, I promise." she laughed.

"All I need is you to get me back safely."

"I got your back. I promise."

Jasmine watched Chance strap black shin guards and front and rear thigh guards that protected his legs from weapons fire and shrapnel. He donned black fatigues over that, then slipped on an outer tactical vest. He put on his utility belt and attached several spare ammunition clips. Finally he strapped thigh holsters to each thigh.

Chance inserted a .45 caliber Colt in each thigh holster, then took down from the rack a Heckler & Koch MP7A1 with a grenade launcher attached. He lifted a heavy camouflaged box from the bottom shelf and carried it all out to his SUV. He returned for his M240 machine gun, and his black Kevlar lined helmet, before heading out of the room and past the control room where Jasmine was waiting in the doorway.

"Aren't you forgetting something?"

Chance turned abruptly and captured Jasmine in an embrace. Staring into each other's eyes, she felt the power of his will and they locked in a long passionate kiss.

"Thanks, but I actually meant your pill," she said, handing him one of the red tracking capsules.

"Well, that's what I meant too," Chance laughed.

"Ok, start heading west on the Pennsylvania Turnpike. I'll give you further instructions once you reach it."

Chance swallowed the capsule, ran down the steps and out the back door, stopping to lock it from outside. Jasmine returned to the control room to make final plans for the raid of the terrorist hideout, as she felt the rumble of his Trail Blazer pulling out of the driveway. All traffic lights were held to green until he had raced through them on the drive to the turnpike. Soon Chance was on the highway headed west.

Once he reached his exit, Chance left the highway and traveled along the main road and eventually spotted a yellow traffic light flashing in the distance.

"Turn left at the next intersection. Then you're going to continue for 9.6 miles. The state troopers have the highways blocked off. I'll alert them that you're there."

Chance slowed his speed just enough to negotiate the turn at the intersection. His tires screeched as the rear of the SUV slid around. He pointed his front tires up the road and gunned the engine, racing ahead until he could see two state trooper cruisers blocking the road. One trooper backed his car up allowing Chance passage. Both troopers waved as he drove through the barricade and the cruiser moved slowly back into place to act as a barrier.

The narrow two lane road was lined with tall, older trees. On his left, he could see flickers of light through the trees, where sunlight reflected off of a small pond. On his right were woods that eventually opened up onto a small neighboring farm. Just past that farmhouse, the woods appeared once more.

"The site is coming up in two miles on the right."

"Rodger that. Give me a visual on my dashboard monitor." Chance glanced at the satellite image of the target farmhouse.

"There's no way to get close without being spotted, but you can possibly use the rig to cover your approach."

"What if it's an active nuke?"

"If it is it'll take more than a bullet to set it off."

Chance came to a screeching halt about a half- mile short of a slight bend that ended before the farmhouse. A quarter mile of plowed farmland covered with a blanket of short leafy vegetation stood between Chance and the house. He calculated the time that it would take for him to cover the distance in the dirt as opposed to a frontal attack from the road.

"Can I have a site report?""

"There are two individuals on the front porch and one at the rear of the house with several people inside."

"What do you think? The front or the side?"

"The side. It's going to be a second or two slower but that trailer will offer some protection."

"How close is the truck to the house?"

"A foot and a half and it's blocking two windows, so you won't have to worry about them firing at you from the side windows. We need you to neutralize that tracking system in that old car. They can see our satellite, so let's make sure that they can't jam it."

"Copy that."

Chance opened the rear passenger door and took his MP7A1 submachine gun, and attached the grenade launcher, then laid it on the front passenger seat. He returned to the driver's seat and buckled the seat belt. After taking a deep breath, he put the Blazer into four-wheel drive, revved the engine, then shifted the powerful vehicle into drive.

Greg parked his unmarked squad car in front of the house and blew the horn, hoping for Chance to come out. Getting no response, he turned off the engine, got out of the car and ran up the steps to the front door and rang the bell. There was no response, but the lock buzzed and he entered, closing the door behind him.

"Yo, Chance, where are you?" he yelled.

"Up here Greg, hurry."

Jasmine met him at the top of the stairs and led him into the control room. He stopped in the doorway, stunned by what he saw. She remained silent, allowing Greg to absorb it all. He silently studied the images on the two rows of monitors. On the screen directly to Jasmine's right was a map, and in the center an icon in the form of a car. The icon remained in the center of the screen while the entire map moved and rotated and shifted in reference to the icon. To the right was another screen with a wide-angle map of the area.

"What's all this?"

"This is how I watch Chance's back."

Greg stepped forward to peer more closely at the monitors. Each computer screen had a different image. Text information continuously scrolled on the screen in front of Jasmine. She touched an icon on the monitor on her left, then touched the large monitor overhead. The image of an empty highway, taken from a camera located on an overpass, appeared. Chance's SUV suddenly appeared, speeding from the bottom of the screen and quickly vanishing off the top. A new view of an empty highway replaced the former image.

"That's Chance?"

"Yes. That was him ten minutes ago. State troopers found Megan Kimble this morning. We figured out where she was being held hostage. He's on his way there to rescue her father, Professor Kimble."

"Where is he going?"

Once more Jasmine touched an icon on the screen to her left, then touched another screen to the left of the one that had showed the view from Chance's dashboard cam as he turned and headed across the field toward the farmhouse. The screen next to it showed a satellite image of a small farmhouse with a semi-trailer parked next to it, and several armed people moved about the property. Chance's SUV sped across the field toward the trailer.

"That's where he's going." She turned and faced Greg.

"That's his truck in the satellite view?" Greg took a step back so that both screens could be seen more easily.

"Is he alone?"

"Trust me. He works very well alone."

"He's still my partner and I need to be there for backup. Where is he?"

Jasmine handed him an earpiece. "Put this on. I'll direct you on the fly."

Greg put the earpiece in. "What next?"

"Just talk like normal."

Greg ran out to his car, but stopped to take his gun out of its holster and remove the clip. He checked his ammo, replaced the clip and put the gun back into the holster. He climbed into his squad car and put the key in the ignition. Turning the key, he began to pump the gas pedal, slowly at first then more violently. The starter whined but the engine refused to start. He got out of the car, opened the hood and stared into the mass of belts, cables and hoses. After jiggling the battery cables, he slammed the hood shut and tried starting the car again. The starter whined and began to fade. Again the engine refused to start.

Greg jumped out of the car and raced back up the steps to the front door. He rang the bell and Jasmine buzzed him in. He ran straight to the control room.

"My car won't start, damn thing," he reported excitedly.

She turned to Greg. "Take mine."

"The Cobra?"

"No silly, my Beetle," she said, frowning.

Greg looked at the image on the map. His body was almost jumping, reflecting his sense of urgency.

"Where's his bike? Let me take that."

Jasmine looked into his eyes and frowned. "He'd kill me."

"The keys. Now!" he commanded.

For the first time, Jasmine saw the same anger in Greg's eyes that Chance had when his targets made him angry. He grabbed her by the shoulder and she leaped up from her seat, ran into her bedroom, took the keys from the nightstand on the side where Chance had slept and handed them to Greg. He turned and ran out of the room toward the steps, then paused.

"His keys were in your room? Hmm."

"Go. No wait."

She ran into the control room and grabbed the helmet that she had worn the night before. After turning on the communications, she handed it to him. "Get started and I'll get a controller assigned to you."

Hunter ran down the stairs, turned and ran through the house and out the back door, letting it swing open behind him. He jumped over the fence rather than use the gate and raced into the garage that Jasmine had already opened. He climbed on the motorcycle, started the engine, circled it around toward the driveway and bolted out of the garage.

After negotiating the bend in the road, Chance continued to accelerate when he drove through the trees. His SUV became slightly airborne as he veered onto the property heading directly toward the middle of the semi-trailer, leaving a trail of dust behind him in the soft dirt. The gunmen on the porch saw the approaching vehicle and opened fire, but their line of sight was hampered by the truck parked next to the house. Chance turned the steering wheel sharply left, causing the rear of the vehicle to slide around, then quickly turned to the right, bringing the SUV to a sudden stop just twenty yards from the house, positioned at a 45-degree angle with the passenger side door facing the porch. The angle of the vehicle gave him some protection from the automatic weapon fire that started to rain in from the front and rear of the house. He quickly grabbed his MP7, exited the vehicle and crawled to the front of his SUV and returned fire. His shots momentarily silenced the gunfire originating from the front porch. Bullets from the rear of the house continued to strike Chance's vehicle. He crawled to the back of his truck and returned a volley of rounds toward the rear door. That barrage of gunfire from the rear of the house ceased, but the gunfire from the front started once more.

Chance reloaded as the shooting started once more from both directions. He crawled to the rear of his truck and fired a grenade at the abandoned car in the back yard. The grenade landed just under the rear of the car and exploded, causing the car to erupt into a ball of fire and ceasing any activity coming from the rear of the house. Heavy gunfire rang from the front of the house forcing Chance to the rear of his bullet-riddled SUV. Chance ran toward the semi and rolled under the trailer to the opposite side, to an open space about a foot and half wide, and rose to his feet with his back against the wall of the house. He removed his .45 from his left thigh holster and fired shots at the rear of the house while advancing forward by sliding along the wall. He saw a figure jump from the porch into the space between the porch and the truck's cab. Chance released a short volley with his left hand from his MP7, immediately dropping the gunman in the space. He fired another shot at the rear just as another figure jumped from the porch, hitting the shooter mid-air in the head, as he fell dead to the ground.

Chance continued to inch his way forward when suddenly the semi's engine started. He fired his MP7 toward the front of the truck but the edge of the trailer blocked his shot. The engine revved up from its idle and the air breaks released with a loud hiss. The rig began to move forward, closer to the house, tightening the already narrow space until Chance's helmet became wedged between the trailer and the house. He released the chin strap, dropped to the ground and rolled under the trailer out into the driveway as the rear wheels came perilously close to crushing him. The truck stopped for a moment and seemed to pick up a passenger from the porch. Chance leveled his weapon at the trailer, then figured shooting may not be wise, not knowing what the payload was. The truck sped out of the drive and turned left, unknowingly headed in the direction where the state troopers had been.

The departure of the semi left Chance vulnerable to gunfire from the windows, and the front porch and the back porch. He took several bullets to the back of his body armor, with one striking him in the hamstring before he could dive over the hood and slide onto the ground on the opposite side of his SUV. Using the SUV for cover, Chance reloaded his MP7, jumped up and fired a volley of gunfire into the two windows.

"Ops. Can you tell what part of the house the professor is in?"

"*There are several people on the upper level, but there are three below grade. My guess is that he's one of the three.*"

Her information was met with silence.

"What are you thinking?"

Chance didn't answer, instead firing at both the front and rear of the house in sequence. He quickly opened the rear door and reached into the back seat, removing the camouflaged box. Opening it revealed a cache of shells all linked together on a metal belt. He repeated the shots to both ends of the house again to discourage anyone with thoughts of trying to get a closer shot. Once again he reached into the back seat and removed a Vulcan Mini gun. He loaded the first shell in the link into the feed block and closed the cover.

He quickly lifted the weapon up over the hood of his SUV resting his elbow on the hood and released a storm of bullets, accompanied by fire and smoke from the multiple rotating barrels. Within a matter of seconds, Chance had riddled the entire side of the farm house exhausting the entire box of shells. The only sounds left were the barrels of his Vulcan spinning to a halt.

Chance smiled at his work while nodding his head with approval, wondering how many holes defaced the entire side of the house. Much of the siding had completely disintegrated while the one remaining piece of glass fell from its pane onto the driveway, breaking on impact. Suddenly the posts holding up the roof on the front porch began to crackle. After a loud snap, the roof collapsed with a huge thud followed by a cloud of roofing material and dust.

"Ops for Hellcat."

"Go Ops."

"What on earth was that?"

Chance chuckled. "That was my little friend."

"It seems to have done the trick. Only one healthy heat signature remains and it appears to be in the basement."

"I'd better get inside." He grunted while putting his gun in the back of his SUV.

He removed his two .45 caliber handguns and limped to the rear of the house. He cautiously climbed the steps and stepped into the kitchen where two critically wounded men lay on the floor. One twitched while the other desperately tried to reach for his gun which was only inches from his hand. Chance shot the twitching man in the head then kneeled over the other and watched him reaching for his gun. He smiled as he pushed the gun to the mortally wounded man who was too weak to even lift it.

"Was it worth it?" He shook his head while rising to his feet and ended his would-be assailant's life with one shot to the head.

Chance continued thru the house delivering fatal head shots to each of the men who lay dead or dying on the floor. Chance holstered his .45 and unsheathed his military knife from a sheath on his belt and gripped it firmly in his right hand. He heard the gunman coughing inside a hallway closet.

"I know you're in there hurt. Toss your gun out and I might spare your life."

A voice called out, coughing. "No."

Chance remained silent but then couldn't resist teasing the injured man. He removed the .45 pistol from his left holster and tossed it into the front of the closet.

"Now I'm gonna kill you with your own gun."

Chance waited patiently until his prey had cleared the threshold, then grabbed him, wrapping his left arm around the man's neck and turning him around. He plunged the serrated knife deep into the assailant's back and twisted it violently. He held the man and wiped the blood from the knife on his clothes before letting the lifeless body fall to the ground. He placed the knife in its sheath, and began advancing up a short hallway, pausing to pick up his .45 from the front room floor.

From the hallway, he could hear a faint cry for help. Immediately, he ran to the doorway leading to the basement and descended the stairs three at a time. Peering into the darkness, he spotted Professor Kimble sitting on the floor, chained to a pole. The front of his shirt was covered with dried blood.

Chance had no reaction when he stepped over the body that lay at the bottom of the steps in a pool of blood.

"Professor Kimble? I'm Chance Barnette. I'm from the Homeland Security Agency. Are you hurt?" Chance asked as he went around the pole and used a universal key to open the lock around the chain. Chance helped the professor rise to his feet and held him by the shoulders for support.

"I'm ok. My daughter, where's my daughter?" he inquired, frantically worried.

"Megan's fine. She's one tough young lady."

"Yeah, she's tough, stubborn and head strong but I do love her to death," Kimble said, his eyes beginning to tear.

"Everything's ok, sir. Don't worry. The state police picked her up a while ago. That's how we found you." Chance turned the professor towards him and began checking his wound. "Let's get you some help."

"No time," the professor replied, his voice choking with emotion. "You've got to stop that truck. It's a nuclear device and they plan to set it off at Independence Hall."

"They want to blow up Independence Hall?"

"No, just contaminate it. That truck is filled with fifteen thousand gallons of water. Right now, it's a cooling system for a mini-reactor with relatively large control rods to keep the fusion process from running away. When they get to the destination though, the driver is supposed to start a timer and get in an escape car that's following them. After ten minutes, the coolant keeping the fuel rods from overheating will run out and make the rods overheat. Once that happens, the fission process will start and run wild. The fuel will then melt the containment housing. When the fuel hits the water, it'll create a huge ground-hugging nuclear cloud. Depending on the wind, it can spread for miles. Any life breathing in the mist will die instantly. And then it will settle and soak into the ground and all the buildings it surrounds, contaminating them. Especially porous brick buildings. Millions will be dead and gone by the time anyone will be able to enter the area again. Like Chernobyl."

"What can do we do?"

"You've got to stop that truck before it reaches the densely populated areas outside of Philly." The professor grabbed Chance's arm. "I purposely had the control rods made smaller than the reactor needed so that the fuel will reach critical mass long before it gets to Philadelphia. I thought it would be better to have it blow before they got to Independence Hall and a heavy populated area. But wherever the melt-down starts, the results are going to be catastrophic."

"Can it be detonated remotely? Or can we bomb it?"

"No, it's a process. If the cycle is interrupted, it wouldn't create a huge cloud but it would spill fifteen thousand gallons of highly radioactive water all over the highway. Some vapor would dissipate in the air, which is dangerous, but the worst is that, if you spill it, the liquid will make its way into the water table and that is definitely catastrophic."

"Honey Bee, did you get all of that?"

"Are you talking to me?" Professor Kimble looked quizzically at Chance, wondering who he was talking to.

"I'm wired for communications. I'll explain later." Chance removed his Colt .45 from its holster. "Do you know how to use this?"

"This is a big gun." Dr. Kimble pulled the slide, released it and pointed at Brandon's corpse lying on the floor, releasing a single bullet into the lifeless body.

Reassured, Chance rose to his feet. "Take care of it. I'll be wanting that back."

"Go." Dr. Kimble prodded. "I'll be ok."

"Did you contact the authorities?"

"Yes, Pennsylvania state troopers are on their way and we're tracking that rig. The escape vehicle is a black Ford SUV, and it's following the truck."

"Tell everyone to stay clear." He turned to Kimble. "Help should be here in a few minutes to get you out of here."

"Go. Hurry. Stop that truck!"

Chance raced up the steps and started to head to the front door of the house. Seeing all the rubble from the collapsed roof of the front porch, he ran back to the rear of the house and out the back door, pausing to spot one more escaping terrorist limping across the field towards the road. He was about a hundred yards away and moving as fast as he could. Chance took careful aim and fired a shot. An instant later, the man fell face first to the ground.

"Hellcat. What do you plan to do when you get to that truck?"

"I don't know, but I've never driven a semi before so you'd better start looking for a truck driver in a hurry"

"Roger that."

Chance ran to his battered SUV, started it up and slammed on the gas, heading back toward the highway. Within minutes, he passed the state troopers who had blocked the road with their cruisers. The truck had collided with them with such force that they had been completely pushed off of the road, and damaged to the point where each was inoperable. He didn't know if any of the troopers were hurt, but there was no time to stop.

"Ops. Better get some help to these state troopers."

"We got it. Just go. And be careful again. Please."

While careening onto the main road at the flashing light, Chance's SUV struck the rear of a passing car, spinning it a full 360 degrees but causing little damage to the SUV. He saw the driver step out of the car in his rear view mirror, so he just continued racing toward the highway entrance where he headed east.

"Have you come up with a plan yet?"

"We're working on it."

"If I can get to the truck, we'll need someplace safe to let it detonate."

"Ok. I'll work with the authorities."

Chance moved to the passing lane, then flipped a switch on the dashboard next to the steering column. The automatic suspension lowered the vehicle, and nitrous oxide was injected into the fuel system. Within moments, the speed of the SUV reached 130 mph. The right front fender of the SUV clipped the rear bumper of a car that did not get out of his lane fast enough. In his mirror, Chance saw the car swerving across the right two lanes of traffic, causing a chain reaction accident in its wake. The SUV was not affected and Chance continued east on the turnpike in the direction of the rig, rapidly closing the distance.

Chance finally caught up with the truck barreling along in the center lane, ramming and destroying cars in its path. Chance flanked the escape car that was behind the truck to verify it. He slowed down a bit, removed a .45 from his thigh holster, reached out his driver's side window and fired several shots into the back window of the black Ford SUV, exploding the glass. Automatic gun fire then rained out from the rear of the vehicle from the missing window. He returned fire and swerved to the far right lane of the highway, dropping behind an innocent passenger car for cover. The Ford swerved into the lane where Chance was driving. Chance swerved sharply over into the left lane while loading a grenade in the grenade launcher of his MP7. He dropped back, trying to lure his foes away from the passenger car that had been caught in the crossfire. When the black SUV moved toward the left lane, Chance sped up and swerved to the right, firing the grenade into the rear window.

He veered sharply into the right lane just as the escape vehicle that had been blocking him from the semi exploded into a fireball and zig-zagged right then left again across the highway, coming to a rest, fully ablaze against a guard rail in the median. He then proceeded to speed forward and pulled alongside of the tractor trailer that, in turn, moved into the right lane, forcing Chance onto the shoulder. He slammed on the brakes, slowing the SUV, then moved back onto the roadway. He tried to get beside the truck on the left side, but now it forced him onto the median strip of grass. He drove on grass for about a tenth of a mile, then pulled back onto the road and tried the same maneuver on the right, but this time when the truck swerved right, he gunned the engine and found himself beside the rig, almost to the door of the cab.

Chance pointed his .45 at the cab when suddenly the truck swerved fully into Chance's lane, forcing him over the rumble strips and onto the shoulder. Sparks and the sound of grinding metal followed as the rig continued to drifting to the right, wedging the SUV between it and the guardrail.

Chance slammed on the brakes as he saw ahead that the guardrail came to an abrupt end at a bridge abutment. The rig continued to drag the SUV along, but the friction caused by the brakes and the guardrail lessened the impact as the SUV slammed into the bridge abutment. The force of the crash pushed Chance towards the steering wheel, but his seat belt instantly tightened and caught his upper body before he hit it. His air bag did not deploy, so he could see the tractor trailer veering back into the center lane and continuing on its way.

"Chance! Are you okay?" Jasmine screamed.

"Yeah, I'm fine." He got out of the SUV and watched the truck as it sped away. "I have an idea. Keep an eye on that truck."

Chance walked to the front of the SUV, and after firing several rounds from his .45 into the front windshield, several holes and cracks covered the entire glass. He leaped up onto the hood and began kicking all of the glass out of the opening, then he jumped off and retreated to the rear of the SUV.

Opening the rear hatch revealed a small latch in the area usually covered by the floor mat. Chance pulled the lever and the bed of the SUV opened up, revealing a cache of weapons. After reloading his .45 he holstered it and reached into his mobile weapons locker and removed an odd-looking handgun with a large barrel. He broke the barrel open, inserted a custom-designed 12-gauge shell, closed it, and then inserted a spring-loaded cam into the barrel. Attached to the cam was a coiled nylon rope.

After securing the rear hatch, Chance returned to the driver's seat, got in and carefully laid the odd gun on the passenger side seat. He backed the Bronco up away from the bridge abutment, and raced it back onto the highway reaching its top speed, 150 mph. The wind ripped across his face now that the windshield was gone.

Within minutes, he had closed the distance to the truck which seemed to be able to go only about ninety mph.

Once Chance reached the rear of the rig, the driver danced the cab, causing the trailer to sway back and forth in an effort to keep Chance from driving beside him again. Chance dropped back and waited for the swerving to stop while grabbing the weapon on the seat beside him. When the rig stopped swaying from side to side, Chance gunned the engine, ramming the rear of the semi's trailer. He set the cruise control and fired the gun right at the rear door of the trailer. The cam entered just above the rear doors and exited through the roof. The spring loaded cam opened up, securing itself firmly to the roof of the trailer.

Chance was relieved that he saw no water escaping. He steadied the steering wheel with his knee, wrapped the nylon line around his arm and activated the nitrous oxide. The vehicle lunged forward, crashing hard into the back of the trailer and throwing Chance out of the front windshield onto the hood. He jumped to his feet and leaped toward the trailer, grabbing the nylon line with his left hand while unwrapping the line from his right arm. He reached the small platform on the rear of the trailer, right behind the doors. Then the rear of Chance's Bronco began to rise, flipped violently into the rear of the trailer, barely missing Chance as it tumbled back and across the highway. It went airborne and flipped over the guard rail.

"*Chance?*" Jasmine yelled frantically.

"Don't even ask. I'm ok."

The terrorists laughed as they looked in the rear view mirror to see the SUV flipping and disappearing over an embankment. Seconds later, the Bronco exploded into a large fireball that rose up over the rim of the embankment.

Chance held onto the rope and began to pull himself up by the cam embedded in the roof of the trailer. After climbing onto the roof, he struggled up on his hands and knees, then looked forward to the front of the rig just in time to see an overpass rapidly approaching. He immediately dropped to a prone position and felt a whoosh of cold air rush over his body as the truck slid tightly under the overpass. Once they had cleared the overpass, Chance cautiously rose to his feet, and began gingerly making his way up to the front of the trailer. Reaching the front of the trailer, he removed his .45 and jumped down between the cab and the trailer. Grabbing the chrome handle attached to the corner of the cab on the passenger side, Chance stepped out onto the running board.

The terrorist in the passenger seat froze in horror when he turned to the side window and found himself looking directly into Chance's intimidating black eyes. Chance immediately fired three shots that ripped through the door, all finding their mark. He opened the door and pulled the limp bloody body out of the cab. The body of the terrorist hit the asphalt and quickly disappeared behind the speeding rig. Climbing into the passenger seat, Chance pointed his .45 at the driver, who immediately smashed his palm against a large red button on a black box attached to the dashboard. He opened the door and leaped from the speeding cab. An amber LED display lit and a clock immediately began to count backwards.

Chance grabbed the steering wheel of the slowing truck and slid into the driver's seat.

"Honey Bee, I've secured the truck. Now what? Did you find me a truck driver?"

"We're working on it. Just keep driving. The troopers have the professor and he's debriefing."

"This day is really going to hell. Just think, it started off in a warm bed..."

"Hellcat... we may have a driver." Jasmine interrupted. Dead air followed, but the silence was soon broken by Jasmine's reassuring voice.

"State troopers are approaching from the east. They can take over when they reach you."

"Do they have a truck driver?"

"Yes, they have a guy who can handle it."

"Negative. There isn't enough time to switch drivers. Just connect me to the guy and I'll do it."

"Ok. His name is Brent. He's a retired Marine who works as a truck driving instructor. We have him on the phone. He has you in one ear and us in the other. We're briefing him as we go, ok?"

Chance continued driving the truck, uncertain where he should be going. He heard three deafening thumps in his ear.

"Chance, this is Brent. Do you read me" Chance responded negatively to the loud yelling into his earpiece.

"I can't hear you, Brent, not so loud," Chance yelled.

"Ok sorry... Can he hear me now?"

"Jasmine?" Chance pleaded.

"He hears you, Brent. Just talk normally. Don't raise your voice."

"Chance, this is Brent," an elderly raspy voice asked.

"How fast can this thing go?"

Brent laughed, "I like this kid. He's direct and to the point.... Well, depending on the weight of the load and the grade of the highway, and then there's a learning curve since you're not familiar with driving a vehicle that size."

"Brent!"

"Ok, about **90 mph** if there's no governor."

"How will I know if there is a governor?"

"Well, it'll only go 55 or so, but then in about an hour... boom! Then you'll know for sure."

"Ok. I get it."

"Ok, hold on a minute. Chance, we have to turn you around and head you west," Jasmine interrupted. "There's an old mine about fifty miles away. You're gonna drive the truck in and when you come out they're gonna blow the entrance to the tunnel. The good part is that it's not far from another mine, with a highway construction crew and a cement plant. They can use that asset to bring all kinds of heavy equipment to seal it permanently."

"And I get out how?"

"They'll put a car inside for you to drive out."

"Just tell them to make it a fast car, will ya?"

"Ok." Jasmine laughed. *"I'm gonna let you talk to Brent while I search for the closest place where you can turn around."*

"Chance. Can you drive a stick?"

"Affirmative."

"That's a good start but here's where it gets difficult. They tell me that the load weighs is in excess of seventy five tons. That's over the limit. It's gonna be a bitch to make it stop to turn around and to get it rolling again. It has 18 gears and you'll have to use all of them. Then we pray that we don't destroy the engine before we get to our destination and that the bridges support the weight, 'cause they usually have a forty ton limit."

"Guys?" Jasmine interrupted. *"Most of the bridges in that area have been beefed up because they move a lot of heavy mining equipment on those roads."* She continued, *"Chance, I found a turnaround about a mile away from your location now."*

"Good. That gives us time to work on your down shifting. Your load is liquid so we'll have to take it slow. Take a look at the shifter. What gear are you in?"

"It says four and eight."

"Ok that's good. Don't touch any buttons and double clutch to the three, seven."

Chance pressed the clutch in and shifted out of gear. He then reengaged the clutch, shifted into gear and released it. The semi slowed with a jerk.

"I'm at the gear that says three, seven."

"Good, now same process down to the one, five gear, but you're gonna have to do it a lot quicker if you're gonna make that turn on time. That load is liquid and it's gonna swish around so we wanna take it nice and slow on that turn."

"Ok, I'm ready."

"Feel the little switch on the front of the shifter?"

"Got it."

"Flip that switch to the down position, and double clutch back to the four eight. We're gonna downshift all the way down to the one, five if we have time."

Just as Chance went back to the four, eight gear, he saw the opening in the guard rail. "I'm here already."

"Chance, you're still going too fast to make the turn with that load," Jasmine informed him. "There's going to be another in about two miles."

"No time, the clock's ticking."

"Swing way out to the right lane and go for it," Brent commanded.

"No, Chance, no chance," Jasmine yelled, realizing the oddity of repeating his name.

Chance removed his foot from the gas pedal, pressed the horn and veered across traffic into the right lane forcing cars off of the road. The rig was still slowing when he steered back across the highway and into a police turnaround that had been paved in the median grass. He hit the brake pedal but felt he'd lose control of the rig, so he attempted the turn anyway. The wheels squealed and smoked against the asphalt. The turn was too wide, as he careened across the opposite direction lanes into the westbound outer shoulder and slid along the metal guardrail trailing sparks and smoke behind him. He down-shifted to the one, five gear, gave it gas and merged back onto the highway forcing the traffic into the left lanes while continually blowing the air horn.

"Wow, that was exciting. I'll save the video for you," Jasmine sighed in relief.

"Ok what now?"

"You've got fifty-two miles."

"Yeah, and about fifty six minutes to get there. Now what?"

"Let's see if this rig has a governor. Get to shifting." Brent ordered. "What gear are you in?"

"It says one, five now."

"That switch in the front is still down right?"

"Affirmative. But it feels like it's gonna shut off."

"Slide the little switch under your thumb back up, and double clutch it back to the two, six gear." Brent paused, listening for the result. "How's that now?"

"Better, but it's still pretty slow and the clock is ticking."

"Ok, now you have to pay attention. Only press the clutch in half-way and slide the switch under your thumb forward. Feel the gears change?"

"Affirmative."

"Okay, slide that switch back, give me a double clutch to three, seven. Half clutch and slide the switch forward. Got the hang of it?"

"So far so good."

Chance glanced in his rear view mirror and saw some Pennsylvania state troopers' cars approaching. The first car sped by, then slowed to Chance's pace. Three other cars remained behind.

"Agent Barnette? This is Lieutenant Vance of the Pennsylvania State Troopers. Do you need our driver to take over? He's in the car next to you."

"No. That turnaround was a little hairy but I've got the hang of it now."

"We're in contact with your people and we're all on the same page. Keep your speed up, drive at your own pace and we'll follow your lead. The road is all yours. We're escorting you to an old mine. The width of the tunnel is big enough for this truck to go up to about a mile inside. They're putting a car in there, so you stop at the car, leave the rig and hightail it out of there in the car. By the time you get there, they'll have the tunnel wired and ready to blow. The charges are gonna explode behind you one by one, right behind you, as you drive out. They're building molding outside the entrance and when the last charge goes off, they're gonna entomb the whole thing with concrete. The highway engineers say that the bridges are all new and because of the mining and construction equipment that they move around in the area, they're capable of much heavier weights. But there's one older bridge over a gorge. There is a steep downgrade on the approach and a steep uphill on the other side. They say not to exceed 25 mph when you cross it. Any questions for us?"

"Not at all. Just give me some space on either side right now. I'm trying to get the hang of driving this thing. Jazzy, can you call Greg and let me talk to him?"

"I meant to tell you. He came by looking for you but his car wouldn't start up again, so I gave him your motorcycle. I see him on satellite and *he's trying to catch up with you. He should be there in a few minutes. Sorry but my car was too slow, and I doubt the Cobra would let him drive her."*

Chance followed the troopers who pulled out ahead of him. They exited the turnpike and headed north on a two-lane road. Chance thought about his missions and the lives that he already saved over the years, and how, due to necessity, his bravery would be kept a secret to his grave. He thought about Jasmine. She knew of his bravery and unlike other women, he wouldn't have to keep his life secret.

"Honey Bee, go P-COM." The background chatter that was ever present while on a mission, ceased.

"P-COM. Go ahead."

"Clear the line and cease recording." For the moment, Chance could hear Jasmine's every breath.

"What is it, Chance?"

"In the bathroom, the other morning. I heard you."

"Heard me what?" Her breath quickened.

"You know what!" Chance laughed.

"No you didn't."

"It's ok."

"Well I heard you talking in your sleep that evening on the sofa."

"Oh no."

"It's ok, 'cause I have one more confession. Before I woke you up, I kissed you. I wanted nothing more than to plant that kiss in your mind."

"The truth of the matter, Jasmine, this is all new to me. The Dean told me that no woman could love men like me because of what we do, and even if we try to keep our lives a secret, she'll find out eventually and be completely disgusted. It confirmed what I already believed, but when he told me, it was too late. The time I've been spending with you has been more like a fantasy than a mission."

"And just think. You could have taken advantage of my goodies all along, silly boy. They were yours for the taking the whole time."

"Now I'm sorry, Jasmine. I'm just not used to a normal life. You've seen what I do. Doesn't it disgust you at all?"

"Remember yesterday, when you heard that lady scream? You went right to her rescue because you have a good heart and you know what's

right. You rescued a whole neighborhood and they all love you for it. You make me feel very safe, knowing what you do."

"When we first met, I thought that you hated me for being a... well, a brute."

"Yes, I was angry because you broke Grady's leg, but I was so looking forward to meeting you for the first time when you came into the gym. I was yours from the first time I heard your voice."

"Jasmine, I know this is a mission, but can we pick up where we left off and make it real life?"

"Chance, nothing would make me happier." Chance could hear Jasmine begin to cry.

"If I survive, that is." Chance looked at the clock that had only fifteen minutes left. "Let's get back to work, Jazzy." Jasmine switched them back to the controllers' airwaves.

"Five miles, Barnette, but you're approaching that bridge. Better start slowing down," Lieutenant Vance informed him, as the patrol cars rounded a curve in front of the semi.

The mountain road began to snake down a very steep incline, S-curving left and right. It was not a road for semi-tractor trailers. Chance downshifted to slow his ascent but the road made a sharp left hairpin turn forcing him to use the brakes. The rig slowed just enough to complete the curve but not enough to avoid scraping against the guard rail, causing the trailer to sway. But as soon as Chance regained control, he reached another sharp curve to the right. He peered out his side window at the valley below with a flowing, dark-water creek running through it. He looked at the guard rail; it was the only thing keeping him from running off of the road and down to the valley below. The trailer tires skidded as he once again used the brakes to slow his ascent. Finally, he could see at the base of the incline the last curve that opened up into a straight 300-foot drop at a thirty-degree angle. An alarm in the cab sounded as he rounded the curve.

"Brent, the brakes are gone," Chance yelled.

"Yeah. I hear the low pneumatic air alarm. Keep downshifting so that you can make that curve."

Chance downshifted three times and was barely able to safely negotiate that last turn. The truck then sped downward onto the last quarter-mile straight stretch of the road leading to the bridge below. It looked small like a landing strip, as it narrowed to just two thin lanes, with raised one-foot wide shoulders on either side. The bridge terminated on its other side at the foot of a steep uphill incline that added a slow vehicle lane. That incline would help slow the truck down, but it would also take precious time to climb. It had a hundred feet straightaway, but then the road made a sharp left turn as it began its ascent up the mountainside. Chance could see that about half way up, the road made a sharp hairpin curve to the right and then the highway vanished into the woods on the top of the apex.

"What's that hill going to do to my time?" Chance asked.

"You're gonna lose a lot of minutes climbing it if you have to slow down. You'll be shifting like crazy. Honestly, what have you got to lose, Chance? I'd go for it."

"Vance did you hear that?"

"I wouldn't advise it. We have to take the word of the engineers who say the bridge is not all that stable for a truck your size."

"Vance, you and the other troopers go ahead. I'm going for it. Stay with me. Brent, I'll need your help." The truck kept picking up speed, heading toward the ribbon of concrete at the end of the road's steep slope. With the trailer swaying behind him, Chance realized that missing the small slab of concrete would result in a 300-foot drop into the gorge below. The speedometer continued to rise until the engine cried for a non-existing nineteenth gear. The truck began to vibrate as it approached the bottom of the hill, gaining more speed. Chance held the steering wheel tight, trying to make sure that he didn't lose control.

The truck slammed onto the cantilevered deck with enough force to make the bridge undulate like a wave, pushing the far end of the bridge's deck section two feet into the air, which caused the middle of the bridge to sink. Each of the police cruisers driving a few hundred yards in front of Chance became airborne as they hit the two-foot drop in the mid-section of the deck. Chance pressed the pedal to the floor, trying to make sure he wouldn't lose speed so the semi could clear the first deck section before it collapsed. He could feel the entire structure swaying beneath him as he fought to maintain control of the rig over the moving stretch of bridge.

The cab of the semi slammed onto the mid-section of the bridge with a loud crashing noise as it went over the two-foot drop. The canyon reverberated with the sound of the semi hitting the decking, and the edge of the bridge crumbled to the valley below seconds after the trailer wheels went past it.

"You still with me Brent?"

"Yep. *Not bad. You barely cleared that one section before it gave way but you should be ok now. Shift to the lower gears when it starts to slow down. You're almost there.*"

Chance didn't have to downshift until he was half way up the hill. Once he cleared the curve the cruisers came back into view.

"*This is Vance. You ok?*"

"Yeah, but I don't think the bridge fared too well."

"*Remind me to write you a speeding ticket,*" Vance laughed. "*We're almost there. Keep it up, buddy.*"

When the truck reached the top of the hill, Chance saw an overpass, and just before it there was an exit leading up to the overpass roadway. He pressed the gas pedal to pick up speed while glancing at the timer. The semi was approaching its downhill speed going uphill.

"Chance."

"Go, Jazzy!"

"*That's your turn coming up. Start slowing down now.*"

Chance realized the exit was closer than it looked. He braked hard, as the truck careened to the right, following the police cruisers up the exit ramp and onto the roadway heading away from the overpass. He passed several huge concrete mixer trucks stopped along the roadside. After a mile and a half, the police cruisers veered off of the pavement onto a dirt road.

They approached the tunnel entrance, passing several concrete trucks parked behind flatbed 18-wheelers stacked high with large concrete pouring forms. Heavy earth-moving equipment had been brought in from a nearby strip mine to reopen the tunnel entrance flanked the two sides, and a crane had already begun to erect the metal forms at the opening. HAZMAT and emergency vehicles were parked on the left shoulder of the roadway.

"*This is it Barnette. Good luck and God be with you.*"

"Thanks Vance. Sorry about your bridge."

"*Don't worry about it. Just get your ass out of that tunnel before they blow it.*"

The dirt road straightened as Chance advanced on the tunnel entrance. The state troopers pulled over on both sides of the road, keeping their blue lights flashing and sirens going. More sirens began to bellow from all of the emergency equipment. A flatbed 18-wheeler sat with its trailer backed up towards the mine entrance to the side, a tarp covering its cargo and its engine idling. The driver wore a white hazmat suit. As the semi rolled forward, the cement and flatbed truck drivers all stood outside their rigs, some on their running boards and some on the hoods of their vehicles. The workers around the tunnel entrance all paused, cleared the roadway and began to cheer as loud as they could. The truck drivers all blew their air horns in support while others waved various size American flags as he drove past. A large flag had been hung above the tunnel entrance, though it was partly covered by the steel structure being erected for the concrete forms. Four fire engines sprayed water into the air creating an arch for the passing semi.

"Is this all for me?"

"Now you're everybody's hero. Not just mine," Jasmine replied tearfully.

"Reminds me more of a funeral."

"You'll be ok. Just get in that car and get out," she responded as she began to cry.

"Hey, Jazzy, don't cry. I'm not dead yet."

"I love you Chance."

"And I love..."

"Chance! Chance!" His last words got cut off as he entered the tunnel.

Thick black smoke bellowed from the exhaust stack on the flatbed with the tarp as Chance drove past. Once inside the tunnel, Chance saw in his side-view mirror that the flatbed began to back into the tunnel, followed by a car with flashing yellow lights.

"Night vision, Jazzy," Chance demanded as he plunged into the darkness, but there was no response.

After a futile attempt to find his headlights, Chance tried unsuccessfully to start his night vision manually using the switches in his gloves. He then realized that the uplink to the satellite was cut off because he was now deep inside the mountain. He ripped the PTM from his face and tried to adjust his eyes to the darkness. The trailer scrapped the walls as Chance tried to negotiate in the dark passageway that was curving slightly, choking off any sunlight from the entrance.

By the time, Chance saw the tail lights it was too late. He locked the brakes and skidded into the car that had been left running for him to make his escape. His body flew up but was stopped by the roof of the cab. He fell back on the seat as it collapsed backwards at an angle. He pulled himself up and looked at the timer: 60 seconds. Chance started to climb out but fell to the gravel floor of the mine from his cab that was now sitting on the trunk of the car.

Chance forced the front car door completely open and it gave enough light to see that the entire rear of the car was crushed and still under the cab. The smell of gasoline began to fill the air as it flowed out of the car's gas tank, which had been punctured by the impact. He could hear the engine of the 18-wheeler back at the entrance. Then a familiar sound that came from behind the rig caused Chance to run to the rear of his truck. He peered into the darkness of the tunnel and got a glimpse of what looked like two lights closely set together. It rounded the curve and rapidly approached. It was Greg, who did a 180- degree skid, ending up directly beside Chance.

"Come on, they're blowing the tunnel any second."

"Hold on." Chance turned a knob under the motorcycle seat that manually activated the NO2. He climbed on the back. "Go for it!"

Gravel sprayed from under the rear wheels as Chance held on tightly while they sped through the tunnel. The flatbed semi that had been backed into the tunnel left very little clearance for the motorcycle on either side. Greg negotiated the space on the left and headed for daylight. The concrete molds on the outside of the tunnel were already put in place. Once they cleared the opening, police troopers pointed at them to continue around a bend in the dirt road where emergency vehicles were waiting. Once there, they could hear the cruisers' radios blasting out the "all-clear" signal, followed by an explosion that collapsed the tunnel entrance.

The explosion set of a geological chain reaction causing the ground to rumble and shake as the interior of the tunnel collapsed. The dust that cleared the opening during its collapse was captured by the huge plumes of water being sprayed into the air by the fire trucks. Boulders rolling down the side of the mountain just above the mine fell behind the steel structure that was emerging at the entrance. Within seconds the only sound that could be heard was that of the pumpers and the water as it hit the ground.

Suddenly a frantic crackling voice rang out from the patrol car. *"Somebody talk to me. Is everything ok? Did he make it,"* Jasmine cried.

Vance lifted the microphone and spoke into it. *"Why don't you ask him for yourself? Uh... while I write him a traffic citation."* he laughed.

"Chance." Her voice crackled and he could tell that she had been crying. *"I thought I had lost you when your message cut off."*

Hunter grabbed the mics. "I saved his ass."

Chance grabbed the mic from a laughing Hunter. "I couldn't get any reception in the tunnel. But I'm ok." He turned toward Greg. "He did bail my ass out," he added, wrapping his arms around Hunter's shoulders.

"That's what partners do pussycat." He laughed in Chance's direction.

"I'm so relieved, happy, joyous, still scared... I don't know what I'm feeling. I need a moment to recover, then I'm gonna sign off, take a shower and get all dolled up. Let's go out and celebrate, Chance."

"After today, I think I'd rather stay home and order in."

"Whatever you want."

"See you when I get home... uh, Mrs. Barnette."

Jasmine began laughing hysterically until her voice disappeared as she signed off. As Chance and Hunter were getting back on the motorcycle, two state troopers approached.

"Great job, Agent Barnette." A man in military fatigues shook Chance's hand. "I'm Colonel Hank Jacobs, Army Corps of Engineers."

A bewildered Greg Hunter looked quizzically at Chance. "Agent?" he asked, his voice rising high. "What are you? Some kind of super-secret agent?"

Chance laughed and shook his head at Hunter.

"It's nice to still be around to meet you. I take it that you're the one that put this all together."

"This is called American ingenuity son. Everybody working together to protect our national interests."

"Can I give you a ride home?"

"Actually, yeah. Driving that semi was a workout. Greg, are you ok taking my bike home without me on the back?"

"Ok?" Greg laughed. "This will probably be my last chance to drive it.... Double-O-Seven?"

"We'll all have to take another route out to the turnpike, given that Mr. Barnette here destroyed my bridge," Jacobs laughed.

The four police cars escorted the late model black sedan and motorcycle along the dirt road to a logging road that led through the forest, eventually terminating back to a paved road that took them to the highway, where Greg launched the bike into high speed until he was out of sight. The remaining three police cruisers eventually dropped from the caravan and returned to their daily patrols, looking for speeders and helping broken down vehicles on the turnpike. To the average person in that part of Pennsylvania, it was a normal day, with nothing special happening.

Jacobs drove past the vacant lot at the corner where the 52nd Street gang headquarters once stood. After turning onto Chance's street, they immediately saw flashing lights from two police cars sitting in front of his house. Two officers flanked the stoop in front of the open front door. Mrs. Johnson was gesturing and talking frantically to some officers. She looked up and pointed to Chance as he ran to the door.

"Officer Barnette?" the sergeant asked.

"What's going on?"

"Your wife has been taken."

"What do you mean, *taken*? A hostage?"

"Yes. We got a call ten minutes ago that she was pulled out of the house at gunpoint, blindfolded. Your neighbors saw the commotion and said the men were masked and armed, holding a gun to her head."

Mrs. Johnson, who was being restrained by another officer, tried to break free and was calling to Chance. An officer stepped into her path, but Chance waved him off.

"Let me talk to her."
"They took her, Chance."
"Who took her?"
Mrs. Johnson began to cry frantically. "I don't know, but I, I, saw them..."
Chance placed a hand on each of her shoulders. "Calm down, it's ok. I'll find her."
"She was fighting.I saw them and was going to run out to try to help, but I saw the guns and it was terrifying."
"Who did you see, tell me exactly?"
"A very muscular man and a woman, yes it looked like a woman, they pulled her out of the house and she was blindfolded, with something in her mouth, and they put her in a white van with no windows. A tall military-looking guy was standing next to the van and after they got her in, they drove away."
"Which way did they go?"
Mrs. Johnson pointed up the street.
"You go home and calm down. We'll find her, don't worry."
"Wait! One more thing."
"What's that?"
"Your friend. He got here on a motorcycle as they were pulling off. I told him and he's the one who called the other police, then he went after them."
Chance grabbed his cell phone from its leather holster and dialed Greg's number, but got no answer. He turned back toward his porch steps as a sergeant put his hand on Chance's shoulder.
"We'll find her, don't worry. The investigators are on their way."
"Thank you," Chance said, then he bolted up the steps into the house and up to the second floor. A young officer who was standing in the living room chased him up the stairs and tried unsuccessfully to grab Chance by the arm. "Wait!" You can't come in here. This is a crime scene." Chance pushed him aside and ran up the steps and into the control room, where two officers were waiting. They immediately grabbed him but were unable to keep their grip.
"It's ok. I'm Officer Barnette and this is my home." He showed his badge.

"This is an active crime scene. The detectives are gonna be pissed, Officer Barnette."

"Sorry guys, but this is personal now."

"What is all this equipment anyway?" one of the officers asked, but Chance didn't respond to the question.

"See if dispatch can find Officer Greg Hunter," Chance barked. "He's missing, too."

One of the patrolmen radioed to dispatch, while the other followed Chance when he went down the hall to the bathroom. He stopped just inside, looked at the officer and slammed the door.

"Give a guy some privacy."

The air in the bathroom felt damp as was the towel hanging on the towel rack. He lifted it from the rack and covered his face with it. He inhaled the smell of her clean body, then wiped the sweat, dirt and tears from his face. He rarely acted out of anger, rarely lost his cool, but now Chance had become pure rage as he flexed his muscles and dropped the towel to the floor.

He opened the door and pushed past the two officers waiting outside the bathroom, and went into Jasmine's bedroom. The eyeliner and lipstick on her dresser were open and the room still smelled like her perfume. Several outfits and a pair of stockings were stretched out on her bed; while on the floor were a pair of black high heel shoes. Chance's heart skipped a beat as he looked at these for a moment, pondering his next move, then he swiftly turned and went back to the control room, tailed by the two officers. The room had been ransacked, and some of the equipment had been damaged. He glanced at the mayhem around, then dropped into Jazzy's chair and rested his face in his hands.

As he sat there peering through the space between his fingers, he suddenly noticed that the monitor in front of him had been faintly turned face down. He removed his hands and pulled the screen upright. He gently pressed the space bar and on the screen, a message appeared 'Session has timed out. Please enter the password.'

"Hey, you can't do that. You're disturbing the crime scene," one of the officers yelled to him.

Chance turned to face the officers with a cold, dark stare. "Let me tell you, you have no idea what's going on here." He turned back to the screen.

The younger officer pointed to the screen. "She's your wife. Try your name."

Chance began to type. C-H-A-N-C-E, then Enter. *'Incorrect Password.'* He leaned all the way back in the chair, far past the point that Jasmine would have approved of. He closed his eyes and suddenly he sensed what she would have done. He sat straight up in the chair and typed the words 'I love Chance' in different variations until he got it with the letters 1 – L – 0 – V – 3 – C – H–@–N – C – 3, Enter.

The screen came alive with activity. Messages were being typed back and forth, with several different conversations going on in the messenger windows. They were flying by so quickly that he couldn't make heads or tails of them, then suddenly the word 'Jazzy!' appeared.

Chance quickly typed, 'I need assistance.'

The words, *'Hawk Requesting a tryst y/n'* appeared on the screen.

Chance typed 'y' in the box that opened up.

'What's up cutie?'

'This is Chance. Jazzy's been taken hostage.'

He saw hundreds of words scroll by on the main screen, then all but two conversations stopped. The typing on the screen slowed to where Chance could keep up with reading them. These were active mission dialogs with several controllers each inputting data. Then a faint chirping sound came from under the desk, but Chance ignored it.

'Put the headset on' appeared on the screen.

Chance scanned the room, finding the headset on the floor.

"What's going on?" said a voice that sounded like a male version of Jasmine, curt and to the point.

"Jasmine's been taken hostage."

"When?"

"About an hour ago."

"Did all you guys get that? *I need Alpha team to check every satellite image within thirty miles over the last hour and a half. Delta team, contact all assets within one hundred miles. Put them on high alert. Epsilon* and Zeta, check all traffic and neighborhood watch cams. X-Ray, get us a satellite overhead. Bravo and Foxtrot, you watching the web traffic, right? Tango, take all the cell phone and short wave transmissions."

Another voice interrupted.

"This is Hackett. Ready two gunships and the director's jet, and clear all airspace. This is about family."

"Hack," Chance jumped in, "what do you need me to do?"

"I would normally say sit tight and let's see what's going on, but I know you can't do that. Gear up now and turn on your transceiver and put your PTM on. Stand by for instructions. By the way, I know it doesn't mean much right now, but great job today."

"Thanks Hack. That was business, but now it's personal."

"I know. We're shifting all of our resources to this. We'll find her, Chance."

"She was just on line about an hour ago, so they can't have gotten too far, could they?"

"Let's not speculate. We'll get the facts and find her."

"If it's who I think it is, they have satellite and probably communications access."

Chance watched the main screen come alive once more, but once more he couldn't keep up as each team continued to update their information. He turned to the officers who were watching in awe.

"Did dispatch hear from Hunter?" Chance turned to the police officers.

"No, not yet. They'll let us know when they do. Who are those guys on the screen?"

Two detectives came rushing into the room. "What are you doing? You're trampling my crime scene." He turned to one of the officers. "Who let him in here? Get him out of here." He grabbed the arm of the chair with one hand and pulled the headset from Chance's head.

Chance jumped up and took the detective by the wrist and twisted it, forcing him to back into the shelving behind them and knocking a small box off that fell to the floor. The uninjured detective looked at Chance, who looked down at the empty box. He looked back at the counter, then the floor again. He put on the headset again.

"Hellcat to base."

"Base."

"You know those red tracking capsules that she makes me take? Do you know anything about them?"

"*They're prototypes that she's developing. They're fueled by body heat. That's why you swallow it. They'll run till they work their way through your digestive system. Once they get in the sewage system they break down in a couple of days.*"

"I don't know how relevant it is, but the box is empty."

"*Good catch. We have the frequency so we can track them from here if one of them gets activated.*"

"Hey, where did all this equipment come from?" one of the detectives asked just as Chance's cell phone rang.

"Everybody shut up," Chance yelled. "It's Hunter." He answered the phone turning on the speaker. "Hey, Greg. Where are you?"

The phone clicked, but Hunter gave no response. The phone then clicked one more time, followed by dead air. He put the cell phone down and leaned back in the chair, and locked his fingers behind his head. He tilted his head upward, staring at the ceiling, then closed his eyes, imagining the scenario. He allowed his mind to see a visual, picturing Jasmine gagged and tied to a chair. His anger continued to intensify until he was again interrupted by one detective, who was listening to his earpiece.

"Barnette!"

Chance leveled his face and swiveled the chair toward the officer.

"Ok, I received orders from the Chief to cooperate with you. Sorry about the mix-up. They told me that they tried to trace the phone location, but no luck. Dispatch will continue to try and let you know if and when they find him. Central is pulling all but four officers from here, two stationed in the back and two in the front. We'll be downstairs. Let us know if you need anything."

"Thanks, guys. I appreciate it."

Chance logged off the screen and rose to his feet. After pacing the floor a few times, he went downstairs, walked past the police posted there and headed for the garage. The door automatically opened before him, and he stared at the open space where his motorcycle was usually parked. He suddenly turned, ran back to the house and bounded up the back steps. In the kitchen, his path was blocked by a sergeant who had been left behind

"Hold on, Officer Barnette. The Chief informed me that he's calling in all of the off-duty officers to sweep the city."

"That's great. We can use all the eyes that we can get. Let's hope that Hunter doesn't try to take these guys on by himself. He's in way over his head."

Chance grabbed the officer's wrist and removed it from his arm. The officer felt a chill, as Chance's black eyes made contact with his.

Chance went upstairs as the sergeant signaled for one of the patrolmen to accompany him. They followed Chance into his bedroom wondering what their desperate colleague was going to do next. He turned and looked at them again, then shrugged his shoulders as he turned back and commanded, "Simon says Open."

As the officers watched, the wall facing the side of the house began to move. The sergeant gasped while a huge grin swept across the young patrolman's face. A section of the wall slid open revealing an arsenal large enough to arm an entire S.W.A.T. team. The locker contained hand guns, rifles, machine guns, hand-held rocket launchers, and armor.

"What the hell...," the sergeant started to stutter.

Chance looked at the officer, pointing his finger at him and addressing him sharply, "You never saw this. Got it?"

"The hell I didn't see it. Who are you? Can't let you leave."

Chance ignored the sergeant and turned to the locker. He removed his PTM from a compartment and put it on his face. The two officers stood in awe, watching Chance strap a holster to each thigh. He took a chrome-plated Colt .45 from its holder and slipped in a full clip that he grabbed from one of several cradles, all containing various clips. After holstering the gun, he removed another, following the same routine and holstered it on the other thigh. He then put on a double shoulder holster and removed a black 9mm Sig from its peg. Before loading a clip in it, he looked at the weapons in his thigh holsters and opted instead to put two chrome 9mm handguns in them. Then he reached up and took down a hanger, from which he removed his Kevlar-lined trench coat, which he put it on.

Chance stepped back and coolly said, "Simon says Close."

"Are you sure you have enough?" the sergeant asked, almost sarcastically.

Chance paused and turned back to the wall, "Simon says Open."

He removed a hand-held rocket launcher and slung it over his shoulder. He then took a submachine gun, loaded it, and turned back to the two officers. "Simon says Close."

"Hold on, Barnette. What the hell is that?" the sergeant said, pointing to the rocket launcher.

"Secure Locker." Chance said, exiting the room.

"This is my job, Barnette. You have to tell me what's going on. The Chief needs to know."

Chance stepped into Jasmine's bedroom and lifted the keys to the Viper from a ceramic bowl on her dresser. He then walked toward the stairs.

"You can't go, Barnette. I told you we'd cooperate with you, but you have to stay here." The sergeant started to try to grab Chance by the arm.

Chance pushed him away and immediately removed a canister from his belt and sprayed the contents toward both officers. A blank stare came across their faces and they both fell to the floor. He reached the bottom of the stairs just as two officers approached quickly from the kitchen in response to the thud they heard. He gassed them as they approached and raced quickly to the back door and into the garage. Chance climbed into the 1969 Shelby Cobra, turned the key and the engine turned over but would not start. Chance stroked the dashboard.

"C'mon, Mommy needs us." Again he tried to start the car, and this time it turned over with a loud rumble that made the garage vibrate. He backed out of the garage, down the driveway, and onto the street, put the car in drive and rumbled to the corner.

"*Ops to Hellcat.*"

"Go for Hellcat."

"*We've found the position of your motorcycle using Lojack.*"

Chance raced off, following the directions from the controller. They guided him to a wooded embankment about two miles from the house. A battered guard rail stood between him and the embankment.

He exited the Cobra and peered over the edge. Fifteen feet below him were the mangled remains of his prized possession. On the guard rail he could see traces of fresh blood and white paint.

Chance jumped over the guard rail and quickly side-stepped down the embankment to his motorcycle. He could see that the front of it had been demolished, suggesting that it crashed into the rail and flipped over down the hill. He reached down and picked up the helmet laying a few feet away. It had been struck by a bullet that had destroyed the PTM circuit inside it, and exited through the rear of the helmet, though he saw no signs of blood inside the helmet.

Chance switched his PTM to thermal mode and looked at the motorcycle engine that still glowed bright red. He scanned the area but there was no sign of Greg.

"There's a camera on a pole at the corner. We're downloading the video to your PTM. We're also checking all of the cameras in the area for additional footage."

In the video, Chance could see a black SUV speed past the spot where the motorcycle crashed. A second SUV followed directly behind. A gunman leaned out the rear passenger window and appeared to be firing a hand gun. Hunter avoided the gunfire, but the SUV swerved sideways and came to a halt. In order to avoid colliding with it, Hunter swerved right, lost control, crashed into the guardrail and flipped over it, disappearing from the camera's sight.

The lead SUV stopped and waited while men jumped out of the second SUV, over the rail and down the hill. Moments later four men returned into the camera's view. Hunter was walking on his own, but with a visible limp. They forced him into the SUV at gunpoint. Both SUV's sped out of camera range.

Chance climbed back up the hill and got into the car, placing the helmet on the passenger side floor. After sitting for a moment, he lifted Jasmine's transponder locater and looked at the blank screen. Frustrated, he tossed it out of the car and peeled off, stopping at the corner to look up at the darkening night sky. He jumped out of the car, walked back and picked up the locater, replacing the cover. He returned to the car, put it on the seat and continued up the street.

Chance drove into the darkness for what seemed to be an eternity to him. His eyes scanned the streets for anything out of place, a clue that could possibly indicate where Jasmine and Greg had been taken to. Some streets were still busy with pedestrians shopping and making their way home for the evening. As if drawn by some inexplicable force, he turned up a residential side street that eventually led to a large parking lot surrounded by industrial buildings. Only about half of the structures were lit up and occupied, while others had rows of gray cinder blocks where windows had once been. Many had bars over the windows.

"Control to Hellcat."

"Go for Hellcat. Any news?"

"*News? Are you looking at it?*" the controller asked excitedly.

"What? Looking at what?"

"*Jasmine's receiver, isn't it alarming?*"

Chance lifted the flashing receiver and he realized he must have broken the audio when he threw it from the car.

"It didn't make a sound, but it's flashing like crazy."

"*That's it. We see you on our satellite image. See the parking lot at your eleven o'clock?*"

"I see it."

"*She's in the abandoned building on the other side.*"

"What's the layout?"

"*There doesn't appear to be any external surveillance, but we can tell you there are two individuals standing on the parking lot side of the building at a loading dock. They have AK-47s and there's no cover as you approach.*"

"Ok. I have an idea. Stand by."

Leaving the car parked in a far off spot, Chance got out, adjusted his coat to make sure his guns were not visible and began walking across the lot toward a three-story brick building facing the street. The back of the building had been defaced with layers of black, white, red, and yellow graffiti in all kinds of gang signs. Chance could see that several tags that had been applied were from the 30th Street gang, signifying that this block was under their control. They were no longer intimidated by the 52nd Street thugs from across town who had lost their headquarters and all of their drug supply along with it. The 30th were now in a struggle for their lives against the drug suppliers looking for payment for their product.

"This appears to be an abandoned factory. Do we have any intel on it?"

"*Here's what we have.*" The controller paused for a moment, then returned. "*It's owned by Roker Industries, a defense contractor. Been vacant about five years. Leased to a company called the Stryker Group, and fully modified so we can't get any type of visual inside, just like the one where the professor and his daughter were being held.*"

"Who are those guys?" Chance asked.

Still don't know and unfortunately we won't be much help on this one either, but backup is on the way.

"Roger, control."

Chance walked on the sidewalk, past the main entrance of the building on the street. Once he cleared the corner of the building, he became visible to the guards. He turned and staggered across the parking lot toward them, as if he was wandering off the street. One guard had his back to Chance while the other, who was smoking a cigarette, was facing him but didn't immediately notice his approach. They seemed to be engaged in a rather raucous conversation, so when they finally noticed him he was within 30 meters.

The guard who had been smoking removed his cigarette from his lips, and holding it between his two fingers he pointed them in Chance's direction. The other guard immediately turned around to face him.

"Hey! What the hell are you doing?"

"Sorry, fellows, I rented a beer and gotta go to the bathroom..." Chance slurred his speech and held up a finger. "Gotta milk the weasel." He turned toward the building and put his hands in front of his fly.

"Just keep moving or you'll be sorry you stopped here to take a leak."

"Ok, ok. Either one of you have a cigarette?"

They started walking in Chance's direction. "Get out of here, you bum."

"Just one cigarette. Then I'll leave you alone."

"Get the hell out of here."

"Hey buddy, all I need is a cigarette, then I'll leave."

The guards, now agitated, stood side by side, both facing Chance and revealing their weapons. The one who had been smoking, angrily threw his cigarette, which bounced off Chance's coat before falling to the pavement. He stepped closer to Chance, who stopped in his tracks and raised his eyebrows. His assailants were now only a few meters from him.

"Whoa, take it easy, sorry guys."

"Yeah, you're going to be sorry you ever stopped here to take a piss." They laughed. One of them looked around to see if anyone was watching. He unholstered a handgun from his waist, pointed it at Chance's head. "Should I kill him now?" He laughed.

"Yeah, shoot him. No one's gonna miss this bum."

In one swift seamless move, Chance pushed the gun to his left, away from his head, grabbed the guard's wrist with his right hand, spun him around and turned the gun on the second gunman, shooting him in the forehead. He then used his left hand to reach into his holster, remove his weapon and dealt a final shot to the remaining gunman's chest.

Chance tossed their hand guns and AK-47s into the hedges next to the building. He then ran up the four steps that led up onto the loading dock at the back of the building. The bays had been bricked but a lone metal door stood off to the side of the dock. He crouched to stay out of the site line of a small square window built into the door, an obvious peep hole.

"I need you to look inside for me," he whispered, removing his PTM and holding the micro camera up to the glass. After a few seconds, he put the PTM back on his face. "What's the situation?"

"The hallway runs the length of the building. There are several openings and it's well lit. A logistical nightmare. I advise you to wait for the breach team."

"That may be too late."

Chance leaned against the wall next to the door, using it for cover, while he removed his coat so he could have easy access to his weaponry.

He raised his Colt to eye level and pushed on the metal door. It was unlocked so he pushed it further and stepped inside, just as Tess exited one of the side doorways. She was turning to walk away and had taken a few steps before stopping, sensing someone. She turned to him just as he approached.

"Stop right there," he said as he closed the distance between them and pointed the gun at her head. Looking at her closely, he was stunned by her beauty, and completely unaware of her fighting skills. "Jeez, I knew we didn't have any guards as good looking as you," she purred. "You are much cuter up close than I expected."

Chance was too distracted to notice the kick that dislodged his weapon from his hand until his gun flew slid into an adjacent dark doorway. Tess took a step back and assumed her fighting stance. Chance readied himself but refused to step backward.

"And you're so buffed." she smiled as she scanned Chance up and down. "I see why your little friend is so attracted to you. A girl's dream, a man who can protect her." A man then stepped out of the hallway behind Tess. He looked at Tess then Chance, then turned and began running down the hall away from them. At the end of the hall, he turned right and disappeared through a doorway.

"See what I mean? The cowards. Afraid of a little contact." Tess reared back and kicked Chance in the side of his face, knocking his PTM to the floor. She immediately followed that with a punch, but Chance caught it in midair.

"Ok, that's the end of your little show," he told her, twisting her arm behind her back.

"You know you're not supposed to hit a girl," she groaned.

"Where's Jasmine?"

"Wouldn't you rather have me Chance?" She grunted as Chance increased the tightness of his hold.

"Where is she?" he yelled in her ear, while tightening his grip even tighter.

"Oh, you mean that weak little bitch?" Tess taunted while forcing a smile, and trying to mask the pain. "I gave her a good old-fashioned ass-whipping. Wouldn't you rather have me Chance?"

He twisted her arm to the point of separating it from its socket.

"Ow, that's enough; she's at the end of the hall, up the steps. But you're probably too late. I don't know what kind of drug that little junkie is on, but I found a handful of red capsules when we snatched her from your home. After I kicked her ass, I shoved six of them down her throat. Stryker didn't even notice." Tess began to laugh.

"You mean the little red heat-activated GPS transmitters?" Chance pointed to the scanner that was now clipped to his belt.

Chance released her arm. Tess's pride turned into anger and she immediately stepped back into her fight stance. Tears from the pain began to roll down her cheeks. The closest door was ten meters down the hall and Chance knew that in the four-foot wide hallway, her only choices were to retreat or move forward and attack. Her expression let him know that she was not the retreat type. Even pain wasn't enough to force her back. It was the same fire that he experienced the first time he met Jasmine in person. Tess took a wild swing at Chance, who was able to move his head away from the punch. He immediately reacted by connecting a hard uppercut to Tess's chin. She reeled backwards, lost consciousness and fell to the floor with a thud.

"See. You got it wrong. You're not supposed to hit *a lady*."

He raced down the hall to its end, turning right and running through a doorway. He found himself in front of a flight of metal stairs, with a metal door at the top, this one without a window. After ascending the stairs, he grabbed the knob and it turned. He easily pushed the door open and entered a large, empty room. Its twenty-foot ceiling made it seem enormous, but it was lit only with a dim incandescent bulb above a doorway on the other side that led to another room that appeared to be cloaked in darkness. The only other light in the room was coming from the full moon that shone through the dirty floor-to-ceiling windows on the far wall.

Chance slowly approached the opposite doorway, but suddenly he was grabbed from behind by someone who pinned him in a full-nelson grip. Two additional guards ran toward him. He slammed his head back, breaking the nose of the man holding him, then flipping him over his shoulder right onto one of the approaching men.

He side-kicked the other approaching guard in the chest, then followed with a fatal punch to the throat which crushed his esophagus. The first guard got up again and, managing to retain his balance and fight back, he grabbed Chance by the left wrist with his right hand. Chance responded by grabbing his wrist, yanking it, forcing him to release his grip, then stepping over his arm and pulling his assailant's shoulder out of its socket. He then delivered an elbow to his temple and a chop to his neck, knocking the guard onto the ground.

Four more men suddenly appeared from the doorway and completely circled Chance while remaining at a distance. They positioned themselves at 3, 6, 9 and 12 o'clock. Chance faked a lunge toward the man he was facing, and the attacker jumped back out of the way. Chance smiled, turned to 3 o'clock to face another assailant, where he faked a punch and the assailant flinched and cowered. He could smell their fear and his next actions were obvious to him. He pivoted and delivered a kick with his right foot to the chest of the man who was behind him at 6 o'clock. He quickly planted his feet and gave the attacker at 9 o'clock a roundhouse kick to the side of his face, followed by a punch to the bridge of his nose and karate chop to the neck. One down. He immediately grabbed the wrist of the man who had been in front of him as he threw a punch, then spun him around while lowering him to the floor and making the others back up. He bent his arm at the elbow and twisted until he heard a snap, then pushed the man's head down until his neck snapped.

With two assailants down he used his legs to sweep the feet from under the attacker at 3 o'clock, then delivered an elbow to his throat. Chance leaped to his feet and hit the attacker at 6 o'clock again, this time kneeing him in the groin. When he bent over in pain, Chance locked his arms around his neck and twisted his body as he fell to the floor causing the guard's neck to snap. The final assailant left, the one at 3 o'clock, jumped up from the floor and took out a switch blade and squared off. Chance backed up to give himself room. He watched his opponent's eyes while trying to gain a positional advantage. The guard eventually lunged at Chance, who leaped backward, limiting the damage as the knife slightly slashed his side. The man continued to slash at Chance until he finally lunged once more. Chance stepped aside, caught the man and turned his body sideways, then grabbed his wrist and wrestled him to the floor, as the knife fell out of his hand and bounced on its blade to land about three feet away. Chance climbed on top of the man and the two tussled and rolled around on the floor.

Chance jumped up and tried to get the knife, but the guard kicked it away. Squaring off again, Chance finally side-kicked the man in the head, then punched him in the sternum, causing him to stumble backwards. As he receded, Chance delivered a drop kick that knocked the assailant out of the second story window on the far wall, while leaving Chance on the ground.

Chance was beginning to feel weak from the fight and the bullet wound which he had received earlier. Before he was able to get up, another figure, Hodges, emerged from the doorway and rushed at him. The large muscular man delivered a well-aimed boot right to Chance's kidney. Though the pain was excruciating, his instincts led him to roll away from the kick, coming to rest on his back. The boot heel had pounded into his torso, causing the air to rush out of his lungs.

Chance managed to unholster a gun and raise it toward his attacker but his hand was immediately kicked by the boot that Hodges had raised to deliver a blow intended for Chance's head but now diverted to the weapon. The gun fell to the floor. Chance quickly rolled towards it, and managed to grab it, but to his surprise the muscle-bound, yet agile, soldier jumped over his body landing on his hand. Chance felt a bone snap due to the force of Hodges' weight who immediately turned and kicked Chance in the rib cage.

The pain disoriented Chance just long enough for Hodges to pull him from the ground by the hair, then deliver a crushing head butt to his chest, causing him to fall to the ground once again. Hodges moved in quickly for another kick, lifting his right foot high into the air for a final strike to the middle of Chance's chest. But his intentions were disrupted by Chance's kick to his right ankle, just as Hodges' body had lifted up onto the ball of his foot. His ankle buckled, causing Hodges to fall hard to the floor next to Chance.

Chance immediately gave Hodges a taste of his own pain by head butting him in the forehead just above his left eye, opening up a large gash. He then wrapped his arm around Hodges' neck. Chance felt his assailant weakening as he choked off the blood supply leading to his brain. Hodges tried to pry Chance's arm from around his neck, but Chance tightened his grip using his broken hand around Hodges' neck.

But the pain in his hand was too great. Chance could feel his finger bones separating and had to release his grip, and Hodges was able to roll away yet again. Both men then slowly rose to their feet and Chance instinctively used his superior speed to kick Hodges in the diaphragm, causing him to immediately fall to his knees. Chance's next kick aimed at the side of Hodges' head was stopped in midair by the stronger man, who rolled, twisting Chance's foot. The pain surged through Chance's ankle but he was able to kick away, falling back through the door that Hodges had come out of. Chance grabbed a chain, which hung from a block and tackle pulley system hanging from the twenty foot ceiling, to break his fall.

Hodges rushed through the door and Chance used the chain to swing toward the charging heavyweight to deliver a flying kick to the jaw of his attacker. The blow only slowed his approach though, and when Chance released the chain and put his weight on his twisted ankle, pain shot through his leg. He was forced to grab the chain once more for balance.

Hodges wrapped his massive right arm around Chance's neck and began to choke off his oxygen supply. Chance grabbed his arm but the pain in his hand kept him from being able to pry it from around his neck. He reached around and fumbled until he was able to grab the chain which hung from the bottom of the block and tackle pulley, and wrap it around Hodges' neck. He then reached for the haul line that was hanging parallel. He felt himself losing consciousness, but was still able to wrap the chain around his forearm and used his free arm to elbow Hodges in the ribs, causing both men to lose their balance, but not their grips.

Chance held the chain tightly and could feel his strength returning, as Hodges' grip on his neck weakened. The struggle had now become one of stamina and the sheer will to survive. Chance was applying pressure from the weight of both men on the haul-line, while his opponent tried to maintain his grip. Chance summoned all of his remaining strength and focused in on pulling the chain causing Hodges' blood supply to his brain to be interrupted completely. Hodges collapsed to the floor, momentarily unconscious.

Chance, exhausted, went in for the final kill. He stood up and coiled the chain around his forearm with the broken hand to compensate for the inability to grip, then grabbing the chain with his uninjured hand he pulled down hard, diving to the ground and hoisting Hodges skyward toward the ceiling, kicking as he was being choked to death by the chain. Chance then jumped up, using the chain to lift himself slightly up, and then fell to the ground again, lifting the now unconscious strongman even higher until the chain block locked in position. He paused to look up at the trickle of blood now dripping from the corners of his lifeless combatant's mouth.

Chance suddenly turned around, hearing a familiar yet weak voice coming from another doorway behind him, but in pivoting, he fell down, unable to fully support his weight on his injured ankle.

"Watch out, he's going to kill you," Jasmine cried out, in a weak and hoarse voice as Chance limped thru the doorway.

Chance instinctively went for his remaining gun, yanking it from its holster in a split second and almost firing it as he turned in the direction of Jasmine's voice. Along the far wall of the very large empty room, Stryker held Jasmine in front of him with his left arm wrapped tightly around her neck. In his right hand, a Glock pressed firmly against her temple. Chance could not believe how helpless she looked. She was tired, dirty and she had been crying, causing the mascara to run black streaks down her cheeks like it was Halloween. Her eye was black and blue and swollen, and there were large red bruises on her arms and legs. Her right hand had been hastily wrapped, but the left side of Stryker's face was badly bruised and swollen, too. Her body was limp and she had no more fight left.

"Chance, he's going to kill you, get out" she tried to scream again, her voice trailing off.

Along the same wall, about ten feet away from them, Chance saw Greg Hunter's motionless body lying on the concrete floor. A fierce combination of adrenaline and anger temporarily masked Chance's pain and allowed him to raise his weapon, but the ribs on the side of his uninjured hand had been broken and he couldn't hold the gun level. Chance looked at Hunter's motionless body lying on the floor. He thought about how easy decisions like this were before he had a friend and before he had fallen in love. Helplessness was a completely foreign feeling until now. In this moment of loss, Chance found his sense of humanity.

"Ok, Stryker, what are you gonna do?"

"You know the drill. Drop the clip out of the gun, or I'll kill her."

Chance tried once more to raise the gun but the pain was too intense.

"Uh uh," Stryker warned, shaking his head negatively. "That would be a bad move." He positioned his head behind Jasmine's. Chance gave in and pressed the release, letting the clip fall to the ground while he began to contemplate his next strategy.

"Now . . . nice and slow, put the gun on the floor with the barrel facing you."

He placed the gun on the floor.

"Kick it to me."

Chance kicked the gun toward Stryker, who soccer kicked it off to the side as it approached him.

"Isn't it funny how love clouds your judgment? In the past, Barnette, you would have never done that." Stryker began to hoot. "The great Chance Barnette gave up his gun?"

"Why don't you let Jasmine go now?"

"That wouldn't be wise. There's nothing more dangerous than a wounded animal. Besides, Jasmine's a prize."

"What's your interest in this anyway? You're a soldier and you're willing to contaminate the place where our nation was born?"

"It was simply a means to an end for me. It probably wouldn't have been that effective anyway. But it is great for business. You see, I work for an elite private security company, and nothing is better for business than fear."

"You're no better than the terrorists."

"The world is always at war, Chance. You know that. We're mercenaries, you and me. Sometimes you fight with the good guys, sometimes the bad. Sometimes they're both the same. You've got to find a way to benefit from it."

"So it's all about money to you? That's all that matters to..."

Stryker interrupted. "I take offense at that. I am a patriot, a decorated soldier. I've fought all over the world in support our values."

"Whose values? What values are those?"

"Ours, idiot. It's our values that people shouldn't look to the government for everything."

"Including security?"

"It's up to each person to hire the best security they can afford, wherever they live."

"Everyone deserves to be safe."

"Everyone deserves food, shelter, and clothing too, but we don't give those away for free."

"You're not a patriot. You're an opportunist."

"And you're not?" He paused. "You know, we know all about the HSA. Hell, we even know your satellite blackout zones and times. That's how we can move around so freely without being detected." He turned to Jasmine. "Don't look surprised. You and your people have no friends in my circles. You live and work in seclusion, all comfortable and safe. And you Chance. You get to be judge, jury and executioner on the people you monitor. You dole out the death penalty wherever you see fit. You hide behind superior technology, lording it over the rest of us. Especially you, Chance. I've been watching you for a long time."

"What do you want Stryker?" Chance demanded, getting an inkling of a new strategy.

"Actually, it's you that I want. You're a hated man, Barnette. A man who's had for business, not to mention some very wealthy enemies that you've made along the way." Stryker paused. "They actually want me to deliver you to the Middle East alive, and I wondered how in the world I could do that. But once I saw you look at Jasmine, I knew I didn't have to capture you. I could just turn her over to them and collect my reward, then they can take you when you try to rescue her."

"Ok, if it's me you want, let her go. I'll go wherever you need me to go," Chance offered, trying to bargain.

"You know as well as I do that it's too late for that. By now, your merry band of hoods are probably right around the corner. We're all going to die here today. Your friend here was the first to die. Jasmine's next, then you."

"No, you'll be the only one to die here today."

Stryker began to laugh. "Do you think he's in love with you?" he asked softly in Jasmine's ear, laughing.

"I *know* he is," she replied, staring him right back.

"You don't know the half of it, Jasmine. For instance, you don't even know your own name," Stryker yelled at her.

"You're crazy. My name is Jasmine Simon."

"No, your name is Zohra Rubin."

"What are you talking about?"

"Sorry, sweet buns," he squeezed her bottom. "Your name is Zohra. Your father was an Israeli soldier and your mother was a Palestinian."

"No, you're lying," she struggled to say.

Chance took a step forward, but Stryker pointed his gun at him as a warning. He quickly turned it back on Jasmine as she started to squirm and attempt to loosen his grip on her.

"You don't even know who you are, do you Jasmine? I do. Your name is Zohra Rubin. Your father was an Israeli soldier and your mother a Palestinian," Stryker repeated, breaking out into sinister laugh. "And all this time you thought you were Colombian."

"I am Colombian."

"Ironic?" he continued without paying attention to her. "Your father was on a covert Israeli mission in Iraq and your mother was visiting her parents in Gaza, when the Israeli army retaliated for a suicide bombing. It just so happened that your uncles were known Hamas fighters and when the army raided the house, they killed everybody including your mother. Yes, everybody but you, because they knew your father would come for you and then they'd kill him to keep him quiet. But your father, being the nasty son of a bitch that he is, ambushed the four soldiers that were holding you and brought you to South America."

"You're lying. My parents were both killed in a fire. Then I was adopted by Richard and Yvonne Simon." She tried to turn to look at Stryker but he tightened his grip.

"No, Zohra. Your father brought you to Columbia. He married a Colombian woman, and she was killed by rebels while he was on a mission. When he got back, you and your half-brother were gone. To this day, he lives in Caracas and thinks you're both dead."

"You're lying."

"No. No. Your people lied to you. Not me. Think back. Remember the orphanage? That's where the rebels took you. Then the US government people came. They were looking for expendable children that nobody would miss. Kids to bring here to train. They found out that your IQ is well above normal and they chose you to come to America. This is how you got here."

He paused to take an inventory of the room.

"As for you, Chance Barnette. Do you have any idea who you are?"

"I know that I'm the man who's going to kill you if you even pull a hair out of her head."

"You just can't suppress that urge. That urge for blood. In your mind, you mask it as justice, retribution, and patriotism, but it's more than that. Something, well, primal. And you know why?"

"No, tell me why."

"You think that the Barnette's are your parents but they just babysat you while the government trained you."

Chance stood in silence while Stryker turned his attention to him.

"It was a little bit harder to get information on you. I had to call in a favor from a very high source but it was well worth it. Someone else was curious about you. Someone in the government and he was powerful enough to get at least some information about you. See nothing riles Americans up more than fear, or maybe a good sex scandal. Lucky for me your rat wasn't happy with the political position he'd been put in. He had a weakness for young women, but then everybody knew about that. But once I found out that every now and then he prefers a young man, so he was more than happy to get me the information that I wanted."

Stryker shook his head and chuckled.

"Ever wondered why you could never form attachments to people, Barnette?"

"No. Never, I had a job to do and I'm about to do it to you."

Stryker turned to Jasmine. "And you thought that you could make him love you. That's the one gene they forgot to give him. He's just not capable." Stryker laughed loudly, then turned back to Chance. "Tell her. Tell her you could never love her."

"I haven't the faintest idea what you are talking about, Stryker."

"Guess you've never wondered why you were usually stronger and faster than your opponents, or how you could get two guns out of the holster and fatally shoot two opponents before they could even un-holster their weapons, or why you're smarter or even why you heal so fast. The list goes on and on."

Stryker looked up at the corpse hanging from the ceiling. "Hell, you don't even have a conscience. Now Hodges here, he was a good man. In fact, he was the best and look at him now. I can only imagine the euphoria that you felt while his life was slowly slipping from his body. You probably could have killed him quicker, but the act of killing him was a moment to savor, right?"

Chance remained silent.

"So let me tell you. What I did find out about you is that you are the result of a government effort to create a super soldier. They knew that it wouldn't be smart or practical to create a whole battalion. After all, who would be able to control a group like that? So they only made a few of your type. I would imagine all of them have or at least would have had those same black, dead-looking eyes." He shook his head in mock amazement and continued.

"Ok, so here's your story now. You were one of these test-tube babies and you got turned over to the startup agency, Homeland Security. You know that the man who pretended to be your "father" was a very well-known psychologist. Well, so was your pretend mother. The government paid them a ton of money to nurture you to be the soldier you are, and I must admit they did a hell of a job."

"You don't know anything about my parents. My parents loved me. They were always there for me."

"Yes they were and that's what got them killed. According to my source, your parents got a little too ambitious in their child rearing. They decided all on their own that they wanted you to have a normal life. The night they were killed they were meeting with a group who was arranging to get the three of you out of the country."

"The accident," Chance mumbled.

"Yes, now you remember. Then you were given to your aunt, who was just another retired agent, who filled in so you'd have somebody when you went home for visits from military school. But she completely lacked any maternal tendencies, and left you hanging," he smirked in delight.

"Now that you know your story, there's only one thing left to do."

"Go ahead Stryker. You'd love to put a bullet in my head."

At that, Stryker pulled the trigger, but Jasmine quickly pushed his arm away and the shot ricocheted off of the wall, grazed Chance in the shoulder. Reeling to the side, Chance heard a second shot, but felt nothing. The second shot that rang out was not the Glock in Stryker's hand, which jammed when he pulled the trigger, but another gun. Stryker had failed to notice that Hunter continued to breath and that he managed to pick up Chance's gun that had come to rest within inches of his body. Although he was struggling to raise the gun, he was able to fire the one shell that Chance had not cleared from the chamber. The bullet tore completely through Jasmine's thigh and came to rest, lodged in Stryker's hip. Jasmine fell to the floor as Stryker let her go in his own pain. With an adrenaline rush, Chance lunged at Stryker and dragged him to the ground. Stryker got to his feet first and fired one wild shot, then limped out through a side door, leaving a trail of blood.

Chance grabbed Jasmine. "Don't you die on me," he told her, fighting back his tears. "Remember, you're not allowed to die yet. I know it hurts, but you're gonna be ok." Through all the pain coursing through her body, Jasmine felt the single tear splash onto her cheek. "You were sent to protect me. I knew it all the time." He kissed Jasmine on the cheek and limped over to Greg, who was now sitting up and trying to lean against the wall.

He forced a laugh then began to speak. "That's twice in one day."

Chance bent over and touched him on the top of the head. "You did well today. Now you're a hero. No more lunch runs for you."

Chance walked back over to Jasmine, bent down and kissed her passionately on the lips. "You know I have to go now."

"Chance, when will I see you again? Will I see you again?"

Stryker had stopped just outside the door when he saw that Chance was not pursuing him. He laid his gun on the floor, took off his belt and wrapped it around his bleeding leg as a tourniquet. He picked up his gun and limped sideways down two flights of metal stairs. Upon exiting through a side door, he found himself squarely facing five masked men dressed in all black. Two of them had their weapons drawn and pointed right at him. He turned around to try to reenter the building, but just as he grabbed the door handle, it was pushed from his grip and slammed shut. Two men dressed like the others stood on either side of the door. One was extremely tall and the other was huge, bigger than Hodges.

"Drop it," the short, muscular one said.

"Who are you with? HSA?" He laughed sarcastically, as he laid the gun on the ground.

His question was met with silence. Two of the masked figures grabbed him by his arms and cuffed his wrists together behind him.

"Guess it won't do much good to ask for my lawyer, huh?" He laughed once more, before cooperating with his captors' silently implied command to enter the vehicle where one of the masked soldiers stood holding the door open. The masked soldiers got into their respective vehicles and the caravan vanished into the darkness.

The first police squad car arrived just as Chance exited the building, his shoulder and leg still bleeding. The officer identified himself as Officer Trudeau.

"Sit down, sir, the ambulance is on the way."

"Upstairs is the missing agent, and police officer Greg Hunter. Take good care of them."

"What about you?"

"Don't worry about me. I'll be fine."

The officer patted Chance on the shoulder and ran into the building. Chance slipped around the building into the shadows and watched as the ambulance arrived. He limped across the parking lot, sticking to the shadows, then walked for another two blocks where he sat down on the curb in front of another abandoned warehouse.

Chance rose to his feet as the late model van approached slowly. He winced while trying to raise his arm to attract their attention. The van stopped directly in front of him and the side door slid open. The inhabitants exited and helped him to climb inside.

"How do you feel?" one of the men asked after the other closed the door.

"Like shit as usual."

"You don't look too bad this time." The technician dialed his cell phone. "The chicken is in the coop."

"Why do I have to be a chicken?"

"Hey... Don't look at me." The other technician laughed.

"They're ten minutes away. Let's get your gear off."

As soon as he had removed his holsters, the van pulled off on the shoulder of the highway. "Here we are."

The two men got out of the van, then helped Chance out. The door closed and the van drove away. A side door on the black semi-trailer opened and a lift lowered to the ground. The two technicians stood on either side of Chance as they were lifted up and stepped into the trailer. Everything inside was white and sterile.

"I'm your nurse, Terry," the woman said as she helped Chance to remove his clothes and climb onto a hospital bed. "You look pretty banged up."

"I've been here before. In fact I've been here a lot."

Terry inserted an IV and hung a bag containing fluids.

"Where is Edwidge?"

Terry smiled. "She's been reassigned. I'll be working on your case until we hire a replacement."

"Why was she reassigned?"

"Don't know." Terry hustled to get the equipment that she needed. "She just requested to be reassigned. Guess the job got to her."

Terry injected Chance with a local pain killer, then proceeded to remove the shell from his shoulder. She filled the wound with gel then stitched it up. Just then, Dr. Busby entered the room.

"Hey, Buzz. Heard you lost your sidekick."

"Yes. Edwidge has been reassigned."

"Was it something I said?"

Busby smiled. "No. She actually didn't like the fact that we keep patching you up and you keep coming back."

"Isn't that what you do for all of your patients?"

"Chance," he paused. "You're our only patient."

"And why is it that I have my own hospital on wheels?" Chance sat up on the bed.

Busby turned to Terry. "Can you give us the room for a minute?"

"Certainly." She walked out and closed the door.

Dr. Busby walked over to a counter and removed a white business card which contained only a telephone number. He handed it to Chance.

"They told me to give this to you when you start asking questions."

"Who?"

"I have no idea. I was just instructed to give it to you when you started asking questions."

"Who do you work for?"

Dr. Busby ignored the question and began once more tending to Chance's injuries. "I advise you to take it easy for a few days, but I know you won't."

"Don't worry about me. I'll be ok. I know how hard to push myself."

"Just don't be foolish. You're not immortal."

"Maybe I am," Chance chided.

"If you were, you wouldn't need me."

"Buzz, I always have a powerful dream that I'm being taken away from myself. Why is that?"

"Have you ever thought that it might be a memory?"

"I've heard that before."

Greg and his hospital transporter, a tall muscular young man, laughed as he wheeled him down the hallway, stopping to let Greg try and secure a date with a young nurse at the nurses' station by telling her that he had been shot several times while trying to rescue some hostages. She replied affirmatively with a smile, writing her phone number on a note paper that Greg pocketed. He pushed him away and down the hall.

"Hey man. I've been trying to get her number for the longest time."

"Ever been shot?" Greg looked up at his new friend.

"Come on. I push sick people around on beds and in wheelchairs all day."

"You gotta get shot man. Be a hero. Then they'll feel sorry for you while they admire you at the same time," he laughed.

Outside Jasmine's hospital room, two uniformed Philadelphia police officers stood along with Brock and Rice. They greeted Greg as he approached, while one of the officers opened the door allowing the transporter to push Greg into the room. Jasmine was sitting up in the bed, chatting with the other controllers on her laptop. The transporter left and closed the door on his way out.

"Be outside when you need me," he reassured Greg.

"Thanks Buddy. Hey when we leave here, you can wheel me by so I can check out Sophie on the eighth floor."

Greg turned to Jasmine, who was glaring at him.

"Oh, no. You shoot me, and now you're already trying to pick women up?"

"You're lucky I was there to shoot you."

"And who is this Sophie?"

"She's a nurse down on the eighth floor." He winked.

"You are such a dog," Jasmine laughed, shaking her head in mock displeasure.

"So check this out, Greggers," she said excitedly as she rose to her feet. "My surgery went well. They threw some metal and some screws in and I started rehab this morning."

"Wow, I'm jealous. I can't even stand on my leg." He got up and stood on his one uninjured leg and they embraced in a hug.

"I've got this on," Greg said, sitting down and revealing a large purple cast on his raised leg. "Plus I'm minus a spleen," he laughed.

"Well I had a concussion."

"Me, too."

"And this, thanks to my friend who decided to shoot me in the leg." Jasmine lifted her gown and showed Greg the scar on her thigh.

"I'm sorry, Jazzy."

"That's ok. Like you said, if you hadn't, we would all be dead now."

"Damn, no more short skirts for lil' Ms. Sexy, huh?"

"Oh please, Greg. The plastic surgeon came by this morning and I'll be back in short skirts in no time. I'm not hiding these legs."

"Soooo conceited." They laughed.

"Well?" Greg's face became serious.

"Nobody has heard from him," Jasmine said, sitting down on the bed. She patted the space next to her, inviting Greg to sit down.

"What are you going to do?"

"I don't know, Greg." Her eyes filled with tears, and though she tried to stop them, they kept coming until they flowed down her cheeks. "I don't know if he's dead or alive."

"I've spent enough time with him to know that if he could be here with you, he would."

Hunter put his arm around Jasmine and she rested her head on his shoulder. "I really love him and I was hoping he felt the same."

Chance entered the front door of the hospital walking with a noticeable limp, his arm hung in a sling. He was met at the door by the police Commissioner and Chief Hallowell, who were being escorted by two uniformed officers as they were leaving the hospital.

"Ah, it's the man of the hour." He placed his hand on Chance's uninjured shoulder. "Where the hell have you been, son?"

"Recuperating. Figured I'd better get things clear with my primary doctor first. You know how picky those insurance companies can be."

The Commissioner and the Chief both stared into his eyes for a moment. "Listen, the city and the nation owe you a major debt, son."

"Thank you, Commissioner, but I was just doing what I was apparently born to do."

"Your director was here this morning and I told him how much this meant to the city. I also asked him if I could keep you in town for a while. Obviously he refused."

"Thank you," Chance said, acknowledging the compliment.

"If there's anything I can do for you, you let me know."

"As a matter of fact . . . you can."

"Anything. Just name it. We owe you big time." Chance took the commissioner by the arm and pulled him aside. "You boys meet me outside." he commanded the officers. "Officer Hunter. They still treat him like an errand boy at the precinct. Without his bravery and police skills, things would not have turned out good at all. Especially for me."

"Ok. I'll see what I can do."

"Listen. I guess my director told you that my identity has to be protected. I want Officer Hunter to get full credit for stopping that truck. He was truly heroic."

"Your people have taken care of everything. On our end we'll make sure that Hunter is the officer who gets credit."

The Commissioner headed out the door, but Chief Hallowell returned and approached Chance.

"Uh... I have a question for you Agent Barnette."

"What is it sir."

"The 52nd Street drug gang bust and blowing up that house. Was that you?"

"Tell me, Chief. Do you really want to know?"

The Chief glared for a moment, then finally smiled. "Maybe I don't. Your wife, Jasmine, or whoever she is, is in room 1020." He turned and exited the building while Chance made his way to the elevators. On the tenth floor, Chance exited and followed the signs leading to the room. The nurses at the station gawked at him as he walked by. One of the officers who was guarding Jasmine's door, pointed to Chance as he approached. Rice and Brock assured him that it was ok, and they sauntered down the hallway to greet him.

"You gonna be ok, man?" Brock asked Chance.

"Yeah. Just got a few more scars to add to my collection. You been taking care of my lady?"

"I've tried to get her to show me her bullet wound, but she called me a nasty man and she slapped me, Chance. She slapped the Dog."

Chance laughed. "I heard that you like a little spanking every now and then."

"Hehehe. Yeah, got that right. Hey Chance. You seem different."

"Different? What do you mean?"

"I don't know. You seem looser. Look, you smiled."

Chance laughed. "I figured some things out. That's all."

Brock nodded his head with a suspicious expression on his face.

"Did you guys get any good intel from Stryker?"

"Name, rank and serial number. That's all that he'd give up. The controllers are trying to trace his steps to see if they can find anything."

"Good luck with that. Where is he now?"

"On vacation I guess. Somewhere in Guantanamo Bay," Brock laughed.

Chance paused and stared at Rice's dark eyes. "Hey, Rice, do you have a hospital?"

Rice looked bewildered. "Huh? You sure you're ok?"

"Yeh," Chance laughed. "Forget I asked that."

"Guess you want to see Jasmine now, huh? She's been waiting for you."

One of the officers opened the door as Chance stepped into the room and saw Greg sitting side by side with her on the bed.

"I've only been gone for two days and you're already hitting on my wife. What a friend!"

The tears stopped and Jasmine jumped to her feet. Greg struggled to stand and fell on the bed while bursting out into laughter.

Chance limped slowly into the room and approached Jasmine with his arms outstretched. Embracing her, he planted his lips on hers in a passionate kiss that lasted longer than he ever thought he could do it. He then turned and hugged Greg.

"Where the hell have you been?" Greg blurted.

"It's hard to explain. It's one of those things you can't ask me."

"Thought you could trust me by now."

"Honestly Greg. I don't even understand things myself."

Jasmine slapped Chance in his uninjured shoulder. "You always have me so worried." She began to hug Chance again, pulling him close to her body and snuggling up to him.

Greg recognized that he had become a third wheel. "Since I can see you're ok, I'm gonna let you guys have some privacy. Stop by and see me before you leave. I'm in Room 815."

Chance grabbed Greg's wheelchair and spun it back around.

"Thanks Greg."

"Chance, you would have done the same for me."

"No, it's not just that. Thanks for being a friend when I didn't even know that I needed one."

Greg gave up a wide smile and yelled towards the door, "Hey, Jay, come get me out of here. We got a mission."

The transporter came in and wheeled Greg out.

"Hey, Hunt. You owe me a motorcycle," Chance yelled as Greg rounded the corner.

"Yeah, yeah, take it out of my hero bonus," a voice answered from the hallway, as Greg was wheeled away.

Jasmine sat down on the bed and picked up a teddy bear that had been sent to her by Hardaway. Her nightstand was completely covered with cards and flowers. The director himself had flown to Philadelphia in his private jet to personally deliver a bouquet of roses, and his assurance that she could have whatever she needed until she was fully back on her feet. Chance sat down beside her, taking her into his arms.

"How do you feel? Are you ok?"

"Well, considering I was dragged down the steps by my feet, tied up and thrown into the back of a van, then got beat up by that she-man, and then shot . . . I feel great. I was more worried about you."

"Yeah. I heard that you did get your ass kicked."

"That's because by then I was tired. Give me a few weeks to recuperate and I want a rematch with her. Is she still alive?"

"Well, I didn't kill her, but I'll bet that she still has a pretty bad headache."

"Chance?" She lifted her head and looked into Chance's eyes. "Do you believe everything that Stryker said?"

"Not everything."

"Well, when the director was here, I asked him and at least what Stryker said about me was true, Chance. He said that he didn't know much about you, and that you were assigned to the HSA by the Department of Defense. He said that he managed to get you permanently assigned to the HSA. I don't even know who I am, Chance." She began to cry.

"And I don't even know what I am," Chance mumbled.

"What did you say?"

"Nothing. I'll tell you later. Jazzy, I have an idea. I know a nice quiet secluded place where we can go to recover. It's quiet and even has a private beach."

"Sounds relaxing. Where is this place?"

"Welcome to my world."

Made in the USA
Middletown, DE
06 February 2016